WALK A
NARROW
MILE

FAITH MARTIN

WORLDWIDE®

TORONTO • NEW YORK • LONDON
AMSTERDAM • PARIS • SYDNEY • HAMBURG
STOCKHOLM • ATHENS • TOKYO • MILAN
MADRID • WARSAW • BUDAPEST • AUCKLAND

Recycling programs
for this product may
not exist in your area.

Walk a Narrow Mile

A Worldwide Mystery/July 2015

First published by Robert Hale Limited

ISBN-13: 978-0-373-26952-5

Printed in U.S.A.

WALK A
NARROW
MILE

ONE

THE MIDDLE OF May was indulging itself with a rare mini heat wave, and Hillary Greene was glad to park Puff the Tragic Wagon under the welcoming shade of a large and beautifully flowering horse chestnut tree in Thames Valley Police HQ's car-park. She locked up her ancient Volkswagen Golf and walked towards the large lobby doors feeling a certain amount of weary lethargy that was unusual for her.

She had not long passed the hurdle that was her fiftieth birthday, but so far her bell-shaped cut of dark reddish-brown hair didn't need the help of a bottle, and her figure, though never trim, still retained the right sort of curves. It was not a physical thing that made her feel so lacklustre, but she was unwilling to dwell on the real reason. Wallowing in self-pity had never been her favourite pastime.

In the lobby, the desk sergeant grinned a greeting at her over the heads of a gaggle of excited officers, dressed in raiding gear. She wondered idly what operation was about to take place, as she headed down into the bowels of the building and the more sedate offices where the Crime Review Team hung their hats. The days of high-octane policing were now no longer her concern. Since retiring as a detective inspector with a full pension over a year ago, Hillary had only recently returned as a civilian consultant to help solve cold cases.

In the rabbit warren below stairs, she made her way to the stationery cupboard that now masqueraded as her office, and logged onto her computer. She stowed away her bag and quickly checked her emails before poking her head in the small communal office where the rest of her team worked. Well, she called them her team. In reality, they consisted of a retired ex-sergeant, Jimmy Jessop, now sixty-three, and regarded by both of them as her right-hand man. The two youngsters who were thinking about joining the force, and were getting some 'on the spot' training by also working in the CRT were, however, absent this morning. It was not an uncommon state of affairs. Sam Pickles was probably at uni, where he was in the last year of doing his BA degree course, but Hillary had no idea where Vivienne Tyrell might be.

'The super in?' Hillary asked Jimmy, who was reading through one of the current files in his in-tray.

'Been in an hour or more, guv,' Jimmy confirmed, and gave her a curious look. 'He's got a DI in with him. Don't know him,' he added laconically, one eyebrow raised in enquiry.

Hillary nodded, showing that she knew what was up, and withdrew. She then walked a few paces down the gloomy corridor and tapped on a door marked SUPT. STEVEN CRAYLE. She waited until she heard his voice call for her to come in and then pushed open the door and entered.

Her eyes went first to Steven Crayle, who was already rising from behind his desk. Just over six feet tall, he had a head of thick, dark-brown hair and dark chocolate eyes. Lean and elegant, he was dressed in a charcoal suit with a cream shirt and pale-blue tie. His eyes watched her carefully, as they tended to do recently. She wanted to snarl at him that she was all right, that she didn't need to be constantly monitored to see if she was about to fall apart, but ruthlessly fought back the impulse.

She didn't *do* hysterical woman.

Instead, she turned her attention to the other man in the room. So this was DI Geoff Rhumer, the man she was going to have to share her case with, she acknowledged to herself grudgingly.

'Geoff, this is Hillary Greene,' Steven introduced them, making it clear that the two men were on first name terms already, and that nice and friendly and cooperative was how he intended that they should all play it. Which made sense, Hillary supposed. Besides, it was how Commander Donleavy had insisted it should be, and if she didn't play ball, she knew the commander was perfectly capable of pulling the plug on her and sidelining her altogether.

So play nice, she told herself firmly. And smiled.

'Hillary.' DI Rhumer held out his hand and she took it quickly.

She knew from having asked around, that Rhumer was fifty-two, a widower with three grown children, and said to be a steady, capable pair of hands. He wasn't dirty, or particularly ambitious, and his rep, if a little stolid, was at least consistent. As a partner, she supposed, she could have had far worse foisted upon her.

Hillary shook his hand and smiled a bit more. He was about an inch or two taller than herself which put him at around five feet ten, with greying hair and somewhat watery blue eyes. 'I know and admire your reputation, DI Greene,' Rhumer said, deliberately choosing to use her former title. 'And I'm really looking forward to working with you. I'm only sorry it's in such circumstances.'

Hillary felt herself thawing, just a little. At least she wasn't going to have to cope with some know-it-all, out to make a name for himself, or some Jack-the-Lad who had problems taking orders from a woman.

Then she gave herself a mental head slap and reminded herself that she was the civilian here now. If anything, she was supposed to be the one taking orders from him. Her new status as an ex-copper still didn't sit very comfortably on her shoulders, and she knew she was going to have watch herself.

'I appreciate that the situation's somewhat unusual and...shall we say, delicate?' she said with a wry smile, and caught Steven nodding towards a chair. She sat down, somewhat amused to note that the two men only did the same once she was seated. How nice it was to be in a roomful of gentlemen.

Of course, Steven was her lover, and since the attack on her a fortnight ago, he was an anxious lover at that, so his behaviour was understandable.

She still wasn't sure about Rhumer. Oh, he was making all the right noises, but he could have a hidden agenda. Only time would tell.

'I think that's a bit of an understatement,' Rhumer said, with a brief smile, revealing slightly nicotine-stained teeth. 'I've been fully briefed by Commander Donleavy, of course, but before we start, I'd obviously like a rundown of the case from you.' Hillary nodded, but wondered how much Steven had said already.

She was wearing a dark-green skirt and jacket, with a white, open-neck blouse, and she had to stop her hand from rising automatically to touch the still red, but rapidly healing scars on her neck.

'You know what we do here, right?' Hillary began, and Rhumer nodded.

'As I understand it, the superintendent is in charge of a team within a team here at CRT, concentrating on high-level cases, nearly always murder cases, that need someone with experience to actively reinvestigate them,' Rhumer said.

'Right. That's where I come in,' Hillary agreed.

Rhumer nodded. 'The super was just filling me in on that. You've only been doing this a few months, but have already solved your first two cold murder cases. Colour me even more impressed than I was before.'

Hillary smiled briefly, in no mood for flattery. 'But you're not here for the cold cases,' she reminded him flatly. 'That's my remit. You're here for the current case that touches on mine.' She did not say it with any undue emphasis but she was nailing her colours to the mast.

In his seat, Steven shifted slightly, but said nothing.

Geoff Rhumer met her gaze steadily and nodded. 'Yes,' he said quietly. 'That's how I see it too. I had the full briefing and the paperwork from the commander yesterday, and I've covered most of it, but I'd still like your take on it before I start thinking out my strategy.' Hillary thawed a little more. So far, so good.

'Right. Well, the cold-case aspect of it is clear cut. We have three missing girls, with a common link,' she began.

'Your stalker,' Geoff Rhumer put in quietly.

'Yes,' Hillary said, her voice perfectly emotionless. 'And he's all yours, of course.' Again, her voice was perfectly flat and even, but Steven Crayle felt the hairs on his arms stand up to attention. The more he learned about Hillary, the more he realized that she was at her most dangerous when she was being calm and reasonable. 'You've heard why Superintendent Crayle and I believe that he's almost certainly working here at HQ, either as a police officer, or as a civilian with access to certain information.'

'Yes, and I agree with your reasoning,' the DI murmured.

'How you and your team set about tracking him down is, of course, your show,' Hillary conceded, still in that same flat, calm voice, 'but you can call on me at any time if you think that I can do anything to help you lure him out and catch him.' She noticed that Rhumer and Steven very carefully avoided looking at each other as she made this offer, and instantly knew why. They'd been talking about her behind her back, and had probably agreed that she was, under no circumstances, to be used as bait. As a civilian now, she could understand their reluctance. The station-house lawyers were probably having the jitters about her suing them if something went wrong. It was how their little minds worked, after all, and the brass had no choice but to listen. It was to be expected, but that didn't mean to say that she liked it.

'Let's be clear on this,' Hillary said, careful to take a deep, steadying breath first; the last thing she could afford to do now was to get emotional. One whiff that she wasn't coping and Donleavy would have her off the case in a flash. And that she was damned well not going to let that happen. 'You may need me at some point, if for no other purpose than to try and establish a dialogue with the little shit, and if that happens, I need you to know that I would have no objections.' She looked Rhumer squarely in the eye. 'Two weeks ago, the man grabbed me from behind in a deserted pub car-park, pulled me into the bushes and held a knife to my throat.' As she spoke, she felt the scars on her neck throb in remembrance, and kept her hands firmly clasped in her lap. She would *not* touch them.

'He cut me, not badly, and I managed to talk my way out of it by convincing him that we were playing some game together. That I was a…a willing participant in his sick little fantasies. I appreciate that it was a close call, and I know that it put me into shock for a short time. But that was then, and this is now. Now I, that is, *we*, have a job to do, and I am perfectly capable of doing it.' She moved her eyes from Rhumer to Steven in a clear and unmistakable message. *And that had better be clear to you too.*

Steven shifted again in his chair but remained silent.

'I appreciate the offer, DI Greene…' Rhumer said, making Hillary shift her focus back to the stranger in the room.

'You'd better start calling me Hillary. I'm not, strictly speaking, a DI anymore.'

'You wouldn't prefer Mrs Greene then?' Rhumer asked, and then smiled as Hillary glowered at him, and held up his hands in the universal peace gesture. 'Fine. But in that case, I'm Geoff.'

'OK, Geoff,' Hillary said, taking a deep breath. 'How it works is this—I intend to try and track down exactly what happened to Meg Vickary, Judy Yelland and Gilly Tinkerton. If, and when, their cases cross the path of your case, that is, my stalker, we pool intelligence and agree a strategy. Sound fair?'

'Yes. I don't see a problem with that, so long as you give me full disclosure.' Hillary smiled.

Steven Crayle felt the hairs on his arms start to dance a fandango.

'At the moment they're still officially listed as simply missing persons,' Hillary swept on, 'but we all know that all three of them are almost certainly dead, and murdered by the same man'—she took a slow, deep breath—'whom we are calling Lol.' Seeing Geoff's questioning look, she sighed deeply. 'It was the name he suggested I use when we had our…little encounter. It stands for Love of my Life, apparently. Which is what he considers himself to be.'

Geoff hid a wince. 'Nasty. And you definitely didn't get a look at him, right?'

Hillary shook her head. 'He grabbed me from behind and had the knife to my throat right away. I didn't dare turn my head. The only description I can give of him isn't of much use. His voice was almost directly in my ear, and yet he didn't feel particularly stooped over, so I would say that he was around your height, not much taller, and certainly not any shorter. He had muscles that went way beyond normal, so he's a body builder. The hairs on his wrist that I could see were dark, so he's not fair-haired, unless he dyes it. His accent was local. He wasn't wearing a watch, so there's nothing on that that we can trace. There wasn't much of use gathered from the scene of the attack forensics-wise either, I take it?' Hillary batted the last question straight to Steven.

'No, nothing much,' Steven agreed bleakly. In his mind's eye he was back on that day nearly two weeks ago. Hillary had just solved the second murder case he'd given her, and he was still at the station, processing the chief suspect, when he'd got her call. At first, he hadn't realized it was her on the line—she'd been breathing hard, and her voice was faint. And her words, when he'd been able to make them out had been disjointed, and not altogether making sense.

But when he'd finally been able to understand what she was trying to say, picking up key words like 'knife', 'bleeding' and 'evidence' he'd realized that their worst scenario had come true. The unknown perp who'd been stalking her for over a month, had finally launched a physical attack.

Steven had managed to get Hillary to tell him where she was—the car-park of a pub in Thrupp. The pub was on the Oxford canal, not far from where she moored her narrowboat, the *Mollern,* which had been her home now for nearly six years.

He had called an ambulance from the office and then raced to the scene, and he and the paramedics had both arrived more or less together.

He could still remember seeing her crumpled form on the tarmac, and running towards her, his heart thumping sickeningly fast in his chest as the ambulance siren blared behind him. He'd seen the blood first—on her neck, soaking into her blouse, pooling around her.

She'd lost nearly two pints, the medics reckoned later, when they'd had a chance to assess her. She'd been semi-conscious, and going into shock. But, typical of Hillary, the next day she'd discharged herself from the hospital, and had been insisting ever since that she was fine.

She refused to have a psych-evaluation, pointing out that she was no longer a serving police officer and could quite legitimately tell the trick cyclists just where to park their bikes. Donleavy had advised him to let it be, telling him that she'd work it at her own pace and in her own way, but Steven was not so sure.

She looked pale to him, and he knew that she wasn't

sleeping properly. And he was not at all convinced that she should be working this particular cold case—even if she was supposedly to be both under his personal supervision and liaising with Rhumer.

'Steven?' Hillary repeated his name sharply. 'Have forensics come through yet on the...on my crime scene?'

Steven sat up straighter and shook his head, dragging his thoughts back to the matter in hand. 'Not much. All the blood was yours so he hadn't nicked himself. And there were no fingerprints on your clothes or any of the other surfaces. A few fibres on your clothes were a match to a dark-blue thread common to many T-shirts, so no help there. There were no saliva traces on your ears or neck'—he paused as he saw that she had suddenly shuddered—'and it was too dry to get any good shoe prints or tyre tracks.'

Hillary nodded. 'So, not much help for you there then, Geoff,' she turned back to Rhumer.

'Doesn't look like it,' he agreed sardonically. 'Tell me how the stalking started.'

Hillary smiled grimly. 'It's been a while since I was on the receiving end of an official interview,' she acknowledged grimly, then held up a hand as Rhumer looked about to demur. 'No, no, it's fine. Let's see—it started off in the usual way, I suppose. Mysterious flowers and little notes and messages. I ignored it, hoping it was harmless and would go away. Then he became bolder—left his little gifts in places where he shouldn't have been able to access—my office, my locker, my car, the narrowboat where I live. In the end, I had to take it to Steven, and we tried to catch the little bastard ourselves. You know how that ended,' she added with a thin smile.

Rhumer nodded. 'The surveillance equipment you set up on your locker led to nothing.'

'Which made us suspect that (a) he wasn't new to this kind of thing,' Steven took up the tale, 'and (b) that he was probably forewarned about our efforts to catch him, making him someone right here at HQ.'

'Right. And then came the escalation,' Geoff said. 'Nasty, that.'

'Yes,' Hillary agreed softly. 'He started sending texts, threatening messages, and finally the crosses.' All three were silent for a moment, thinking about the crosses. Geoff Rhumer opened his file and took out the set of photographs of the roughly-made wooden crosses, three in all, and all bearing a set of three initials.

'This was the first one he sent you right—the one with the letters JOY on it,' he clarified.

'Yes. Although I was very dim about it, and didn't immediately twig that they were the initials of a person,' Hillary admitted drily. 'My first thought was that he was calling me a killjoy. Then I asked the computer nerds to run a programme on missing girls called Joy. Nothing came up. Then I finally got around to thinking of them as initials, and they came up with....' She paused, giving him room to jump in.

'Judith Olivia Yelland,' Geoff Rhumer obliged.

'Right. A little while later I was given the second cross, and the initials MJV, giving us Margaret, known as Meg, Jane Vickary. And the final cross, GGT for Gillian Gale Tinkerton. Known as Gilly.'

'All of them missing, and two of them known to have complained about a stalker before they disappeared,' Geoff said, reading from the notes.

'Right, got it. Which is how you made the connection between the missing girls and your stalker.'

'Which is when we went to Donleavy, and he called you in,' Hillary said.

'And here we all are. Ain't that grand?'

Steven leaned forward on his desk. 'Geoff, it goes without saying that we need to work hand in glove on this. As Hillary said, she will keep you apprised of any leads she gets tracking down the last known movements of our missing women, their backgrounds, and anything else she may come up with. But in return, we need to be kept in the loop about what your team come up with in tracking down Lol.'

'Fine by me,' DI Geoff Rhumer said firmly.

Hillary caught Steven's eye and nodded reluctantly.

It all sounded clear enough. Even so, she could still see trouble ahead. Maybe DI Rhumer was only making the noises she wanted to hear in order to keep her pacified. Maybe Donleavy had secretly given him, and maybe even Steven for all she knew, a set of far different instructions.

Maybe they thought she was still traumatized by the attack on her and needed babysitting.

Whatever the true state of affairs, she would just have to smile and nod and play nice and, in the meantime, just get on with it. Because she had a job to do, and neither Donleavy, the oh-so-accommodating Geoff Rhumer, or even Steven, were going to stop her from doing it.

Once again she fought the impulse to stroke her still sore scars, and smiled briefly. 'Right then, I'd better get started.' Steven said nothing as he watched her get up and leave. When she was gone, he was silent for a moment, then caught Geoff Rhumer watching him.

'What?' he demanded.

'You and her an item then?' Steven smiled reluctantly.

'That obvious, is it?'

Rhumer shrugged and smiled. Then frowned. 'You're worried about her?' Steven Crayle's already grim smile became even grimmer.

'Wouldn't you be? In my place?'

'Oh hell yes,' Rhumer agreed.

HILLARY GLANCED ACROSS at Jimmy, who was strumming his fingers idly against the steering wheel as they waited for a traffic light to turn green. They were in Jimmy's modest little runabout on their way to Kingston Bagpuize where Judith Yelland's parents still lived.

She had briefed Jimmy on what was happening back at the office, and the old man was obviously still thinking things over.

'So this all comes from Donleavy, right?' he asked eventually, as they pulled away from the lights and headed away from Oxford.

'I'm surprised he let you anywhere near it, to be honest.' Hillary smiled kindly. So that was what was puzzling him.

'Oh, it comes with a lot of strings attached, believe me,' she reassured him. 'And it wasn't easy convincing the commander to see it my way, either. And if I were still a serving officer, you're right, I wouldn't have been let within even sniffing distance of the case, let alone given this much leeway.' She sighed heavily.

'As it is, they're trying to keep me on a very short leash.' And she explained the new working arrangement to her deputy.

'So anything we come across that leads back to Lol,

we have to hand over to this Rhumer bloke?' Jimmy asked carefully, shooting her a quick, questioning look. Hillary knew why he was being so wary, of course. He was wondering just how far she was willing to play ball with the DI being foisted on her by the brass. And the fact that his loyalties clearly lay with her, made her feel both uneasily proud and at the same time protective of him. The last thing she wanted was to get Jimmy in trouble because he was listening to her, and not to Steven. She knew how much this job meant to him. She'd feel perpetually guilty if he were fired because of her.

'Yes. But I'll decide when, and I'll do the telling. Everything we learn goes through me first,' she said. 'That way, anything ricocheting back is my problem. But that shouldn't be hard—I'm not going to let the youngsters in on this for a start. They're to know nothing about my stalker at all, and it's going to be a purely need-to-know basis on the missing persons case as well. The less they're in the loop, the better I'll like it.'

Jimmy nodded quickly in agreement. 'I'm with you there, guv. I think Sam would be able to handle it all right, but that young minx we've been lumbered with wouldn't know how to keep her mouth shut if she had sewing lessons in buttoning lips.'

Hillary smiled briefly and stretched her arms over her head. She hadn't realized how tense she'd felt, until now. It seemed as if she'd been waiting for months, instead of just a week, for Donleavy to give the go ahead for her to head up the cold case aspect of the assignment, and now that it was finally underway, she felt a trickle of unease.

Was she really up to it?

She caught Jimmy looking at her again, and wondered

if he was thinking the same thing. Or was she just being paranoid now?

Oh, she knew she had a good rep for having guts and gumption at the station house. Being awarded a medal for bravery tended to do that for you. But Hillary knew, in reality, that it did, in fact, mean very little in any way that counted.

She'd been given the medal when a raid she'd been on had gone wrong, and her old friend and one-time superior, Mellow 'Mel' Mallow had found himself in the line of fire from a fleeing gunman. She'd had only a split second to react, and in that time had managed to shove him out of the way, and take the bullet instead. It all sounded very melodramatic and gung-ho when other people talked about it, but in reality, Hillary knew differently. For a start, the bullet wound had been anything but fatal—indeed, she'd come within a hair's-breadth of being shot in the arse! And the flesh wound had quickly healed anyway.

More than that, though, the stress had been minimal. She'd reacted purely on instinct, and it had all been over—quite literally—in a flash. A few days in hospital, one or two bad dreams, and that had been that.

Nothing to it really. Anyone would have, and could have, done the same thing. It had required very little in the way of true grit or backbone.

What was happening now, though, was a totally different matter. Lol was subjecting her to a prolonged, sustained and nasty psychological attack. And she knew her nerves were beginning to tighten up like piano wires in response—as much as she tried to stop it from happening.

She wasn't sleeping well either, which made her feel

sluggish, as if she was constantly playing catch-up with herself, and the world around her. Worse than that, she kept reliving that moment in the car-park when she felt the super-sharp blade of the knife slice into her neck. The blade had been so sharp, all she'd felt was the slightest of stings—and then the far more terrifying ooze of her own blood running down her neck and into the narrow valley between her breasts.

The lightest warm breeze on her skin reminded her of the feel of his breath on her neck. She would never forget his voice either. The moment she ever heard it again, she'd recognize it. Which was good, of course. But constantly hearing it repeated in her mind, when she was trying to concentrate, was far from good.

No wonder Jimmy looked at her and wondered. If that was, in fact, what he was doing.

'So, what do we know about the Yellands then, guv?' Jimmy asked now, sounding very much the same, pragmatic assistant he'd always been.

She told herself that she had enough on her plate to start inventing problems that might not even exist, and shrugged briefly, focusing her mind on the case at hand.

'Not much. At the time, very little follow-up was done on any of the three missing girls, because nobody thought it was a priority,' she admitted.

'So we've got very little to go on?'

'That's right,' she agreed. 'But in a way, that might be an advantage. We're starting from scratch for a change, which means we won't be going over old ground, or having to rely on an original investigation's preconceptions.'

'Fine by me,' Jimmy said. And put his foot down to pass a trundling tractor.

THE YELLANDS LIVED in a small bungalow just before you entered the village proper, and Jimmy parked beneath a pale-pink flowering cherry tree. The sky was that bright azure of approaching summer, and the sun, approaching noon, was beginning to get that bake-you-dry edge to it.

Hillary removed her jacket and left it in the car. The bungalow was one of those neat, yellow-brick ones, set in a skimpy but well-maintained garden. A mat in front of the door bore the legend WELCOME TO OUR HOME.

The windows sparkled cleanly and the double-glazed pvc frames were snow-white. As she pressed the door-bell it set off a cacophony of excited yips from within. Beside her she heard Jimmy sigh.

'I'll bet they're those little rat-on-rope things that like to show you their teeth and'll have your ankles, given half a chance,' he predicted dourly.

Hillary grinned, then quickly wiped the smile from her face as the door was opened. The woman looking back at them was in her late fifties, Hillary gauged, with a carefully dyed blonde perm, and was wearing a silvery-grey summer dress and matching sandals. She was free of make-up, but wore a nice gold watch and several rings with semi-precious stones set in them. Her face though, was tight and pinched, and she looked like one of life's constant worriers.

'Yes?' she asked faintly.

Hillary introduced herself and Jimmy, and they both showed their IDs.

'Are you Mrs Yelland? Frances Yelland?' Hillary asked.

The woman, who was already looking a little bewildered, looked even more so. 'Yes,' she agreed uncertainly, as if she'd been asked a trick question.

'We work for the Crime Review Team for the Thames
Valley Police, madam. We're here about your daughter.
She is still on our files as a missing person. I don't suppose she's turned up, has she?' Hillary asked. And then
had one of those weird, almost *Twilight Zone* little moments, when she wondered what she'd do if the other
woman smiled and said that yes, as a matter of fact,
she had.

Probably faint, or start laughing and not be able to
stop, she supposed.

Of course, Frances Yelland said nothing of the kind.
Instead, she took a sharp breath, and then sighed. 'You'd
better come in then,' she said, with a quick glance around
to see if any neighbours were watching. None were. In
this day and age, Hillary could have assured her that
most people were too busy working or trying to sort out
their own dysfunctional lives, to care about their neighbours' woes.

'Max, my husband, is in the back garden tying up
the runner beans. Since he retired he's been growing all
our own vegetables. They all say that it's so much better for you, and good for the environment too.' Frances
Yelland opened the door and stepped back. Hillary and
Jimmy entered, glad to get into the relative coolness of
the tiny hall. From another room, they could hear tiny
snouts sniffing under the door, and Jimmy for one was
glad that the mutts had been shut away.

Without another word, they were ushered through
to a small, tidy lounge in shades of apricot, cream and
mint green. 'Please, sit down. I'll make us some tea and
get Max.' Hillary glanced around, her eyes halting on
the mantelpiece, where a whole range of family photographs was arranged. She saw a wedding photograph of a

much younger Frances and a handsome man staring solemnly at the camera. There were several baby pictures, then those unmistakable school photographs, where a travelling photographer comes and takes a head-and-shoulders shot of every kid, regardless of whether or not they wanted their photograph taken. The Yellands had three children, she knew from the file, but there were only photographs displayed of two of them: a boy and a girl.

And the girl was not Judith. Did they already think of her as dead? If so, did they know something that she didn't? Or was it just too painful for them to be constantly reminded of their missing child?

'You notice there aren't any pictures of our MisPer?' Hillary said quietly to Jimmy, who followed her gaze and grunted quietly in assent.

Just then Frances came back with a tea tray, and an older version of the man in the wedding picture.

'My husband, Max,' she introduced him nervously. Hillary could tell by the way that she looked for approval from her husband, that Mrs Yelland had lived all her married life very much under the thumb. It made Hillary's hackles rise, and she forced herself to smooth them back down.

She was not a marriage guidance counsellor, she reminded herself firmly.

Maxwell Yelland was lean, not particularly tall, and had silver hair and pale-grey eyes. He was still a handsome man, even though he'd never see sixty again. He glanced at Hillary, then at Jimmy, and then back at Hillary again. He took a seat, and then accepted a cup and saucer from his fluttering wife.

'I understand this is about Judith? Do you have news

of her?' he asked, but without any sense of urgency. He looked, if anything, more wary than concerned.

'No, sir. I'm afraid not. But we're investigating her case, along with that of several other missing women, and we just have a few questions for you, if you don't mind.' Hillary sensed Frances Yelland was now hovering nervously behind her, and wished that she could see her face. 'Mrs Yelland, perhaps you'd like to take a seat?' she said, half turning in her chair and indicating the sofa space available beside her husband.

'Oh yes, of course.' Frances Yelland responded with immediate obedience and sat down beside her husband, then took a sip from her teacup.

Hillary could feel Jimmy tensing up beside her. Just as she had, he'd picked up on the atmosphere in the house. And didn't like it.

'When was the last time you saw your daughter before she disappeared?' Hillary asked, directing the question at Mrs Yelland, but in fact watching her husband closely.

'Oh not for a while.'

'A few weeks?' Hillary hazarded.

'Oh no. Much longer. Months, wasn't it, Max?'

'Yes. Nearly a year, I would have said.' He spoke with a concise flat tone that was probably designed to hide some strong emotion. But what it might have been, Hillary had no clue. But Max Yelland's grudging co-operation wasn't about to put her off.

Instead she nodded. 'That seems rather a long time. Had there been some sort of a problem?' she asked delicately.

Max Yelland smiled bleakly. 'Nothing specific, Inspector.'

Hillary didn't bother to correct him about her lack

of official status. 'But you would say that matters were somewhat…strained…between you?' she persisted doggedly.

'My daughter was always a wayward child, I'm afraid,' Max finally admitted, pausing to take another sip of his tea. 'Unlike our other children, she became difficult. Defiant. It started when she was a teenager and, alas, she simply never grew out of it. When we heard she'd left her flatmate in the lurch with the rent and gone off somewhere, frankly, we weren't really surprised.' Hillary glanced across at the missing girl's mother, wondering what she had made of this harsh assessment of her daughter, but she was studiously sipping her own tea and avoiding meeting anyone's eyes.

'I see,' Hillary said. 'So you don't know if her behaviour had changed in the months before she disappeared.'

'No,' Max agreed shortly.

'And she never talked to you about being afraid of anyone, of being pestered by strange phone calls, or letters or gifts?'

'I doubt Judith would have objected to being given gifts, Inspector,' Max said, still in that same pedantic, careful tone.

'She always was materialistic. We tried to drum that out of her, but without success. Sunday School was wasted on her, I'm afraid. Meredith now,' Max said, looking with pride at one of the photographs on the mantelpiece, depicting a beanpole-thin woman with her mother's hair and eyes, 'she volunteers at several different charity shops. I doubt that Judith ever knew the meaning of the word.' Hillary smiled briefly.

No wonder it had been noted in her file that Judith Yelland had left home at the age of seventeen. 'I see. And

I take it you haven't heard from her in the three years since she went missing.'

'No. And I really rather doubt that she is in fact missing, Inspector,' Max said with a tight smile. 'I think you'll find that she's simply shacked up somewhere with some man. Judith always did take the easy options in life. Why work, if you can play, that was always her motto.' Hillary nodded again. She could see that there was no way that Judy Yelland would have gone to her parents for help when she began to be stalked. Her mother was too timid to be of any help, and her father far too judgemental. She would have been well and truly on her own.

It was also as clear as day that she was going to get nothing of use in this arid environment.

'I see. Well, thank you for your time.' Hillary put her cup down, noting that Jimmy eagerly followed suit.

Frances Yelland shot up from the sofa and showed them out. But, on the doorstep, she cast a quick look over shoulder, then leaned forward and all but whispered, 'When you do find her, you will let me know that she's all right, won't you?' Hillary felt as if someone had just sucker-punched her, and she had to force a brief smile.

'Of course we will, Mrs Yelland,' she promised softly.

But never had a promise seemed so hollow.

TWO

'BLOODY HELL, GUV,' Jimmy said, as they climbed back into the car. 'That place gave me the willies.'

'Yeah, me too. It's not hard to understand why their daughter legged it, is it?' she agreed.

'If she wasn't missing the way she is, I'd be inclined to say that she'd just written off her family as no-hopers, and decided to get herself a new life,' Jimmy opined.

Hillary sighed. 'Back to base. We need to get the admin underway. Set up a case file number, get the murder book started, and work out some way of relaying our data to Geoff. What we want him to know, that is.'

'DI Rhumer going to be a problem, guv?' Jimmy asked sagely.

Hillary sighed again. 'Not sure yet. Let's hope not.'

VIVIENNE TYRELL LEFT Kidlington's Thames Valley Police HQ that lunchtime with a spring in her step. She was twenty, pretty rather than beautiful, with long dark curly hair and pansy-velvet brown eyes. She'd been working in the CRT for nearly eight months now, still unsure whether the police force was for her and if she should apply to join properly when the opportunity arose. She was, however, still a little bit infatuated with Steven Crayle. But even there, she was beginning to see the writing on the wall as far as the handsome, sexy superintendent was concerned. He'd always played hard to get, and now she was being forced to admit that he hadn't been playing, so much as meaning it. He was never going to ask her out. And ever since Hillary Greene had joined their team, things had gone from bad to worse.

She simply couldn't see what a gorgeous guy like Steven saw in her. She was older than he was for a start, and here Vivienne gave a mental snort. Who'd have thought the super was into cougars?

As she walked into the local pub, she began to smile in anticipation though. At least it wasn't all bad news on the romantic front now that things were looking up. Tom might be just a humble PC, but at least he was young and fit. In both senses of the word! He must work out every day to get the pecs he had!

OK, having the hots for a forty-year-old had been fun while it lasted, but Tom was closer to her own age. And she loved his green eyes.

She glanced around the crowded bar and saw him stand up and lift an arm to attract her attention. He'd managed to snag a window seat, and through the open windows, a hanging basket of flowers provided some floral colour for the dark interior.

She approached at an easy hip-swinging stride, knowing that many male eyes had turned to look at her. She hoped Tom noticed it too. It wouldn't hurt to remind him that she was hot, and that he was always going to have competition.

'Hiyah,' she said cheerily, slinging her bag onto the bench seat and sliding in beside him. She was pleased to notice that he that already had her favourite drink— a cinzano and lemonade—waiting for her on the table. 'Boy, am I glad to get out of that place. I feel like a mole, working down in the basement like that. I tell you, as soon as I can get out of there and into somewhere better, I'll be off.'

Tom Warrington smiled stiffly. And the moment you are, he thought silently, you cease to be of any use to me, you silly cow.

'Have a drink, and tell me all about it,' he said instead, forcing a sympathetic smile to his face and nudging her glass closer. 'I asked for ice, just how you like it.' He watched her sip the silly drink, wondering what it was that Hillary drank. It would be something classy and simple, he knew. Perhaps a good wine? Or something more straightforward and no-nonsense perhaps, just like herself. A G and T?

'We've got this new guy in, but I don't know why,' Vivienne said, taking a sip and giving a sigh. 'Him and Hillary and Steven were closeted together nearly all morning. But nobody's telling us nothing.'

Tom forced himself to relax in his seat. 'Oh? Who is he, then, this new bloke?'

Vivienne shrugged. 'DI Rhumer. Geoff, I think I heard his first name was. Funny thing is, I got the feeling that he's on the job. I mean currently, like, not a retired old fart like Jimmy.'

Tom felt his heartbeat quicken. Yeah, that made sense. The CRT only dealt with cold cases. But they would need to call in someone else to work on an on-going crime. Even so, he felt a shaft of anger lance through him. It should be just between Hillary and himself; that's how she would have wanted it too, not to have some stranger brought in to spoil their fun. It couldn't have been her idea to bring in an outsider.

He knew who was to blame—that bastard Steven Crayle. The superintendent wanted Hillary for himself—

that was obvious. And because he was her boss, he could insist on them bringing in someone else to ruin it all.

But they wouldn't let him. Hillary was more than a match for this DI Rhumer and Crayle put together, of that he had no doubt.

He smiled across at the silly, fatuous girl beside him, and forced himself to lean closer and put an arm around her shoulder. In deference to the warm May weather, he was wearing only a short-sleeved T-shirt under his police jacket, and he was pleased with the way his muscles showed as he flexed his arm.

He saw Vivienne notice, and saw the way her dark-brown eyes registered admiration. Silly little twit.

The skin on his arm tingled, though, when he remembered it draped around Hillary Greene's neck. Over and over again, he was reliving that moment when he'd stepped up behind her and held her hard against him.

He heard again her quick intake of breath.

The way she quickly realized she couldn't physically fight him and had become quiet and clever.

The way she'd tried to play him.

The fun they'd had. The touch of his knife against her skin. She'd barely flinched as he'd drawn a fine, oh so fine, line of blood in her skin. Anyone else would have panicked, or started begging, or behaving in any number of disgusting ways.

But not his Hillary. She was class, through and through.

Tom Warrington felt a delicious warm wave wash over him as he remembered how magnificent she'd been, as he'd always known she would be, after all that time watching her and adoring her from afar.

Wanting her. Playing the delicious, torturous, waiting game. The first move had been his. Now it was her turn.

'So what's the queen bee been doing?' he asked, forcing himself to use Vivienne's nasty nickname for her. Vivienne, who was nothing more than a wannabe, and who didn't even have the sense to realize that she was being given the opportunity to learn at the feet of a master. Sometimes, Tom found it hard to keep from snapping her stupid, vapid little neck for her.

'Oh, she and Jimmy went off this morning to interview some people over a missing girl. Oh yeah, that's what we're working on now apparently—not even a proper murder. But some missing girls. I mean, who cares?' Vivienne said, taking a large gulp of her drink. 'They've probably all run off to be with a bloke, right? I mean, that's what usually happens, yeah?' Tom absently twirled a lock of her hair around his finger.

'What's the name of the couple?' Vivienne shrugged, and snuggled up closer.

And to Tom's fury said smugly, 'Oh, I can't remember. It's not important, is it? When are you and me going to get together seriously, then?' Tom fought back the urge to slap her. But really, she was right in a way—it didn't matter. Whichever set of witnesses Hillary had talked to, it meant the same thing: she'd made her move. She'd begun trying to track him down. She was on his scent.

The thought made him shudder with delight.

Beside him, Vivienne giggled, believing it to be a reaction to her flirting. Tom Warrington smiled with forced patience and reached for the menu. She was his eyes and ears in Hillary's camp, he reminded himself, so he needed to keep her sweet.

'What do you fancy to eat then?' he asked.

BACK AT HQ, Hillary reached for the Vickary folder.

Margaret—known to all her friends as Meg—Jane

Vickary. According to her file she was thirty-two years old at the time she was reported missing. Photographs of her showed her to be a rather glamorous woman with long, tawny hair that looked so casually untidy it had to have been carefully cut and arranged to look like that by a top flight hairstylist, and large grey-green eyes. In nearly every snapshot and photo they'd been able to accumulate of her in the last few days, she seemed to be always fully made-up with highlighter, blusher, mascara and eye shadow. It was hard to see past the mask to the woman beneath. Did she secretly fear that she wasn't as beautiful as she needed to be?

She'd been married but then divorced from one Brian Vickary. No children. Had the divorce undermined her self-confidence?

Hillary sighed, knowing from experience that it was pointless to speculate before getting the facts. But so far, the first of their missing girls had a bad family situation behind her. Now she needed to find out if the second of their missing women also had a difficult situation behind her, courtesy of a bad marriage and a messy, damaging divorce.

Perhaps her stalker liked damaged, vulnerable women? Or was she just trying to force a pattern where there was none? After all, nobody could think of *her* as vulnerable, could they? A veteran, battle-hardened middle-aged ex DI with the hide and disposition of a grumpy rhino?

She picked up the folder and walked on through to the communal office. 'Jimmy?' she said, ignoring the quick, hopeful look that Sam Pickles gave her. He was a good lad and coming on well, and would be an asset to the police force once he'd graduated and been properly recruited and trained, but right now he was out of his league and needed to be kept on the sidelines.

'I want you to keep on researching the three missing persons' backgrounds, Sam. The more information we have, and the more diverse it is, the easier it'll make our job in finding out what happened to them.'

'Right, guv,' Sam said, but looked enviously at Jimmy who was following Hillary out of the room. Although he'd worked with the police long enough to know that research and paperwork were the bread-and-butter of crime solving, like Hillary, he preferred to be out and about actually talking to people and getting a feel for a case.

Outside, Hillary followed Jimmy to his car and slipped into the passenger side, where she carried on reading the folder, relaying bits of information to Jimmy as he drove.

'According to this, Meg was a legal secretary at Kane, Boltham and Kane.'

Jimmy whistled. 'Top notch solicitors, those. Only cater to the well-heeled. If you're an Oxford don caught doing something naughty, they're the people you'd run to screaming "fit up".' Hillary nodded, also being familiar with the firm.

'Want to stop off at their place first, guv?' he asked, as he indicated to go around the Woodstock roundabout on one of the city's northern-most main thoroughfares. 'We'll be going through Summertown any minute.'

Hillary thought about it for a moment, and then shook her head. 'Maybe later, when we know more about her. For the moment, I want to interview her flatmate, the woman who reported her missing in the first place.' Georgia Biggs was still living at the same residence in a converted Victorian pile in Botley, but they were unlucky. Nobody answered the doorbell. However, a nosy neighbour was able to point them to the dental practice in town where she worked as a hygienist.

Finding the usual trouble parking in the fabled city of dreaming spires, they had to hoof it a quarter of a mile to the practice. And the moment Hillary pushed open the door to a narrow hallway with an even narrower flight of stairs leading upwards, they could hear the nerve-grating high whine of a drill. When she pushed open the door at the top of the stairs, the smell of disinfectant, peculiar to dental surgeries everywhere, set her teeth automatically aching. Beside her she heard Jimmy mutter something dire about hating these places.

Hillary grinned. 'Never mind, Jimmy. At least you're not here to get your root canals a good seeing to.' The old man muttered something even less repeatable, but Hillary was already smiling at the receptionist and reaching for her ID.

'We were hoping to speak to a Miss Biggs. Strictly routine, nothing to worry about,' she said automatically.

The woman, fifty-something with a fine coiffeur and deep crows' feet around her eyes, smiled uncertainly. 'Georgie? She's got a patient in with her at the moment, but she should be out soon. Would you like to take a seat and wait?' Further in the room, a guppy confronted her, swimming bug-eyed and fan-tailed in a large fish tank. Watching him, and several of his piscine friends, was a wide-mouthed boy of about five, who began to wail piteously when a door opened and he was beckoned inside by a patient-looking man in his sixties.

'Poor little bugger,' Jimmy said, then reaching for a magazine on dog-breeding, added heartlessly, 'rather him than me though.' Hillary was still grinning about that when a door opposite opened, and a plump blonde

woman wearing the prerequisite white coat ushered out
a man and walked him to the reception desk. She then
gave a classic double-take towards them as the receptionist whispered something to her, and then approached
them warily. She had the slightly puzzled, worried but
intimidated look a lot of members of the public wore on
their faces when confronted by the police. Well, the in-
nocent ones, anyway.

'Police?' Georgia Biggs asked tentatively. She had a
round, pleasant but just a touch plain face, with somewhat protruding blue eyes.

'Yes. We're here about your flatmate, Meg Vickary,
Miss Biggs,' Hillary said at once, hoping to allay at least
some of her anxiety.

'Oh Meg.' Then she went pale. 'You've found her.
She's dead, isn't she? That man did something to her.'
Hillary felt Jimmy snap to attention beside her, like a
pointer suddenly spotting a pheasant in the undergrowth.

Hillary smiled gently. 'No, we haven't found a body,
Miss Biggs. I work for the CRT, and we're currently re-
investigating Meg's disappearance. We just have a few
follow-up questions for you. Perhaps we could talk in
your office?'

'Oh yes, of course. Sorry, it's a bit small.' The room
they were ushered into was small, with the obligatory
and ominous black vinyl dentist's chair taking up most of
the space. Both she and Jimmy gave it a wide berth, and
in the end it was Georgia Biggs who parked her plump
rear end on it, whilst Jimmy and Hillary stood leaning
against the walls.

'When you said "that man did something to her",
who did you mean, Miss Biggs?' Hillary asked, getting
straight to the point.

'Oh, Marcus of course.'

'Marcus?'

'Marcus Kane. Her boss.' Hillary nodded slowly, as if she knew all about it, and glanced across at Jimmy, who was rapidly taking notes in his own idiosyncratic shorthand.

'Why would you think that, Miss Biggs?' she said, beginning the mining process for information gently.

'Oh, please, call me Georgie. Everyone does.'

'Did Meg not get on well with her boss? Is that it?' Hillary pressed.

Georgie laughed harshly. 'Rather the opposite, Inspector,' she said, and Hillary didn't bother to correct her about her title. Since retiring from the force, strictly speaking, she was no longer entitled to it. But she'd grown so used to hearing it over the years that she quite liked to hear it aired now and then. And it sure as hell beat being referred to as Mrs Greene. She'd been in the process of divorcing her corrupt husband when he'd died in a RTA. She was still pondering whether or not to revert to her maiden name, but somehow couldn't seem to drum up the energy to tackle the paperwork involved.

'Meg and Marcus were something of an item,' Georgie Biggs said, with a certain snap to her voice.

'You didn't approve.'

'He was married. With kids.'

'Ah,' Hillary said. 'That old story.'

Georgie sighed. 'He kept telling her he was going to leave the wife and kids when the time was right, stringing her along. But guess what?'

Hillary nodded. 'The time was never right.'

'You got it,' Georgie agreed. 'The kids were too young, their wedding anniversary was too close, or it was Christmas in a few months' time. You name it, he came up with it. I kept telling her to get out from under, but….' She shrugged helplessly. 'I don't know what she saw in him. I thought he was creepy.' Jimmy glanced up at the word. Hillary wasn't surprised. It was a word bound to twang any copper's radar.

'You met him?'

Georgie flushed. 'No.' She sounded puzzled for a moment, as if for the first time realizing the inconsistency of it, then shook her head. 'It's hard to explain. It's just something I picked up from the things that Meg used to say. But then, any married man having an affair with his secretary has got to be a scuzz-bucket, right?' Hillary nodded. But had to wonder, what did that make the secretary?

'When she went missing, you reported her as missing straightaway?' Hillary carried on smoothly.

'Yeah, I did. If Meg was going to spend the night away she always told me, see? And after the second night, I knew something was up. I didn't like the way she just vanished without packing a case or saying anything. Especially when the flowers stopped coming.' Hillary felt her spine grow cold.

'Flowers?' she repeated. Against the opposite wall, she saw Jimmy stiffen too.

'Yeah. She'd been getting these bouquets of flowers and cards and stuff. I thought at first they were from him—Marcus, but she said they weren't. She said she'd got a secret admirer. She thought it was funny. To be honest, I did wonder if she'd been sending them to herself, you know, to try and make Marcus jealous.' Hillary smiled, but it felt tight on her face.

'Did she get any threatening phone calls?'

'No. But she got some text messages. She showed me a couple. I told her she ought to go to the police, but she just shrugged it off. She said it was probably just some poor loser who knew her from around, you know? Someone with a crush on her. Like the guy who sold her the newspaper in the supermarket, or the mail courier who biked stuff to the office, someone like that. She didn't take it seriously.' Georgie Biggs shifted on her dentist's chair. 'You have to understand, Meg was one of these women who could have been a model. The sort you see on telly, selling shampoo, waving their fabulous hair about. Well, OK, maybe not quite that gorgeous, or young, but pretty damned close, you know? In a league of her own around here, at any rate. She was used to attracting male attention. It's why I can't understand why she'd waste her time on a loser like Marcus.' Hillary smiled, but could think of several reasons. If Marcus Kane worked for one of the top firms of solicitors in the county, he'd be earning a fair whack, for a start. And married men with kids usually meant middle-aged men ripe to have a mid-life crisis, and dump the current wife for a younger, more glamorous model.

'Tell me about her marriage to Brian Vickary. Did she talk about it much?' she decided to change tack.

'No, not really. I think it really hurt her,' Georgie said, with a frown. 'She used to go all pale and tight-lipped whenever I mentioned him, so I stopped asking.'

Hillary nodded. 'Doesn't sound as if the marriage was a happy one. Well, obviously not, if it ended. I don't suppose you know where I can find Mr Vickary?'

'Sorry, not a clue. Although his name and number might be in Meg's private papers. I still have all her stuff parcelled up at the flat. I don't quite know what to do with it, you see. Her parents are dead, and I can't sell it. What if she comes back?'

'I'd quite like to have someone look through it, if I may, Georgie. If I arrange a time, could you be in?' She looked across at Jimmy. 'Ask Sam if he can pick it up. I want all her private papers, diary, address book, anything he thinks significant.' Jimmy nodded and made a note. 'Don't worry,' Hillary carried on, turning back to Georgie Biggs, 'we'll give you a receipt for it, and you can have it back when we're finished with it.'

Georgie nodded. 'Anything to help. Do you really think you'll find her? Now, I mean? I mean, if you're looking into her case again, is it because you have new evidence?'

Hillary didn't want to look her in the eyes and see the hope there, but forced herself to do so. 'We're certainly going to do all we can to find her, Miss Biggs,' she said.

And meant it.

Back outside, they walked back to the car. It was the start of rush hour, and they were stuck in the usual, horrendous tailback that began almost at the end of St Giles, and reduced them to a crawl the entire length of the Banbury Road.

Hillary sat frowning thoughtfully in her seat. From time to time, Jimmy cast her a questioning glance.

'Penny for them, guv.'

Hillary sighed. 'I'm not sure. Something about that interview didn't sit right with me, Jimmy. You pick up on anything off?'

Jimmy pondered. 'Don't think so, guv. You think she was lying? I have to say, she didn't strike me that way.'

Hillary shook her head, still angry with herself for not being able to pin it down. 'No, it's not that. Like you,

I think she was being pretty straightforward. But still, something wasn't right.'

'Well, she certainly had it in for her friend's boss,' Jimmy said, trying to be helpful. 'Probably a bit of jealousy there. The dentist lass was pretty enough I suppose, in a way—if you like 'em blonde and plump, but I reckon her friend knocked her into a cocked hat and she knew it.'

'Yes. Considering she never even met him,' Hillary said, 'she seemed really down on him,' and then she snapped her fingers.

'That's it. Say you had a pal who was having an affair with a two-timing but probably harmless married man, but who'd also picked up some unknown admirer who sent her anonymous text messages and flowers. And then this friend suddenly went missing, wouldn't you be more worried about the stalker than the married man?'

Jimmy crept the car forward a few yards then changed back down to neutral. 'Dunno, boss. Married man with a wife and kids and a good job and a reputation to lose could be far more dangerous than some unknown infatuated jerk. I mean, from her point of view. Georgie Biggs had no way of knowing that her pal had caught the attention of a real nutter, did she?'

Hillary sighed. Jimmy made sense. 'No. I suppose you're right.' Even so, something about it still felt wrong.

Or maybe she was just off her game. She didn't want to think that the nightmares and the almost inevitable loss of some of her self-confidence after the attack on her were affecting her judgement. But it was possible.

She felt her hand creeping up towards her neck to massage the scars there, then forced her hand back into her lap.

Behind the driving wheel, Jimmy Jessop pretended not to notice, and inched the car forward another few feet.

BACK AT HQ, she climbed from the passenger seat and stood at the open door of Jimmy's car, glancing towards the entrance to HQ before deciding to go straight to her own car and then back home to her narrowboat, moored at the nearby village of Thrupp. It was clocking off time, after all, and she was going to have to get used to keeping to civilian hours. She was a strictly nine-to-five girl now.

'First thing in the morning then, Jimmy, we'll go and speak to Brian Vickary. See if you can track down an address for him, yeah?'

'Not Marcus Kane, guv?' Jimmy asked in surprise.

'He'll keep,' Hillary said. 'Unless you think that a responsible citizen like one of Oxford's top solicitors is also our stalker, that is?'

Jimmy grunted and gave a wry smile. 'Sorry, guv. I keep forgetting we already know who our man is. I mean, not his name, but…hell, you know what I mean.'

Hillary did. 'It feels like an ordinary case, doesn't it, and we're trying to find our killer amongst the vic's friends and family? Yeah, I know. But the truth is, our man is probably here somewhere,' she said, nodding toward the large police HQ.

Jimmy sighed. 'You really think Rhumer and his team can track him down from this end?'

'Let's hope so,' she said, forcing her voice to remain noncommittal. 'In the meantime, we try and see if we can get a sniff of the bastard, via our three missing vics.'

Jimmy nodded. 'See you in the morning then, guv,' he said, and watched her walk away. When he was sure

she was gone, he got out and walked down to the basement to confer with Steven Crayle.

He wanted to make sure that Hillary would have
someone watching over her tonight—whether she knew
about it or not.

WEDNESDAY DAWNED BRIGHT and clear and, despite her efforts to keep civilian hours, Hillary found herself at work
an hour early so that she could sit at her computer and
type up a report of their activities for Geoff Rhumer. She
printed off an extra copy for Steven and left it on his desk.
She knew that he had an early meeting with Commander
Marcus Donleavy, who was not particularly happy to have
been talked into letting Hillary head up the missing girls'
inquiry. That meant they were going to have to babysit
him all the way, which they'd agreed was Steven's job.

There was, as usual, no sign of Vivienne, who arrived
any time she chose, but usually before ten. Her argument
that because she wasn't a 'real' copper, and wasn't being
paid a real copper's wages because of budget cuts, meant
that she had more flexibility than those that were, had
some merit, Hillary supposed. But she noticed that, despite being in his last year of a BA course, and still not
being paid a fair wage, Sam Pickles still managed to put
in the hours required.

Hillary would be glad when the little madam finally
decided to call it a day, and go off and pursue a job in
PR. Or the beauty trade. Or whatever.

Jimmy came in with a mug of canteen coffee and the
latest address of Brian Vickary.

'Had the lad do some finger walking before he clocked
off last night,' Jimmy confessed, sipping his coffee. Al-

though he could use a computer when he had to, Jimmy tended to avoid it when at all possible.

Hillary nodded and began reading the file, giving him time to finish his much-needed caffeine fix.

'Says here he owned his own double-glazing firm.' She spoke out loud in case the old man hadn't had time to study it himself yet.

'Went bust though when the bankers tossed the world economy to the wolves, guv,' Jimmy said, tacitly letting her know that he'd been a good boy and done his homework. 'Been unemployed on and off for the three years since.'

Hillary winced. 'He's only thirty-two.'

Jimmy shuddered. 'Tell me about it. Makes me glad I've still got this little gig, I can tell you,' he said. Over at his desk, Sam chortled at Jimmy's choice of words. He thought the old man was probably trying to sound with it, and he found it oddly touching that it only succeeded in making him sound even more of an old fart.

Jimmy ignored the youngster's mirth.

'He's just down the road in Begbrooke, guv.' Hillary nodded. The small village, distressingly situated beside a busy dual-carriage way, was literally only a few minutes' drive away.

'Well, since he's having trouble getting work, I dare say we'll find him at home then,' Hillary agreed.

'You fit?' Jimmy hastily gulped the last, still piping hot dregs, from his mug, making his gums wince in protest, and nodded gamely.

BRIAN VICKARY LIVED in a pre-fab bungalow that looked something like a beach hut. Tucked away far from the road, it appeared to be damp and somehow sagging. Even in the bright May morning, it looked as if it should be condemned. An identical bungalow beside it had a FOR LET sign. Hillary guessed that the landlord owned both, which meant that Vickary didn't even own the place.

A come down indeed for a man who'd set up and run a highly successful company, not so long ago. According to Sam's research, Victory Glazing had rented offices in Banbury, and had employed four workmen/fitters and two office staff.

Hillary rang the bell, realized it was defective, and banged on the door instead. The paint was peeling, and she was still wiping the knuckles of her hand when the door was yanked open suddenly and aggressively.

'Hello? Whatever is you're selling, I don't want it.' The man who answered needed a shave, and was wearing an open-topped white shirt with grubby collar, and black, shiny trousers. With a mop of brown hair and large grey eyes, he was though unequivocally a handsome man.

The whiff of beer coming off him at not even ten o'clock in the morning wasn't quite so attractive.

'Mr Vickary?' Hillary showed her ID. 'We're here about your wife, sir. Can we have a few moments?'

'Don't have a wife,' Brian Vickary shot back at once. 'Got an ex-wife though. I suppose you mean her?'

'Yes, sir.'

'I heard she went missing. Wanna dig up the back garden? Help yourself.'

Hillary smiled pleasantly. 'Thank you, sir, but I think we'll give the cadaver dogs a miss for now. Just a few questions, like I said.'

Brian's grey eyes regarded her steadily for a moment, and then he gave a reluctant grin, exposing white, even teeth. His smile was attractive too, and Hillary could understand why a woman with good looks of her own might have chosen him for a partner.

'OK, fair enough I suppose,' Brian said mildly. 'Come on in. Mind the mess. But you're wasting your time. Meg will just have found herself some other mug to feed off. She's probably living it up on the Costa del Sol somewhere with a big, fat, ugly sugar daddy. Or do people still go to Spain now the bubble's burst?' he asked, with probably automatic and inconsequential charm.

Hillary smiled obligingly.

As he was talking, he led them through into a tiny living room—which was indeed messy. The floorboards underneath her had an oddly spongy feeling, and she half-expected to put her foot through one of them. Two of the walls were badly affected by damp, and the wallpaper was peeling off.

'Welcome to Casa Vickary. My other home's a chateau in Bordeaux.' Brian grinned, then abruptly sobered. 'We used to go there you know. France. And Florida, and places like that. Twice a year, when the business was good.' Hillary nodded, but didn't want to give him time to start getting maudlin.

'I take it the break up wasn't amicable, Mr Vickary,' she said, sitting somewhat gingerly on a couch. Whilst it didn't actively have broken springs digging into her backside, it wasn't exactly welcoming either.

'No,' Brian said succinctly. Then, 'Do you want a beer? I'd offer you tea, but I don't have any milk. Or sugar. Or teabags, probably.'

'Thank you, sir, we're fine,' she said. 'Can you tell me why you broke up? Was there another man? You seemed to think your ex-wife wouldn't be lacking for male companionship.'

'What? Oh no. No, it wasn't a man that broke us up, I'll say that for Meg. She played fair. I met her when I was twenty-five, and I thought she was the most gorgeous thing on earth. I'd just got the business up and running, and she fancied me, and thought my prospects were good, as they say in the old-fashioned novels. So...' He shrugged. 'We got spliced.'

'Sounds reasonable,' Hillary said.

'So it was. For a while. Quite a while, actually. It was good. Like I said, the company took off, we went on holiday twice a year, had a house on the outskirts of Banbury in the green belt, with a bit of a view. Two nice top-of-the-range cars.'

'Again, it all sounds very reasonable.'

'Right. Till it all went tits up and I lost the firm. Bloody bankers. 'Course, in a recession, the first things that are cut back are the non-essentials. People who'd been thinking of getting double-glazing, or adding value to their properties with conservatories and patios, suddenly realized that putting food on the table and petrol in the car are higher priorities. I lost two of my fitters, then one of the girls in the office. Started taking on more and more of the admin myself. Working crazy hours to try and keep it afloat. Meg started complaining how she never saw me, how the money wasn't there anymore to do the Town and take in a show and have a meal, blah, blah blah. And as the money got tighter and tighter, so did the expression on my dear wife's face.' Brian had wandered over the window and was staring outside. Now he turned back and gave them a savage grin. 'And when the firm finally went, so did she.'

'You lost the house?' Hillary guessed.

'Mortgage providers took it back, the bastards.'

'The cars?'

'Had to sell one of them. Hers, obviously, since I needed mine. And lo and behold, I come back one day from a particularly vicious interview with the bank manager, and no more wife. She moved out to live with a friend. Female, before you ask. I got a nice solicitor's letter serving divorce papers about a week later, and that was it.'

'You never tried to see her? Talk her into coming back? No sending her flowers, or letters begging her to return?' Hillary asked casually. 'Most men try to save their marriages, if possible.'

Brian Vickary cast a bleary, attractive eye her way. 'Are you kidding? Me, beg? No way. Besides, I considered myself well rid of her. If she couldn't stick by me through the bad times, who'd want her?' He cast a look around at the ramshackle bungalow and gave a sudden burst of laughter. 'You know, when I heard she'd gone missing, I was seriously pissed off. I had this fantasy, I guess, about starting up a new business after coming up with the big new idea that was going to make me millions. Then I'd buy a top-of-the-range Porsche—her favourite car by the way—and I'd drive it by her house wearing a load of bling and with an even better-looking girl in the passenger seat.' Brian Vickary laughed again. 'I'm going to get another beer. Sure you don't want one?'

Hillary shook her head. 'Just a few more questions first, sir,' she said firmly. She had a feeling Brian was working himself up to a binge, and she needed him sober for just a little while longer.

'You weren't at all worried, then, when you heard she'd disappeared. You didn't think, perhaps, that she was a victim of foul play?' she asked curiously.

'Meg?' Brian snorted incredulously. 'Nah. She was nobody's victim, Meg, believe me. She had a way of getting what she wanted. When I heard she was working in some posh office I knew damned well what her game was.'

'You think?' Hillary asked, deadpan.

'Sure. Getting into the boss's trousers. Mind you, I did bump into her once, just the once, in some trendy bar. About a year after the divorce it would be. It was a mate's thirtieth, and he was buying. She just came swanning over, as if nothing had happened, and began chatting. Said she was working for a solicitor or some such. Bragged a bit about her salary, her nice flat in Oxford. My mate was well up for it, I could see, though I tried to warn him off. She hooked him like a prize carp, flirting, showing off the cleavage, giving it with the chat.' Brian mimed with his fingers the universal symbol for gabbing. 'She could really talk, could Meg. Wind men around her finger. She had my mate panting about her tales from the office. A boring bloody solicitor's office, I ask you! But even that she could make into a tale. She told my mate she knew no end of West End villains, men who made the Kray twins look like cissies, who'd been got off by one or other of the QCs her bosses hooked them up with. Had my mate believing that she visited them in their Spanish villas and South American hideaways for freebie holidays all the time. And he was lapping it up, poor sod. I could see she was laughing up her sleeve at him. She only did it to rile me, I suppose. Show me what I'd been missing.' Brian suddenly realized what he was saying, and who he was saying it to. For a moment he looked nonplussed, but then he laughed again. 'Honestly, straight up, I didn't lay a finger on her. That was the only time I saw her—and if you still want to dig up the garden, the offer still stands. It'll be a way of getting some free gardening done anyway. It's a bit of a jungle out there.'

Hillary smiled. 'I'll keep it in mind, sir. In the meantime, if you think of anything else…' She handed him one of her cards.

Brian Vickary saluted her with it, and walked them to the door.

Hillary let him get back to his beer.

If Brian Vickary was her stalker she'd eat her hat. If she had a hat.

THREE

Tom Warrington took his lunch hour early. Since he'd volunteered to be posted back to admin he had more flexibility with his working hours than he had when he'd been on the beat, provided he could keep on the good side of the dragon, a civilian clerk who thought she owned the records office.

He left HQ and drove through Kidlington, which was either one of the country's largest villages, or a small town, depending on who you spoke to, and headed to the nearest Park and Ride. He didn't like using it, since he always felt vulnerable without instant access to his car, but since parking in the city was about as easy to do as win the Lottery, he had little option.

Getting off the bus in St Giles, he made his way to the covered market, just off Cornmarket Street. He felt more anonymous here than in a jewellery store in town, where CCTV tended to proliferate too much for his liking. He felt a stab of conscience for the lack of taste implicit in his choice, but he knew that Hillary would understand. He couldn't make things too easy for her after all! Besides, she knew how much he cherished and rated her.

And despite the rather dark, smelly and less-than-salubrious surroundings, the large, cosmopolitan market was quite capable of producing some very good quality items if you were prepared to put in the time and effort to look for them.

And Tom was. He'd been on the lookout for such an item every day this week, and he felt his heart rate quicken as he prowled the aisles of the last remaining jewellery booths he'd yet to inspect. Most was tat and he avoided that fastidiously. He didn't like the bright, the brash and the costume stuff; that would be an insult to his Hillary, although he might pick up something to keep that stupid cow Vivienne Tyrell happy.

He quickly pushed thoughts of the wearisome girl aside and concentrated on his task.

Since he wasn't sure what Hillary's favourite gem-stones were, he'd decided to stick with something classic and simple in gold. The high-quality stuff, naturally. He eyed lockets of all kind, and was sorely tempted by some of the antique silver ones especially. Although not gold, they had the quality and uniqueness associated with ar-tisans long gone, and he thought that she would appre-ciate both the workmanship and the class.

But lockets, by their nature, needed something inside them—a photograph of a loved one, or a lock of hair.

Tom grinned at the impossibility of either of those: she'd be on to him like a lioness on an impala.

So he skirted the lockets, rejected the gems, and fi-nally found what he was looking for in a dimly lit booth almost at the back near one of the many exits from the market. The stallholder was a foreigner of East European extraction by the sound of his accent, a middle-aged man with a cadaverous face and blank blue eyes.

The item was made of a beguiling mixture of old gold, white gold, and gleaming buttery yellow gold: two love-hearts, one in solid white gold, the other in lattice-worked yellow, both joined by a finely moulded old gold arrow.

It was perfect. On a simple but substantial, good-quality box-style chain, it was understated and chic, obviously old and perfectly made.

'And the message couldn't be clearer.

Beaming with delight, he paid out the £200+ for it without a flicker of protest. He'd made sure that the booth owner wouldn't be able to pick him up out of any line up easily by wearing sunglasses, and a baseball cap pulled well down over his forehead. He paid in cash, obviously, and spoke as little as possible.

If the stallholder had any suspicions, his blank eyes hid them well. He counted the money fast, and without being asked, retrieved an old leather, velvet-lined jewellery box from under the table and carefully arranged the pendant inside.

Although it clearly wasn't the original box for the piece, it had faded writing on it in gold, and Tom liked the way it added a touch of class to the whole enterprise. Perhaps the booth owner had sensed that the young man buying such a love token was well and truly smitten and was a romantic at heart. Or perhaps his radar for danger had just insisted that he wanted Tom gone quickly—and perfectly satisfied with the transaction.

Either way, Tom left Oxford smiling.

Back at HQ, he donned a pair of fine leather gloves and used plain A5 paper and one of the record office's computers to type and print out a message.

MY DEAREST HILLARY
A GIFT FROM THE HEART. PLEASE WEAR
IT AND THINK OF ME. I CAN'T WAIT UNTIL
WE MEET AGAIN.
LOL.

He read it and smiled. Lol was what he'd told her to call him when she'd asked him his name, that glorious day in the car-park in Thrupp, when he had finally been able to put his arms around her and could breathe in the wonderful perfume of her hair, and luxuriate in the fast beat of her pulse under the forearm that he had draped around her throat.

Lol, short for Love of your Life.

He whistled as he popped both the note and the jewellery case into a plain brown envelope. He used water to seal it, so there would be no chance of lifting his DNA from the saliva, and resisted the urge to write her name on the front, even using plain capitals. She was just too good to give her any leeway at all.

He was sure that the jewellery booth owner had collected a vast range of old jewellery cases over the years, and any attempt by his bright and beautiful girl to trace the origin of the locket from that was doomed to failure. And if he'd read the body language of the foreigner correctly, even if some uniformed plod did do the rounds of the jewellery stalls with a picture of the pendant, he was unlikely to admit ever having seen it before. Let alone selling it. His sort liked to avoid having anything to do with the police.

It was an irony that wasn't lost on Tom.

HILLARY SPENT HER lunch hour in the canteen, which was hardly fine dining with Jimmy and Sam, whilst contemplating the paperwork in front of her.

The last of the three missing girls, Gilly Tinkerton had, in some ways, the slimmest file of them all. 'She's a bit of a cipher, our Gilly,' Hillary said, tapping the folder, the contents of which were, once again, the result of Sam's handiwork. 'You weren't able to come up with much,' she added without censure, and looked across at the young lad with a questioning smile.

'Sorry, guv, there simply wasn't much to be had. All the regular stuff was there, but…' He shrugged.

'Right. Just the easily verifiable.' Hillary nodded, eating a ham and tomato sandwich whilst studying the data. 'Aged twenty-nine, two years ago when she was first reported missing. About five feet six, plumpish build, red hair and freckles. Big blue eyes according to her old school photos.' Hillary grinned, shoving the file around so that Jimmy could see.

'She must be about twelve there,' the old man guffawed, nodding down at the file's one and only photograph.

Sam flushed.

'Sorry, guv, I just couldn't find anything more recent. None of her family and friends seemed to have any. She was a bit camera shy they all said, on account of her being fat, I reckon,' he added carelessly.

Jimmy snorted a laugh. 'Not interested in political correctness then, sonny? I thought that's what you modern lot all went in for like good little boys and girls. And if you want to impress the brass you should stick to it, that's my advice. What is it called nowadays? Corpulently challenged, is it? Or rotundly handicapped?'

Hillary laughed and took back the file. 'You couldn't find anything more official even?' she asked Sam. 'Driver's licence?'

'She's never driven, as far as I can see. Never took any lessons or passed a test—officially, at any rate. So she never had a driver's licence issued. Mind you, that doesn't necessarily mean that she wasn't out and about driving around in a car anyway. From what people said, I don't think she had much interest in observing the law, guv.'

'Oh, a criminal record?' Jimmy said, perking up. 'She's bound to have official ID then.'

'No, Jimmy, I don't mean it like that,' Sam said, spearing a chip and chewing vigorously. 'She's not a villain. Just one of these so-called "free-spirits" you get nowadays. Someone who's not all that interested in living by the rules.'

'Oh right. New Age clap trap,' Jimmy grumbled. 'In my day they were called hippies, and were always stoned at rock festivals.' Sam and Hillary exchanged more grins. Jimmy pretended not to notice.

'Right, Jimmy,' Sam said kindly.

'Well, perhaps her family can help us out in other ways, even if they don't have a decent photograph of her. They still live in Brill?' she asked, naming a village that sat atop a high and, locally famous, hill.

'Yeah, guv, the address is recent,' Sam promised.

Jimmy, sensing his boss was impatient for the off, quickly gobbled up the last of his fried-egg sandwich and reached for his mug of tea.

Twenty minutes later they were headed for the other side of the market town of Bicester, where they hoped to put some flesh on the bones—so to speak—of the third of the stalker's victims.

Deirdre Tinkerton turned out to be one of those roly-poly women with red cheeks and a naturally cheerful disposition that you expect to see playing as an extra on *The Darling Buds of May*. She had salt-and-pepper hair rolled back in an untidy bun and big blue eyes. She also had a rolling Oxonian country burr in her voice, and seemed determined to reinforce the stereotype yet further by an-swering the door dressed in a flowered apron, and with flour sprinkled up her arms to her elbows.

She looked at Hillary's ID card without touching it, waving margarine-smeared fingers as a mute explana-tion and looked at Hillary with a trace of fear.

'Is it our Gilly? Lumme, you ain't found no body, have you? Don't tell me it's my little girl?' Hillary hastily re-assured her that that wasn't the case, and gave her the same standard line as she was giving to all the witnesses.

'Nothing like that, Mrs Tinkerton. We're just look-ing at Gillian's case again.' She gave a brief description of what the Crime Review Team did, and of her role in it as an ex-copper.

'Oh right. Like with those three old men on *New Tricks*,' she said, mentioning the name of the popular television programme that showcased the solving of cold crimes. Hillary and Jimmy smiled and agreed that they were indeed, just like that.

'Come on through then. I'm just doing the baking for the month,' she said, as she led them through to the kitchen, her usual bonhomie quickly restored. 'I does a freezerful at a time, see. Right now it's rhubarb—com-ing up a treat it is, and Les has got an allotment full of it. Good thing we likes rhubarb, I say! You want one?' she added, pointing to one of six already made and waiting to be baked pies, lining one of the work surfaces.

The Tinkertons lived in what had once been a coun-cil house but was now obviously privately owned as a large kitchen extension had been built. Hillary smiled and declined the offer with real regret. Just how long was it since she'd tasted a homemade fruit pie?

'Ah right. Can't be having bribes, I 'spect it is,' Deirdre said, but with her eyes twinkling at Hillary as she reached for her rolling pin and began rolling out a roughly circular shape of pastry.

Hillary noticed Jimmy watch her carefully when she reached for the rolling pin, and then slowly relax, and silently approved of his caution, which spoke of years of experience and instinct. Although it was almost impossible to regard this woman seriously as a threat, no doubt Jimmy had, in the past, had equally unlikely women come at him with a rolling pin! All beat bobbies were called out to domestics, after all, which were notoriously unpredictable.

'So how can I help then, my love?' Deirdre asked comfortably.

'Would you mind giving that pan a stir and stop it from sticking? Has this got anything to do with that nice, young, redheaded boy who come round asking about Gilly and wanting a photo of her? He reminded me a bit of that other nice young constable who came the very first time, asking about our Gilly. Good-looking lad he was too.' Hillary, obligingly stirring a vast pan of pink and green stalks with a wooden spoon, nodded with a smile. Sam would be chuffed to be regarded as 'good-looking' she had no doubt, even by a woman old enough to be his grandmother.

'My colleague, Sam Pickles. Yes. He told us you weren't able to find a recent photograph of Gillian.'

'No. We don't go in for cameras much in our family. Never could get the hang of 'em myself, and Les is no good with one either. And Gilly never was the sort to primp and preen much and want her picture took.'

'You haven't heard from Gilly recently, have you, Mrs

Tinkerton?' Hillary asked cautiously, feeling strangely wrong-footed by the woman's easy-going manner.

Deirdre frowned. 'No. But you know I'm not that worried about it, to be honest. Our Gilly never was much good at writing—I was the same at school myself. Never could spell worth a damn.' Hillary nodded.

'But she never phones?' she prompted persistently. She was puzzled by Deirdre Tinkerton's distinct lack of worry. Her home was clean and cosy and had a nice atmosphere about it. And in direct contrast to the impression that she'd got from the Yellands, she was sure that Gilly Tinkerton had been well loved and reared with generosity. And had been very much a wanted and valued child.

'You have other children, Mrs Tinkerton?' she asked curiously.

'Lumme, yes, my love. Three of each—three girls, three boys. Gilly is second youngest.'

'You don't seem to be all that worried about her, Mrs Tinkerton,' Hillary said at last, keeping her voice bland. Even so the woman stopped rolling out her pastry and cocked an intelligent eye her way.

'That's because you don't know our Gilly, and never did know her, whereas I know that girl like the back of me 'and. Not hearing from her is just her way. She probably don't even realize how much time has gone by. Always a dreamer. Never had no sense of time, or thought for what other people might be thinking neither.' She suddenly laughed. 'To be honest, she often has no sense, full stop. She went off with a band of them gyppos in caravans and camper vans or what have you a while back, even. You know about that, right?' Hillary did.

'A little. She spent a few years travelling, I think?'

'Right. I reckon she thought it was as close as she was gonna get to running off and joining the circus. That's what she wanted to do when she was little, you know,' Deirdre said, with an indulgent chuckle. She gently nudged Hillary away from the stove and nodded in satisfaction at the softening fruit. 'Ah, just need to cool down a bit.' She took the pan off the stove and set it to rest to one side.

'I blame them books she read as a kid. About some elephant packing its trunk and what not. You ask any of my other kids what they wanted to be when they was nippers, and they'd have said that they wanted to be astronauts, or train drivers, or actresses or nurses or whatever. Gilly always wanted to run away and join the circus.' Deirdre Tinkerton sighed and carried on somewhat pragmatically. ''Course, there ain't any circuses any more, can't afford to keep runnin' I reckon, and even if there had'a been, our Gilly wouldn't have been any use to 'em, Lord love her. She couldn't ride a horse, and she was built too much like me to swing from a wire. She didn't have no beard neither, and her dad threatened to wallop her backside if she came home with so much as a single tattoo.' By now she was openly laughing, and Jimmy was also holding a hand over his mouth as he pretended to take notes.

'So when she upped and left just after her eighteenth birthday with this band of gyppos none of us was surprised. We were just glad and relieved when she came back. Les was half-expecting her to come back with a nipper or two, but she didn't. 'Course, that never surprised me so much. For all she's got her head in the clouds half the time, she's also got it screwed right on her shoulders. If'n you see what I mean.'

Hillary smiled, thinking that she knew very well what

Deirdre meant. 'She was well able to take care of her-self, you mean. She might not have had book-learning, but she was canny, like a fox.'

'That's it, my love,' Deirdre said approvingly, and reached for some battered tin plates and started laying out pastry in them, carefully trimming the excess from around the edges. 'So now she's gone off again, I ain't worried this time neither.' Well, that explained her easy manner, Hillary thought. And instantly felt guilty. For this mother truly believed that her daughter was all right. But was now the time to tell her differently? Would it be needlessly cruel to shatter her convictions? Hillary thought that it was—especially since they didn't have any concrete evidence to go on.

'When she left the first time, did you hear from her then?' Hillary asked carefully.

'Not for ages, no, love. Gilly don't like modern tech-nology stuff—not computer mad, see, like all her little nieces and nephews. I swear, some of the gadgets they use make my 'ead swim.'

'I see.'

'Gilly was always good with her hands, see,' Deirdre swept on, anxious to make her understand. 'But not so good with living in the everyday world, like. She was shy as a kid, something terrible. She could knit a treat by the time she was ten though. Crochet too, and em-broidery. And when she got older she took up painting— lovely little country scenes and what 'ave you. There's one over there.' She nodded her head towards an unin-spired and not very good watercolour of weeping willows surrounding a small pond full of ducks. But the compo-sition showed the artist had at least some eye for form. And the colours showed a hearty verve.

'Very nice,' Hillary said. 'Before she left, was she acting jittery at all?'

'Oh, yes, love, I knew she was getting itchy feet. I said to Les, "You just wait and see. Our Gilly's gonna be off again soon". And she was.'

'Did she ever mention being bothered by anyone?'

'Whaddya mean, love?' Deirdre asked, retrieving the saucepan and smoothing in a good dollop of cooling rhubarb into one of the pie cases.

'I mean was a man pestering her?' Hillary asked.

'Oh, him. Yeah, Gilly did say someone fancied her. She got a bit giggly about it. Flowers and Valentine cards came for her, and all that sort of thing.'

'Did they frighten her?'

'I don't think so. I think it pleased her. And I thought it did her self-confidence a bit of good, having a lad take a fancy to her, like. But she got sort of impatient with him for not coming forward. She said it was all very well having a secret and anonymous admirer and what have you, but you couldn't hug and kiss a love letter, could you?'

'So to your knowledge, she never had any real contact with him?' Hillary pressed.

'That's right.'

'Do you still have the letters?' she asked hopefully.

'Lumme, no. I reckon she took most of her stuff with her. Not that she had much. Didn't believe in possessions, she didn't. She said worldly goods just weighed you down.'

'She packed her bags?' Hillary said sharply, clearly taken by surprise.

'Well, yerse, I think so,' Deirdre said slowly. 'Like I said, she never had much. But a few of her favourite clothes were gone. And some money she'd earned from making and selling some of her own jewellery at Bicester market. Beaten copper she said they were. Bit bulky for my taste, but she sold enough to get by.'

Hillary nodded and glanced at Jimmy. No doubt they were both thinking the same thing: it didn't quite fit the pattern. Both Judith Yelland and Meg Vickary had vanished without any sign of premeditation.

'Did Gilly have a bank account? Credit cards, that sort of thing?' Hillary asked sharply.

'Oh, no, love. Gilly didn't hold much with the…whatchamacallit—how did she put it? Being part of the establishment. That was it. She always kept her money close. Said banks were in league with the Devil—well, as good as.' Deirdre laughed again. 'I reckon most folks would now think the same thing, right?'

Hillary nodded and agreed. 'So what do you think happened to her, Mrs Tinkerton?'

Deirdre's smile faltered just a little. 'Maybe she found some more gyppos to run off with. Or she's gone abroad to where they live in them big tent things. She mentioned them once or twice. Out in Israel or some such place. I told her she didn't want to be going out and messing in them sort of places. Can't really remember what they're called now.'

'A kibbutz?'

'Some word like that, I reckon. Oh, she'll have found herself some sort of comfy little hideaway somewhere— she was always good at landing on her feet. Bit like a cat, like that. You'll see, she'll be fine.' And Hillary could see that Deirdre Tinkerton truly believed it. Apart from a lingering doubt perhaps, which was surely both natural and inevitable, that's what Gilly's mother genuinely believed.

'OK. Well, thank you, Mrs Tinkerton. We'll be in

touch if we think of anything else we might need to know.'

'That's fine, my love, call any time. Sure you don't want one?' Deirdre nodded to a freshly crimped rhubarb pie.

Hillary sighed, but again declined.

She was silent in the car as Jimmy drove them back to HQ. Once again things had taken an unexpected turn. Even though it was early days, she could sense that this case just wasn't going to play by the rules.

Gilly, it seemed, had planned to leave. Her mother was sure she'd packed up at least a backpack's worth of stuff. And her mother was also convinced that she was safe and alive somewhere. Was that just a case of so much for a mother's instincts? Or was she in denial and simply unable or unwilling to think the worst? Or was it not Deirdre Tinkerton's thinking that was at fault here?

Hillary twisted unhappily on her seat.

'You seem a bit pensive, guv,' Jimmy said suddenly, glancing over at her.

Hillary sighed in acknowledgement. 'I don't like the way this case is going, Jimmy,' she admitted at last. 'This is the second time I've felt something is a bit off. Like we're not seeing the whole picture. Or we're approaching it from a wrong angle. Or…oh, I don't know. Perhaps I'm just a bit off my game.'

'That's understandable,' Jimmy said quietly.

Hillary sighed impatiently. 'It's not just the stalker. There's something else…oh forget it. It's early days yet.'

Jimmy nodded. 'You'll get there, guv. You always do,' he said. And if his voice sounded just a tiny bit unsure, neither of them acknowledged it.

BACK AT HQ, Geoff Rhumer was waiting for her outside her ex-stationery cupboard. She unlocked the door and waved at the tiny office space. 'I'd offer you a seat, but you can see how it is.'

The DI grinned. 'No worries. Just thought I'd keep you updated. We've got a trace installed on both your office phone and mobile, so if he calls or texts we might get lucky.'

Hillary nodded, but said nothing. They were both very much aware that her stalker was unlikely to be caught out so easily.

'I've also got my team started on trying to run-down any likely looking lads on staff here.' He handed Hillary a folder with three full sheets of names. He grimaced. 'I know. Even with narrowing down the criteria, it's still a lot of possible suspects. We've kept it to men aged between eighteen and forty, and physically fit. But as you can see, that doesn't eliminate a whole lot. We're going to concentrate on those who worked MisPer or sex crimes, since the shrink who's doing the profile on him thinks that's more likely where chummy would have gravitated.'

'These are the ones highlighted in yellow?' Hillary asked.

'Yeah. Could you take some time and go through them, see if any names stand out? Although the shrink seems to think it more likely that chummy won't have had any prior contact with you. He said something about the pathology of it being wrong. But still….'

Hillary nodded in understanding. 'Yeah. I'll go through them all carefully tonight and let you know if anyone sets off alarm bells.'

Geoff nodded. 'Anything your end?'

Hillary gave him a brief rundown of her activities, and concluded grimly, 'So, nothing that's standing out so far.'

'OK. Well, we'll let you know if anyone acts twitchy at interview. We're using a cover story of missing inventory as our reason for sniffing around, but I don't know how long that'll hold water.'

Hillary nodded. 'It won't fool him for a minute.'

Geoff shrugged. 'That's not really the point, is it?'

Hillary smiled wanly. 'No. I don't suppose it is.'

STEVEN CRAYLE STOOD and stretched, glancing at his watch as a knock came at the door. It had just gone 6.30 in the evening, and he was more than ready to call it a day.

'Come in.' Jimmy Jessop stuck his head around the door. 'Just wondered if I needed to keep obbo tonight, guv,' he said quietly.

'No. I'll see to it tonight,' Steven said flatly. 'I'm going over to her boat for supper and I'll be staying the night.'

Jimmy was careful to keep his face utterly neutral. 'OK, guv. See you in the morning.'

Steven sighed as the door closed. Of course, he knew that it was all over the station by now that he and Hillary were an item, but he was not so sure what the consensus was. He had an uncomfortable feeling that most of them probably thought she could do better.

At first, he and Hillary had deliberately cultivated the rumour of their affair in an attempt to try and flush out Hillary's stalker. But somehow the lie had become a reality, and Steven, after some initial misgivings, was glad that it had.

And was becoming even more glad the longer it went on. The fact that she was older than he worried him not

at all. And he found her no-nonsense independence re-
assuring, rather than emasculating. But the fact that he
sometimes found himself envious of her success and reputation, however, did cause him a few sleepless nights.

He left HQ and drove the short, barely five-minute
commute to the neighbouring village of Thrupp, situated on the Oxford canal. He parked next to Hillary's old
Golf, as usual, impressed by the beauty of the scenery.
Kidlington and work was only a stone's throw away, yet
here along the tow path, where yellow iris were beginning to bloom, and ducks were proudly showing off the
first of the season's ducklings, it was a different world.
The evening sun made even the khaki-coloured water
of the canal glitter like silver gilt and the gentle chug-
chug of a passing narrowboat added to the sense of calm.

The more he visited Hillary on her narrowboat, the
Mollern, the more he could appreciate why she chose to
live in such a cramped, narrow environment. There was
also something nestlike and comforting about living in
such a cocooning space. And knowing that you could just
cast off a rope and take yourself and your home miles
away whenever you felt like it, was so liberating that
it was unbelievable. Since they'd been together, they'd
spent most weekends chugging up north to Banbury, or
going south to Oxford and beyond.

Now he walked to the grey-painted boat, with its black
roof and white and gold trim. Hillary had already explained to him that *Mollern* was the old country word
for heron, and that her boat was painted to reflect that
water bird's colouring. In contrast to the cheerful boats
that favoured the more traditional green, yellow, blue and
red, it was an elegant-looking boat and, as he approached

it, he saw the back metal doors open and Hillary's head with its distinctive chestnut hair, appeared.

'I thought I heard footsteps. It's herb omelette, salad and warm fresh baked bread. With some peach ice cream for dessert.'

'Sounds ideal,' Steven said. 'We got any of that white wine left?'

'Still in the fridge,' Hillary assured him. She watched him come aboard, amazed, as she so often was, that someone so tall and elegant seemed not to mind the fact that his head was always barely a scant inch away from the ceiling.

She watched him take off his jacket, slip off his tie and shoes, and make himself comfortable in her favourite chair. The sight of him brought a lump to her throat. He was both sexy and gorgeous, and fast becoming an ever-growing presence in her life.

And she still didn't know what she really felt about it.

She broke the bread apart and put butter on the table, then mixed the eggs. Steven poured the wine.

They ate easily and comfortably, with trays on their laps in the intimate sitting area, then, after washing up, watched the sunset go down from the roof of the boat, where they lay flat on their backs, watching the swallows swoop and dart.

Hillary was listening to a blackbird serenading in the nearby willows when she felt Steven stiffen beside her. She too sat up quickly, and saw what had attracted his attention.

A young man was strolling down the towpath, holding a padded envelope and clearly checking the names of boats. He wore black motorcycle leathers and stopped when he reached the *Mollern*. He smiled up at them.

'Hillary Greene?' he asked. He was about twenty, around five feet five, and had impressive acne on his chin.

'Yes.'

'Package for you.' Hillary reached down and took the envelope.

'Can you sign just there and there please?' he asked, handing over one of those machines that had a mostly blank grey screen but with a black-outlined box and affixed stylus. 'Where the Xs are,' he added helpfully.

Hillary signed and half-listened as Steven began questioning the courier. He made sure to get both his name, the name and address of the courier company, as well as the young lad's immediate superior, before he let him go.

They waited until the puzzled lad was gone before she turned the padded envelope over thoughtfully in her hands and studied it. It had her name and the name of her boat and nothing more. She glanced at Steven.

'What do you want to bet that whoever the customer was, he paid in cash, and probably got some little kid to hand deliver it the courier's office?' she asked.

Steven smiled grimly. 'No bet. Do you want to call in the bomb squad?' he asked seriously.

Hillary thought about it seriously.

'No. But let's be careful.' If they called in the bomb squad it would be all over HQ tomorrow. And for DI Rhumer's investigation to stand any chance of catching her stalker, he needed to keep it on the Q.T. as much as possible.

She held the envelope far away from them, dangling it over the edge of the boat and out over the water. If it did hold something nasty, maybe she'd be able to drop it in the water before it did any real damage. Then she had a sudden, appalling thought.

'What if it's anthrax or something?' she said. 'It mustn't get into the water system.'

'Open it flap side up. That'll keep the contents inside.'

Hillary did so. Nothing flashed, banged, or shot out at her, hissing. She peered cautiously between the two sides of the envelope, then reached in and drew out an old-fashioned jewellery box.

She opened it.

Inside, was a pretty, antique pendant of two love-hearts joined together by an arrow. Over her shoulder, Steven looked at it grimly.

'Any message?' There was: in the envelope, obviously computer printed:

From Lol.

'Well, that gives us something to play with, at any rate,' Steven said, trying to keep the mood upbeat. 'First thing in the morning, Rhumer can start trying to trace that.' He nodded down at the pendant.

Hillary shuddered, snapped the lid shut and handed it over.

'What say we finish off that bottle of wine and go to bed?' she asked savagely.

Wordlessly, Steven reached an arm around her and held her close. He kissed the side of her neck. 'Now that's an offer no man in his right mind would refuse.' After a tense second, Hillary Greene smiled.

FOUR

THE NEXT DAY, Hillary got in to work early. She'd slept badly again, and once the sky began to get light just after 4.30, she'd left Steven sleeping in their narrow fold-out bed and had spent the next few hours going through Geoff Rhumer's list. She paid special attention to those men he had highlighted as having worked in either MisPer or on sex-crime cases involving rape or sexual attacks on women.

A lot of the names were familiar to her for one reason or another, of course. She had worked out of the HQ at Kidlington for most of her working life, and during the years, she'd come across many of the men named. Those she knew, she put a small neat asterisk by the name and a number, and on a separate page wrote out anything and everything she knew about the man, both from her own personal knowledge, or from what she'd heard about them through the general scuttlebutt on the grapevine.

Some she recalled simply for winning football or rugby matches and being a minor celebrity for a week, whilst others had a rep for being a bit of a lad with the ladies, or the horses, or the booze. A lot had worked on some of her cases where she had needed extra manpower doing the scut-work and labour-intensive jobs that higher-ranking members of her team wouldn't have had time for. She spent a lot of time mulling over those particularly, since it might have been possible that she'd inadvertently ticked them off or somehow got on their bad side, but she honestly couldn't recall a problem with any of them.

Of the others, some she knew to speak to, others just to nod to, others had names that recalled some incident, but not a face to go with them.

She made detailed notes of everything and anything she could remember, because when you were dealing with a crazy any detail might matter. And she knew that as well as DI Rhumer.

For all she knew, her stalker could have targeted her because she happened to beat him to a car space at HQ. She might not even have been aware that he'd been competing for the same space. Or she might have seen a group of men, and greeted one by name, and one of the others had felt slighted. Anything could set a crazy off.

But as she walked into HQ and sought out Rhumer in his office, she didn't hold out much hope for the list in her hands.

'Hello. Heard you had more contact last night.' Rhumer greeted her with a thoughtful smile, and she quickly filled him in on last night's events, although it was clear that he had already been briefed, probably by Steven.

'And here's your list,' she concluded, handing it over. 'As you'll see, I've made notes. But nothing stands out.'

Rhumer sighed and thanked her, and quickly began to glance through the lists. 'So, what's on your agenda today?'

Hillary smiled. 'Keep on plugging. I'm going to concentrate on Judy Yelland today, the first girl to go missing. There was no joy at all from her parents—and I mean that literally.'

Rhumer nodded. 'OK. Be careful,' he added, and grunted a short laugh as Hillary gave him a mocking look.

'Right. Grandmother. Suck eggs. Got it.'

'I'd still rather have my job than yours.' Hillary grinned, nodding at the long list of names. 'It'll take you and your team weeks to work through that lot.'

'Don't I know it,' Rhumer groaned. 'But we'll start with those both of us have marked, and who knows? We might just get lucky.' Hillary left him to it, thinking that they bloody well needed a bit of luck.

Geoff Rhumer reached for her list. Towards the bottom of the alphabetical list on the last page, was the name of Thomas Warrington. It was neither highlighted in Rhumer's yellow pen, nor did it have an asterisk with a corresponding note in Hillary's hand.

'TELL ME AGAIN who it is we're seeing?' Jimmy asked, as he headed towards the Glory Farm area of the market town of Bicester.

'Ruth Coombs. She was the friend of Judy Yelland who reported her missing,' Hillary said.

'Right, right, I remember. Didn't the chap who took the original report think that she might well have had something to do with the girl upping sticks in the first place?'

Hillary nodded. She'd re-read Judy Yelland's sparse file before collecting Jimmy for the off. 'Yes. He found her pushy and domineering. Reading between the lines, he had the feeling that she was the sort who liked to be boss, and even marked down in his notes that if Coombs had been his friend, he'd have done a runner too.'

Jimmy snorted. 'Sounds like we're in for a barrel of laughs then.'

Hillary nodded. 'It'll certainly be interesting to see if time's changed things any.'

'And besides, you always like to make your own judgement calls, right, guv.'

'Always, Jimmy.'

RUTH COOMBS WORKED in shop on a small industrial estate that specialized in selling camping and outdoor gear. They parked near a large stock of propane cylinders, Jimmy eyeing them warily as they passed.

'Had a bad experience with gas, Jimmy?' Hillary teased. Living on a boat, she was used to using gas cylinders for all her cooking and heating needs.

Jimmy grunted something dire about rather being electrocuted than being blown to bits, or burnt, as they pushed on into the shop. It had seen better days, and décor wasn't a particularly high priority, but at least it had several customers who were all shopping seriously. She supposed, in hard economic times, that cheap camping holidays were better than no holidays at all.

She waited to pass a man with an enormous beer belly who was stocking up on barbecue fuel. Given the vagaries of the great British summer, she had to admire his optimism if nothing else. When he moved to one side and they were able to get past, she headed for the only member of staff she could see in the place, a big-boned brunette serving behind the counter.

She held out her ID. 'Excuse me, I'd like to speak to a Miss Ruth Coombs. She does work here, I understand?'

'I'm Ruth,' the woman said at once. She turned and suddenly barked out, 'Hey, Joey, come out here a minute,

will you?' to someone out of sight behind the partition
walling behind her and a moment later a thin, bespec-
tacled man appeared. Ruth told him to mind the till,
and inclining her head imperiously for them to follow,
quickly led them round the back.

She was tall, and strode rather than walked. Jimmy
gave a mock Nazi salute to her back. She was wearing
a pale-blue nylon overall that was obviously the shop's
own uniform, and sneakers.

She led them to a cubby-hole that held a stockpile of
fire lighters, storage heaters and single gas rings. It also
boasted a kettle and a big tin of industrial-sized instant
coffee.

'Is this about Judy?' she asked flatly. From the file,
Hillary knew that Ruth Coombs was thirty-five years
old, but she looked marginally older than that, mostly
because her brown hair was already beginning to silver with grey. Her dark-brown eyes watched them with
a hard, steady glare that almost defied them to deny it.
'It has to be about Judy, right?' she asked, before either of them could say anything in response. 'There's
no other reason for the police to come calling. Not that I
expected anything from you people after all these years,'
she added, this time with obvious belligerence.

Hillary instantly understood the reason for it. 'I'm
sorry if you feel we've been failing to do our job, Miss
Coombs. I can assure you, Miss Yelland's case hasn't
been forgotten. The Crime Review Team periodically
reinvestigates cold cases,' she said, not quite accurately,
but definitely in no mood to give this hostile witness any
information about the current state of affairs.

Ruth Coombs sighed and leaned back against a chipped Formica work table.

'So, what can I do for you?'

'I don't suppose you've ever heard from Judy since you reported her missing?' Hillary began with the stock question.

Ruth snorted. 'Of course not. I'd have been back on to you lot like a shot if I had. I'm not stupid, so please don't treat me as if I am!'

'I can assure you that wasn't my intention,' Hillary said, responding to the other woman's heat with a cool, neutral tone. 'What can you tell me about Judy, and about what happened just before she went missing?'

Ruth looked at her steadily. 'OK. Fair enough. But I can tell you right now, the same thing as I said before: Christopher Deakin is behind it all.'

Hillary nodded. 'This was Judy's boyfriend at the time. You told the DC in Missing Persons that you thought he was acting suspiciously.'

Ruth flushed. She had an odd sort of face—at times she looked attractive, and at other times she looked downright plain. Now her eyes began to glitter, and the heightened colour made her look suddenly vivacious. Hillary wondered, suddenly, whether Ruth was single or living with someone.

'Before Judy went missing, I know they'd been having some rows,' Ruth said, her voice once more belligerent, as if she was expecting Hillary to call her a liar.

'They'd been seeing each other for some time?'

'About a year. He was married, of course, still is, but that didn't stop him. Or her, for that matter.' Hillary caught a whiff of something besides a bad attitude in the woman's voice. Pain perhaps? Spite? Obsessive, at any rate. It was definitely something interesting.

'You didn't approve?' she asked guilelessly.

'If a man doesn't intend to be faithful, he shouldn't get married,' Ruth said flatly, crossing her arms across her ample chest. She shot Jimmy a sour look, but Jimmy had far more sense than to look up from his notebook let alone make a comment.

Hillary thought that although Ruth's simplistic views were obviously heartfelt, she must have led a somewhat sheltered life if she thought them universal. Once more she wondered about the state of Ruth Coombs's love life.

Closet gay? Had she, in fact, been in love with Judy? Or was it thoughts of Christopher Deakin that made her face flush with heat? And, if so, had she been jealous of her friend?

'I understand you told the constable in Missing Persons that Judy had complained of a stalker?'

Ruth nodded reluctantly. 'Some guy was sending her flowers and cards and what have you. Making nuisance phone calls. Judy had just changed her number.'

'She never said who it was?'

'She didn't know. It wouldn't surprise me if it wasn't Christopher's wife playing games.'

Hillary blinked. 'Mrs Deakin knew about her husband's affair with Judy?' she asked sharply.

Ruth's glaring gaze faltered slightly. 'Judy didn't think so,' she admitted, grudgingly. 'She was convinced that they'd kept it all such a secret. Who knows, perhaps it was Chris himself who was doing it.'

'Why would he do that?' Hillary asked, confused. She was finding it hard to follow the younger woman's thought processes.

Ruth sighed. 'I don't know. It was all a mess between Judy and Chris, I know that. Love's young dream wasn't all that dreamy any more, that's all I know. And then, out of the blue, Judy just vanished into thin air.' Ruth's glare was now back. 'You tell me that that was all a co-incidence.'

Hillary nodded slowly. 'When was the last time that you saw her?'

'I already went through this. Judy came over the night before for a drink and to talk about Chris, and moan about her life, and how she needed her life to change. She went to work the next day, because I went to the shoe shop when I didn't hear from her, and her boss there said she went to work in the morning, but didn't come back from her lunch break. I think she went to meet Chris and he did something to her.'

'That's a serious allegation, Miss Coombs.'

Ruth shrugged. 'I call it like I see it. I never liked or trusted Christopher Deakin,' she added, far too ada-mantly.

No, but you wanted him, Hillary added silently. Call it a hunch, or a copper's instinct, or sheer feminine intu-ition, but she was willing to bet there and then that was at the root of this woman's angst. And still was. Had she kept in contact with Deakin? Somehow, Hillary thought that she had. Had she tried to take up where Judith Yel-land had left off?

But even if she had, could it have had anything to do with Judy's disappearance?

Then she gave herself a mental head slap. Of course it didn't. As interesting as all this was, even if some sort of twisted love triangle had existed between Judy, Ruth, and Christopher Deakin, it was Judy's unknown stalker they needed to find.

'Did Judy ever mention seeing a man following her perhaps?' she asked hopefully.

'No,' Ruth said flatly.

'You said he made nuisance phone calls. Did Judy ever tape them to take to the police, or did you ever answer the phone when you were around her place, and hear his voice yourself?'

'Sorry, no.'

'Did Miss Yelland keep the cards and envelopes they came in?'

'No, she binned them the moment they arrived.'

Hillary sighed. 'All right. Well, thank you, Miss Coombs. If we think of anything else we might need from you, we'll get in touch.'

'Huh. I shan't hold my breath,' Ruth Coombs said flatly.

Back at the car, Jimmy grinned at her over the roof. 'Well, guv, I reckon the original flatfoot had it right: if you had a friend like that, wouldn't you do a runner?'

Hillary smiled wryly.

'Did you get the distinct impression that she wanted Judy's boyfriend for herself?'

'Hell yes, guv. Talk about a frustrated man-eater.'

Hillary shook her head wearily. 'This case has got more twists and turns in it than a game of snakes and ladders.'

'Where to next, guv? This Deakin guy?'

'Might as well,' Hillary said. 'He might have a better angle on his girlfriend's stalker. You can see why she wouldn't confide in our Miss Coombs, but a girl might well cry on her boyfriend's shoulder. Perhaps she did catch a glimpse of our man, and told him all about it.'

Jimmy snorted. 'If she did, he never came forward and told us about it when she went missing,' he pointed out.

'He's married, remember?' Hillary said sardonically.

CHRISTOPHER DEAKIN, ACCORDING to all that Vivienne had been able to dig up on him when she could spare the time, was thirty-three years old, married to a woman named Portia, and had twin boys, now aged eight. Hillary wasn't surprised to note that it was the wife who had the money. With a name like that, it was almost inevitable. But to give Deakin his due, although he'd started out life on a council estate in Milton Keynes, he had successfully managed all of his wife's money, a portion of which he'd invested in setting up his own business, a small television production company. According to the taxman and various other financial sources, the company was moderately and steadily in profit.

Specializing mainly in producing television adverts and news/documentary segments for local television, they had their offices not far from the BBC office building on the Banbury Road in Oxford.

Once they'd found it, this small slice of the so-called glamorous world of show biz turned out to be a rather nondescript yellow-brick, two-storey building with a small car-park and a view of a rather scrappy rugby field. But the grounds of the building itself were well maintained and the interior was clean, freshly painted in pale apricot and populated with helpful staff.

Within five minutes they were ushered into the office of the man himself.

Christopher Deakin was a touch over six feet tall, with

very short blond hair and hazel eyes. He was lanky, but wore a good suit that did much to make him look elegant. He wore a plain watch and tie. He was good-looking in a Daniel Craig sort of way—with a touch of the rough-hewn about him that gave him a certain distinction. Hillary could see why Judy, his wife, and Ruth Coombs had all fallen for him.

He smiled at her a shade uncertainly however, and her first instinct was that here was a man made of straw, rather than steel.

'Hello. You're the police, Lizzie said?' he asked, half-rising from behind his desk but then subsiding again as Hillary waved him back down. She flashed her ID, introduced herself and Jimmy and gave the usual spiel.

Christopher Deakin paled visibly at the mention of Judy's name, and nervously readjusted his tie. Until then, Hillary thought that nobody ever did that, outside of bad television shows and old-fashioned crime novels.

Deakin managed to give them a shaky smile. 'Please, sit down. I'll make no bones about it, hearing Judy's name again after all this time has shaken me up a bit.' Hillary nodded, unimpressed. No doubt he was well aware that he'd given himself away, so becoming open and honest all of a sudden was probably a good move on his part.

'You were having an affair with her, Mr Deakin?' she asked, almost casually but stating it as a fact. She had the feeling that if she gave him just a little leeway he'd instantly start trying to justify himself or explain how nothing could possibly be his fault, and she just wasn't in the mood for a whining display.

Christopher winced a little, then took a deep breath

and nodded. 'Yes,' he confessed. 'You've been speaking to Ruth, I imagine,' he said, with a sad, small smile.

'You were still seeing her when she went missing, in fact?' Hillary clarified, not wanting to get to the Ruth Coombs conundrum just yet.

'Yes.'

'But you didn't come forward.'

'There wasn't really an investigation, was there? I mean, nobody from the police called on me. And the first I heard about Judy being reported missing was when Ruth called, demanding to know where she was.' Christopher sighed heavily and swung slightly to and fro on his black leather swivel chair. It was a subconsciously childish gesture that sat oddly on a grown man.

'At first, I thought it was Ruth typically over-reacting. I kept expecting Judy to get in touch.'

'But she never did,' Hillary finished for him flatly.

'No.'

'And still you didn't come forward.' Christopher held out his hands, fingers widespread in the universally what-can-you-do gesture. Hillary noticed his hands were clean and well kept, and that he'd had a recent manicure.

'What was the point? I didn't know where she'd gone.'

'Did your wife know about her, Mr Deakin?' Again, the television producer went distinctly pale.

'Portia? Good grief, no,' he said fervently.

No bonuses for guessing who wore the trousers in that relationship, Hillary thought wryly. Then gave herself a quick admonishment. She was not here to score points off this man—just find out what he knew. She deliberately let her voice become softer and a shade more coaxing. This, she was sure, was the best way to handle the likes of Christopher Deakin.

'Can you tell me how you and Judy met?' She smiled gently.

'We met at a party, actually,' Deakin said, relaxing a little. 'A friend of a friend was holding a big barbecue and Judy was helping out with the serving. She did odd jobs at weekends to get more money—she didn't particularly like her job at the shoe shop; she didn't particularly get on well with the manager and she was always complaining that she was on minimum wage. So she was always on the lookout for ways to earn some extra cash.'

'And you hit it off over the hot dogs, so to speak,' Hillary said, with another encouraging smile. She felt a bit like a primary schoolteacher egging on a slightly backward pupil.

'Yes. She was one of these people who seemed really sunny and friendly, you know? Uncomplicated. She was pretty too, and…my wife can be rather…. Oh hell, I'm not going to go into the whole my-wife-doesn't-understand-me cliché. Let's just say, we met at a time when I was feeling needy.'

Hillary nodded. Something told her that this man was always going to be needy. 'You'd been seeing each other some time, I understand.'

'Oh not so long.'

'Ruth said it was nearly a year,' Hillary said, with just a hint of reprimand in her voice. She was not surprised when he responded instantly.

Christopher blinked and quickly backtracked. 'Was it really that long? Yes. I suppose it was, now that I think about it.'

Hillary smiled gently. 'A year is a long time for a young woman in love, Mr Deakin. After a year, they start to assume things. Did Judy ask you to leave your wife, for instance?'

'No, never,' Christopher said at once, looking truly alarmed now. 'She knew the boys were too young and that they needed both their parents. Judy said that she knew what it was like not to have a good home life. She didn't seem to have got on with her own family, and the last thing she wanted to do was split up mine.' He was leaning forward in his chair now, his elbows on the table in his urgency to get his point across. 'You don't understand how it was between us at all if you think that's the sort of relationship we had. It was nothing like that. She wasn't some demanding bimbo or home wrecker. We were good together, honestly we were.' His voice level had risen by both a decibel and an octave by the time he'd finished.

'OK, OK, I understand,' she said soothingly. 'Did Judy ever mention having a stalker?'

Deakin hesitated for a fraction of a second, then said, 'No.' A lie. Interesting.

'Did she ever give you the impression that she was in trouble? That she was feeling suicidal maybe?'

'No!' Deakin said, sounding honestly shocked now.

'Do you have any idea where Judy might have gone? Did she mention friends, or people abroad maybe, anywhere she might go if she just wanted to get away for a while?'

'No. I thought about it, of course I did. I thought of nothing else for weeks—well, both Ruth and I put our heads together to try and think where she might have gone, but neither of us could come up with anything.'

'It sounds as if you and Miss Coombs were united in your worry for her.'

Christopher shifted uneasily on his chair. 'Yes. We were.'

'Are you still in contact with Ruth Coombs, Mr Deakin?' she asked casually.

Christopher shot her a quick look. 'Not really. Why do you ask?'

Hillary smiled neutrally. 'When we talked to her, she seemed to find you a fascinating subject.' Deakin again went pale. Hillary was beginning to find it a very interesting phenomenon with this excitable, weak but attractive man.

'Oh, that's just Ruth,' he said, with a brief, somewhat pitifully false laugh.

'I found her rather....' Hillary paused, let the silence deliberately lengthen just enough to get him nervous again, and finished quietly, 'Well, let's just say that I thought she had a forceful personality.' She baited the hook carefully and waited to see if he'd bite.

'Ruth?' Deakin said casually. 'Oh, Ruth's all right. She was Judy's best friend.'

'So you had no trouble with her?' Hillary asked curiously.

Again Deakin gave a brief laugh. 'No. Why should I?' Another lie. But why was he going out of his way to protect Ruth?

'All right, Mr Deakin. If you can think of anything that can help, please contact us.' She handed him one of her cards, and rose.

Christopher looked pathetically grateful to see the back of them and leapt off the chair eagerly to escort them to the door. Hillary said nothing until they were out of the building and heading across the car-park.

'That guy made a cat on a hot tin roof look like positively laid back, guv,' Jimmy snorted, the moment the electronic doors swooshed shut behind them.

'He *was* all over the place, wasn't he?' Hillary agreed.

'And he was lying nearly fifty per cent of the time,' Jimmy added darkly.

'Yes. But didn't you find the lies far more interesting than the truth?'

Jimmy grunted. 'He knew about the stalker.'

'But why deny it? Surely if your girlfriend goes missing, and you're a married man and the police come a-calling, you would want to emphasize the fact that there were other suspects out there,' Hillary said. 'So either he's got no sense of self-preservation—or something else scares him more than we do.'

'That'd be Mrs Deakin, guv. If they divorce, she'd have the kids and take her dough with her.'

'Hmm. Maybe. But that still doesn't explain why he kept quiet about the stalker.'

'I reckon he just wants the investigation to go away. I mean, the more we dig into Judy's life the more likely it is something will come to the ears of his missus.'

'Yes, it could be that. He struck me as the kind of man who'd do anything to avoid something unpleasant, rather than tackle it head on and get it over with. And he does seem to be the ostrich type anyway.'

'Huh? Oh, burying his head in the sand, you mean? Yeah. He doesn't have a lot of backbone does he?' Jimmy said with a touch of contempt.

'That might also explain why he wanted us to think that everything was hunky-dory between him and Ruth Coombs,' Hillary mused out loud. 'But he has to have known that Ruth suspected him in Judy's disappearance. And a man would have to be blind and deaf not to pick up on the vibes she was giving out. He has to know Ruth's got some serious hang-ups about him. What's more, it wouldn't surprise me if she hadn't kept in touch all this time. Maybe even did a bit of stalking of her own.' For a moment, as Jimmy searched his pockets for his car keys the two of them thought about that little scenario.

'But he wouldn't want to rock the boat, would he? If he complained about Ruth to us,' Jimmy pointed out, 'we'd be obliged to do something about it and again, the missus might get to hear about it, and wonder. And then there's the chance that Ruth could go postal in which case the whole Judy/Christopher lovey-dovey connection comes to light and lover boy's out on his ear.'

Hillary sighed. 'You know, there's something about Mr Deakin that makes my whiskers twitch. If it wasn't for the fact that we know it's the stalker we're after, I'd set the kids on to delving into our Mr Deakin's activities like a flash.'

'He was twitchy all right,' Jimmy agreed thoughtfully. Then he sighed. 'Bloody hell, guv, you've got me doing it now.'

'Doing what?'

'Thinking that this case is going all screwy on us.' He unlocked the doors and they slipped inside Jimmy's car. Hillary felt her hand wandering up to caress the fading scars on her neck and abruptly snatched her hand back down and into her lap.

'Back to HQ, Jimmy,' she said flatly. 'I need to re-read the notes and try to get an overview on this case before it runs away from me completely.'

Jimmy grinned. 'It wouldn't dare, guv,' he said confidently. Hillary only wished that she could feel the same amount of confidence.

IT WAS NEARLY four o'clock, and Hillary was starting to see double. She'd read and reread all the case files until she was sure she could quote the damn things from memory.

But nothing was gelling. The stalker was still a phantom figure about as real as a handful of smoke. All three girls seemed so different in their personalities and background. Even the circumstances of their disappearances didn't really seem to hang together. Gilly Tinkerton, a scatter-brained, hippy type whose own loving mother wasn't that particularly worried about her. Meg Vickary, ambitious, maybe a man-teaser with an eye to the main chance. And Judy, who'd grown up in a frigid family unit and had turned to a man of straw for comfort. As a group, they just made no sense. What was it about them that attracted the same stalker? Weren't they supposed to go for a certain type—a look, or a commonly shared pathology?

Although she didn't set much store by profilers and shrinks in general, she supposed gloomily that at some point she was going to have to go to the man Geoff Rhumer was using and ask for his input. But that was for another day. Knowing shrinks, he'd take one look at her scars and start trying to get her to 'emote' about that day in the car-park. And she wanted to do that about as much as she wanted to watch her toenails atrophy.

She sighed, and reached for Judy Yelland's file again, reading the initial reports. The WPC who'd called on the Yellands had had her head screwed on right, and had nailed the atmosphere of the place perfectly. WPC Mandy Dern. Hillary stared down approvingly at her neatly written notes and suddenly realized that she'd seen that writing before. She quickly checked the other files.

Not Meg Vickary—yes. She'd been the one to investigate the original Gillian Tinkerton case.

She re-read the WPC's notes on Mrs Tinkerton and nodded in vindication. Once again, WPC Dern had hit the nail on the head. It might be a good idea to catch up with WPC Dern and see what she could remember about the two cases.

Reading between the lines, it was clear to Hillary that although WPC Dern hadn't been surprised at Judy Yelland walking away from her old life, she'd been a little more worried over Gillian's defection, although she'd been reassured by Mrs Tinkerton's belief that she'd just gone 'gad about' as Deirdre Tinkerton had put it.

Hillary was just about to call it a day, and was actually bending down to retrieve her handbag from the bottom drawer of her desk, when something tugged so hard in the back of her mind, that it had the physical result of shooting her upright on her chair again.

What was it?

WPC Dern. And something Deirdre Tinkerton had said. Hillary sat very still and ran her mind back over her time at the Tinkerton household. What? What had she said…? Something about Sam Pickles being handsome. No, that didn't make sense.

Yes. Yes it did.

Instantly she was back in the kitchen with Deirdre Tinkerton making her rhubarb pies. And Deirdre saying something about that nice young man who had come the first time to ask about Gilly.

Quickly, Hillary snatched the Tinkerton file and riffled through it. No, she was right—WPC Mandy Dern had been the only officer assigned to do the rounds of people who knew Gillian Tinkerton. Which made sense:

WPC Dern had worked MisPer for nearly eight years now. So even back then, she'd have been an experienced hand for her sergeant to employ and on low-priority cases like missing adults, they wouldn't have assigned more than one person anyway.

So who was the 'nice young man' who'd gone calling on Mrs Tinkerton?

Her heart pounding, Hillary got through to MisPer, and spoke to the case officer. He had to call up the details on his computer of course, but he quickly confirmed what she already knew. No male PC had been sent out to interview Mrs Tinkerton. Hillary thanked him and hung up.

Her eyes shining brightly for the first time in weeks, she grabbed the case files and hot-footed to Steven's office.

Was it possible that they'd caught a break? Had Lol finally made the mistake of coming out of the woodwork far enough for them to catch a real glimpse of him at last?

FIVE

STEVEN LOOKED UP as Hillary knocked and came into his office. His spirits did that little 'lifting' thing that they did whenever he saw her. And he had to admit, it was slightly alarming. Since he and Maureen had divorced, there'd been other women of course, and, like all men, who'd once been married and then found himself unexpectedly free, he'd enjoyed a few years when it seemed that his youth had been returned to him.

But the novelty had long since worn off. With a nineteen-year-old son at university, and a seventeen-year-old daughter still living with her mother, he now considered himself to be both experienced and battle-hardened when it came to managing his love life. In recent years, his encounters with women had been few and far between, and not particularly successful.

And then Hillary Greene had been forced upon him professionally, and the next thing he knew he found himself feeling just a little bit giddy whenever she was near.

Just what the *hell* was all that about?

He tensed, and all personal worries were subsumed as he noticed the tight, expressionless look on her face. It was a look that he had learned from sometimes bitter experience that she used as a mask to cover some strong emotion. One quick look at her glittering eyes told him that this time it was either fury or excitement.

'I think the bastard might have shown his hand,' she said, in response to his questioning look.

Instantly he sat up straighter. 'How?' She placed two files down in front of him, pointing out the reports from WPC Dern. Quickly, she went through the salient points with him.

'So if WPC Dern was the only one from MisPer to talk to both Judy Yelland and Gillian Tinkerton's family, who is this "handsome nice young man" Deirdre Tinkerton was talking about?'

'You think it might be her stalker?' Steven said. 'Taking a bit of a risk, isn't he?' he asked, knowing that one of his key roles in their professional life was playing devil's advocate.

'We know he likes to take a certain amount of those,' she pointed out bitterly. 'Maybe he's the kind who just can't help but play games,' she concluded. 'I need to get back to Deirdre Tinkerton and get more details.'

'Whoa!' Steven said, knowing that she was not going to like what he said next but determined to say it nevertheless. 'You mean we need to fill Geoff Rhumer in on this, and *he* needs to get over there and see if Mrs Tinkerton can come up with a photo-fit. Better yet, he can gather together photos of his top twenty list of suspects and see if she can pick him out. Tracking down the stalker is his priority, remember. Getting leads on his victims is your job.' Hillary opened her mouth to argue, caught his eye, and quickly snapped her mouth shut again. She hated it when he pulled rank on her, but, at the same time, she found it as sexy as hell.

'Yes, sir,' she snapped.

Steven's dark-brown eyes flared. Damn it, he hated it when she 'sirred' him, but it made him go hot all over.

'Glad we got that sorted then,' he said, with a sweet smile.

Hillary smiled back just as sweetly. 'I'll get on with interviewing Gillian's sister then, sir,' she said smartly, and before he could issue her with any more smart-arse orders, she turned on her heel and left. Her back was ramrod stiff.

Steven, robbed of the last word, watched her go. Then he had to smile. Tonight was certainly going to be interesting.

TOM WARRINGTON DROVE his car down a deserted and ever-decreasing farm track until it ended in the traditional wooden five-barred gate. There he parked and walked across the field to his copse. He'd known the landowner since he was a small boy, when he'd first discovered the small area of slightly boggy land in the dip of a field where some scrubby bushes had helped to make a wonderful den.

Since then, he'd made the place his own in a far more interesting way. The farmer, fed up with having his farming equipment stolen, and even some of his sheep rustled, had no objection to a uniformed copper being seen every so often walking across his land, and he had no objection to Tom planting some silver birches in the copse. The land was too boggy to plough, and he'd taken Tom at his word when he said he liked to go there to bird-watch and chill out.

Now, as Tom walked across the field, a portable battery-powered laptop in one hand, he felt his mood change.

It always did when he came to visit his girls.

He pushed his way into the green, cool space, listening to the birds twitter in agitation in the elder bushes. He ignored them and sat on the driest part of the small copse, on a mossy bank.

He patted the ground under one of the weeping willows.

'Hello, ladies. I'm back. You know I never forget to come and visit.' He imagined them all as if they were lying around him, sleeping. Or maybe sunbathing. All smiling at him.

He sighed, and opened up his laptop.

He stared at the blank screen and took several deep breaths. He knew Hillary was under constant observation now. Both that old-timer she went around with, Jimmy Jessop, and that lanky sandy-haired boy Sam Pickles were taking it in turns watching her boat, as were a handful of other old men and some of DI Geoff Rhumer's team.

It was frustrating, but understandable, and he tried not to let it get to him.

Tom had taken special note of Rhumer, he had done so ever since Vivienne had told him about the new mysterious DI who had so many conferences with Hillary and that waste of space Crayle, and he had to admit to feeling rather insulted at the quality of the man they'd put on his trail.

He'd done some careful digging into his background. Once again, volunteering to work Records and Admin had paid off, and he'd been able to research quite a bit about Rhumer on the QT. The man was strictly a second-rater. He'd made no big mistakes in his career, but then again, he'd busted no big cases either. He was a plodder. A reliable pair of hands.

Tom had, at first, been inclined to take it personally.

Then, after thinking about it for a while, he'd understood what had happened, and he began to feel much more cheerful about it. It was Hillary's doing, of course—what else could it be? Since she was so tight with Marcus Donleavy, the commander was bound to have let her pick whoever she wanted to be on her team, which meant she'd chosen Rhumer on purpose. After only a few seconds Tom could see her reasoning.

Rhumer was a nothing and a nobody, which is just what she wanted—someone who'd never be able to keep up or give them any bother. A high-flier might spoil their fun and get in their way. But the likes of Geoff Rhumer she could handle with one hand tied behind her back.

It was just like her to be one step ahead of everybody else. But he mustn't let her think she could do the same with him. As delicious as it was to play the game with her, he had to make sure she never gained the upper hand.

Now he smiled as he began to type.

My wonderful darling Hillary
When are you going to get rid of all your body-
guards? Don't you know I long to guard your body
myself? But don't worry—we'll meet again soon.
I know you're busy right now (and I hope you're
having fun playing with the presents I gave you)
but don't forget about me, will you?
All my love, forever. Lol.'

He smiled and saved the missive. Later he would print it out then take it to the centre of Oxford and post it. It wouldn't do to send it electronically—she worked for the CRT, where modern technology ruled. They'd be on to him like a shot, no matter how clever he was. Besides, he rather liked courting her the old-fashioned way and he was sure she'd appreciate it.

He sighed and stretched, then got up and looked around at the young silver birches he'd planted. 'Don't worry, ladies, I'll be back to see you soon,' he promised them.

He left the copse and drove back towards HQ reluctantly. The dragon in the office would notice if he was late, and she was an annoyance who was beginning to irritate him almost as much as that silly little twit, Vivienne Tyrell.

Perhaps, one day, he'd remove the officious clerk from the world as well, just so that he could have the relief of not having to see her pinched, middle-aged face looking disapprovingly at her watch whenever he came into the office. Or maybe not. Perhaps that would just be petty, and spoil it all. He had, after all, his standards to maintain. And he didn't think Hillary would approve of him indulging himself by simply knocking off annoying, pointless people.

She had more class than that.

And she would be right: it was a little tacky, after all.

HILLARY MADE AN appointment to call on Gillian Tinkerton's sister later that day. Sitting in her office, feeling restless and mentally calling Steven Crayle all the nasty names she could think of, she couldn't help but wonder how Geoff Rhumer was getting on.

He'd be with Mrs Tinkerton by now surely? What was she saying? Did she remember her caller clearly? It had been years ago now and she knew from experience just how unobservant most people were unless they were the sort who were good with faces. Just how visual was her memory? The thought that she might soon have a face to put to her enemy was making her itch.

She had Rhumer's mobile phone number so she could easily call him. She had the phone almost in her hand when she realized what she was doing and stopped herself. She knew how annoyed she'd be if some other officer kept looking over her shoulder all the time she was trying to do her job, and demanding to be kept up to date. Rhumer would quite likely tell her to sod off and let him get on with it. And who could blame him?

She put the phone away and sighed, rubbing her hand over her neck. The scars were healing, weren't they? Catching herself obsessing about those marks on her neck yet again, she snatched her hands away and gave herself a firm mental head-slap and grabbed the first folder on her desk.

It happened to be Meg Vickary's.

Right. Time to talk to Meg's boss, the much married Marcus Kane. It would be interesting to see what his take on their affair was, and if it matched the account Georgia Biggs had given them. Somehow she rather doubted it. Cheating husbands, in her experience, tended to be good at justifying their actions and sugar-coating even the most unpalatable pill.

She grabbed her bag and decided for once to leave Jimmy behind. If Marcus was a woman's sort of man—and he sounded as if he might be—he might respond better to talking to a woman on her own.

She quickly checked her appearance in the ladies loo. She was wearing a white skirt and a white and orange floaty-type blouse. Her rich chestnut-coloured bob had been recently trimmed and highlighted at the hairdresser and she looked good. She'd kept off the weight, and her figure looked as trim as it had done in years. Although she kept her make-up to a minimum she knew she wasn't being particularly vain in thinking that nobody would put her age at fifty.

She also knew that a lot of her new found 'glow' could be laid at the door of a certain sexy, elegant superintendent. Damn, he could be so infuriating at times. Being her boss and having a certain amount of power over her was an added aphrodisiac that she could do without. The man got under her skin easily enough as it was, without having that added advantage.

She wondered if he'd be coming over to stay, and hoped that he was. She was beginning to need his arms around her at night.

Then she gave herself another, even harder, mental head slap for mooning about like a silly little girl. She was fifty, for pete's sake, not fifteen.

Grumbling, furious with herself, she stalked across the car-park towards Puff.

She didn't notice the well-built young man with cat-green eyes watch her go past, a man who was instantly intrigued by her tense, angry energy. Nor did she notice the yearning in his body language as he fought the urge to follow her.

He was standing too far away to draw her attention, but Tom Warrington knew that he could cover the distance between them within a matter of seconds. For once she was on her own, without either Jimmy or Steven Crayle by her side. But it was too risky here.

His fists clenched with the effort it took him to force himself to keep on moving towards the entrance to the HQ.

What a tease she was. She didn't even give him so much as a glance! But she must feel his presence. She must know what she was doing to him.

Then he smiled. Bloody hell, she was good at this game. She had him tied up in delicious knots without so much as lifting a finger.

He went on into admin, breathing heavily and carefully avoiding the civilian clerk. At the first opportunity he would print off his letter to her. She would read it soon. He hoped the words would keep her awake at night.

As Hillary drove away to talk to a cheating husband, Tom Warrington began to hum softly to himself.

He wondered what he could do next to impress her.

HILLARY WALKED ALONE along the Summertown pavements, doing her best to avoid the usual tourists and students who always seemed to be clogging Oxford's streets, but, as she made her way towards the offices of the upmarket solicitor's office, she felt unusually lethargic which couldn't entirely be put down to the spell of hot weather.

She was not sleeping properly for a start. Even worse, she was beginning to feel as if this case was getting the upper hand. She just couldn't seem to get the proper grip on it that it needed. It had never happened to her before and she didn't like it.

Had she lost her nerve?

When she'd been attacked, it had scared her, left her bleeding and in a state of shock. But that hadn't worried her—she was human, not some magazine super-hero creation. If you were cut with a blade, you went into shock and had nightmares about it. That she could deal with.

She'd returned to work as soon as she could, and she had more or less twisted Marcus Donleavy's arm into letting her work at least on the periphery of the stalker case. She had, in fact, got back on the horse after being thrown, like a good little girl.

But could she ride the damn horse now that she was on it? That was what was really giving her nightmares. Or had she let that bastard win?

Feeling vaguely depressed, she entered the offices

of the law firm where Meg Vickary had last been seen alive and well.

Marcus Kane kept her waiting, which exacerbated her already bad mood. But, as she listlessly scanned a *Homes & Gardens* magazine in the swish waiting room, she tried to be philosophical about it. It was only to be expected, after all. He was telling her that big, bad solicitors such as himself had nothing to fear from the police. In fact, he probably regularly dined on the constabulary for breakfast.

He was also making the point of just how valuable his time was, whilst she could presumably waste hers willy nilly. The me-big-important man, you little-nobody was a ploy that was old as the hills, and had been used against her so often that it now barely registered on her psyche.

But maybe he was also informing her, and not so very subtly at that, just how unimportant Meg Vickary was to him as well? Because Hillary had made a point of telling his secretary just what her visit was all about.

Either way, when she was finally shown into his office, she was in no mood to take prisoners, and she moved with her most graceful sway. Her smile was strictly one of her feminine best.

The man who was rising from behind his desk to greet her was of medium height, with dark hair and blue eyes. She knew from Sam's notes that he was forty-seven years old, and had been married for nearly twenty years to the very rich, senior partner's only daughter. They had no children. She had assumed that was Mrs Kane's choice, or was maybe down to a medical problem of some sort, because she rather thought that a man like this *would* have wanted to have children, if only to reinforce his power base. A woman with children was far more likely to look the other way when it came to marital infidelity, because she'd be far less willing to seek a divorce. Also, producing grandchildren for the powerful senior partner would have earned him extra brownie points. Or perhaps they were just one of the growing number of couples who had chosen to enjoy their youth for as long as possible and have children at the last minute.

As expected, Marcus Kane's blue eyes widened just slightly as they took her in, and a definitely interested look crossed his handsome face but was quickly suborned. No doubt even Marcus Kane's libido could be held in check by the knowledge that she represented the police.

She showed him her ID, and briefly explained her civilian status and the work she did for the Crime Review Team.

'Yes, Jenny said this was about Meg,' Marcus acknowledged, waiting until she was sitting down in the chair opposite his desk before retaking his own seat.

'Jenny would be Meg's replacement, yes?' Hillary said, slipping in the knife right away, not wanting to give the slippery sod time to draw breath. 'No doubt that makes her even more curious about what happened to Meg,' she swept on with a charming smile. 'It can't be easy to step into the shoes of a woman who simply vanished.'

Marcus Kane's own charming smile tightened. 'I can't say as I ever thought about it like that,' he conceded.

'No? Your secretary goes missing and you don't give it much thought?'

'That's not what I said,' Marcus responded stiffly. 'Of course we were all concerned when Meg left.'

'But she didn't exactly leave, though, did she, Mr

Kane?' Hillary pointed out at once, not willing to let him get away with anything. He was desperately trying to keep this civilized, and to understate the seriousness of it, and she was damned well not going to let him. 'She didn't hand in her notice in the usual way, or tell anyone where she was going. She didn't pack a bag, cancel her milk, or withdraw any money from her bank. She just—poof!—vanished.' Marcus drew in a long slow breath.

'Yes. It certainly appeared to be a spur-of-the-moment thing.'

'Her flatmate reported her missing,' Hillary said, letting the intended criticism sit for a scant second, before sweeping on, 'so you weren't surprised when she didn't turn up for work one day as expected?'

'I assumed she was unwell, of course. What else was I to think?'

'Didn't she usually phone with the usual excuses whenever she threw a sickie?' Hillary asked innocently.

'Of course. I mean, not that she ever lied, I'm sure. That is, whenever she was off work, I'm sure it was because of genuine illness,' Marcus said, aware that he was stumbling over his words, and beginning to flush with anger. Words were his stock-in-trade after all, and dealing with intense, potentially dangerous situations was what he was paid well to deal with. He shouldn't be letting this bloody woman walk all over him like this.

He squared his shoulders. 'By the time I realized something untoward might have happened, I received a visit from a member of the Missing Persons department. It seems that her flatmate, as you said, had reported her missing. Naturally, everyone here in the office cooperated fully.'

Hillary nodded. 'Very commendable, sir, I'm sure,'

she said blandly. 'How long had you and Mrs Vickary been having a relationship?'

Marcus drew in a long, slow breath. 'As I told the constable at the time, the, er, affair between Margaret and myself wasn't that serious. And I would appreciate it if you didn't bandy that information about, Mrs Greene. I know it's been a long time now, but I would still rather my wife didn't get to hear about it.'

'Yes, sir, I'm sure you would,' Hillary said amiably. Now the bastard had called her *Mrs Greene* he had really put his foot in it. At some point she was going to call on Mrs Marcus Kane and have a really long chat with her.

'It would only upset her,' Marcus Kane stated, 'and, like I said, it was never serious between Meg and me.'

'Miss Biggs seemed to think that it was.'

'Who?'

'Meg's flatmate. Apparently Meg told her all about you. According to her, you and Meg were a very hot item indeed and deeply in love. In fact, Meg was just waiting for you to leave your wife.' Hillary gently cocked her head to one side. 'Is that true?' she asked, sweetly curious.

Marcus Kane began to sweat. 'Of course not! I think there must be some mistake. Either this Miss Biggs has got the wrong end of the stick or Meg herself seriously misunderstood the situation. And before you make any more snide comments,' Marcus rushed on, 'I can assure you that Meg wasn't the sort to misread anything. She was hardly a simpering, retiring wallflower, Mrs Greene. She was an experienced divorcee who knew exactly what she was doing, how to get what she wanted, and just how the land lay.'

Hillary looked at him for a moment or two in complete silence. 'So, the affair was strictly light and casual?'

'Absolutely.'

'You never intended to leave your wife, and Meg knew this?'

'Absolutely. She never asked me to leave my wife.' He looked at her so steadily and openly as he said this that Hillary knew at once that he was lying. Whenever anyone became so palpably honest, it always set her radar pinging.

'Of course she asked you to leave your wife, sir,' Hillary said amiably, making it a statement of fact, 'but I fully accept that you told her that such a move was out of the question.'

Marcus opened his mouth to deny it, then thought about it, and sighed. 'Look. I don't know why Meg upped and left in the way that she did; it certainly made a lot of trouble for me, I can tell you—which, knowing Meg, was probably the point. I don't know where she went, or who with, but I can assure you, I had absolutely nothing to do with her disappearance.'

Hillary nodded. 'Let's just get the facts straight, shall we, sir? Miss Biggs seemed to think that the relationship between you and her friend had soured somewhat, by the time Meg disappeared. Would you say that was true?'

Marcus shifted uncomfortably on his seat. 'I suppose you could say that the affair was coming to its natural end,' he conceded cautiously.

'And Meg wasn't happy with that?' Hillary asked sharply. Marcus Kane shrugged, a shade helplessly.

'A lot of women who start affairs aren't happy when they end. But, like I said, Meg was a big girl, and well able to take care of herself. I can assure you, I hardly

broke her heart and left her devastated. Meg was the sort
of woman who came armour-plated.'

Hillary nodded. She found it interesting that both Meg
Vickary's ex-husband, and her boss and ex-lover were
both singing from the same hymn sheet where Meg's personality was concerned. Was she really the hard-headed,
hard-hearted woman as they were both anxious to por-
tray her? Or did they both have guilty consciences that
made them want to remember her as being that way?

'Did Meg ever say anything about being stalked?'
Hillary asked abruptly.

Marcus looked genuinely surprised. 'What? No. Why?
Was someone bothering her? Oh hell, her body hasn't
been found has it? Has she been killed by someone?' He
was now quite pale.

But Hillary was wondering why it had taken him so
long to come to that conclusion. Surely hearing that the
police wanted to see him about a missing woman, he
would have jumped to that conclusion long before now?
He was a solicitor after all, and regularly came to the defence of criminals. He would know—and who better—
that many women were killed by the men in their lives.
And yet, for some reason, it had never occurred to him
that something like that had happened to his conspicu-
ously absent lover.

The fact that it hadn't, told her something unexpected:
either Marcus Kane was a superb actor, or there was
something about Meg herself, or Meg's disappearance,
that he knew and she didn't.

'No, sir, nothing like that has happened,' she said, realizing that he was staring at her and still waiting for an
answer to his question. 'But, surely, a man of your experience must have thought at some point the worst might

have happened? Unless you happen to know something that we don't?' And for the briefest of moments as she spoke, she saw something sly and secretive flash in those handsome baby-blues of his. Something that seemed to both amuse him, but worry him slightly as well.

Then the smiling, urbane solicitor was back.

'What? No, of course not. As I told you, I have no personal knowledge of where Meg is or why she left.' Hillary nodded slowly. Now he was hiding behind words—which was something of a stock-in-trade for people of his profession, she thought grimly. So he had 'no personal knowledge' of where she was or why she had left. That was a very careful phrase. He might not *know*, but she would have bet a substantial sum of money, that Marcus Kane could make a bloody good guess.

Or rather, that he *thought* he could.

But the truth was actually the other way around: *she* knew something that *he* didn't. *She* knew that an experienced stalker, who was almost certainly a killer, had sent Hillary Greene a wooden cross with Meg Vickary's initials on it, which meant that Meg Vickary, along with Judy Yelland and Gilly Tinkerton were almost certainly dead and long gone.

But clearly this man thought that something else entirely had happened to Meg Vickary. But what, and what had made him think so?

But did it really matter in the end, what it was that he thought?

Suddenly Hillary felt very tired. She'd got what she'd came for. She didn't think that Marcus Kane had had anything to do with Meg's disappearance, despite what Georgia Biggs had come to believe. More importantly, she was sure that this man was not her stalker. Or even had any idea that the stalker existed.

Hillary sighed. 'If you can think of anything else that might be relevant, please let me know, sir,' she said flatly, handing over one of her cards.

She saw the startled look in his eyes as he realized that the ordeal was suddenly and unexpectedly over, but couldn't even summon up the energy to feel smug.

For now, she would let Mr Marcus Kane keep his secrets. She couldn't see how they could possibly be important.

Later, she'd come to realize that she'd got that rather wrong.

GILLY TINKERTON'S SISTER Rebecca Frost, lived in a terraced row of neat cottages in the village of Woodeaton, not far from the Oxford suburb of Headington. Older than Gillian, she was married with four children, and when Hillary called on her at 4.30 that afternoon, she'd just completed the school run.

As she showed Hillary into a small parlour with an original fireplace and a large-screen HD television dominating one corner, she could hear youthful squeals coming from the slightly overgrown garden out the back.

'Sorry about the mess,' Rebecca said, bringing in a tray bearing a jug of lemonade and tall tumblers. Ice jangled deliciously against the glass. She was a short, dumpy woman who would obviously turn into a mirror image of her mother before she was much older. 'Lemonade?'

'Yes, please.' Hillary accepted a glass and took a long cool drink. As she did so, she noticed Rebecca glance at the scars on her throat and then look away.

'So, this is about Gilly?' Rebecca said with a bright

smile. 'Mum told me that you'd been round. She said there was nothing to worry about though. You haven't got any reason to think something has happened to Gilly, right?'

Hillary caught the anxiety in the tone and smiled, forcing back the usual feelings of guilt. 'We don't know for sure what has happened to Gillian, no,' she said, ironically aware that Marcus Kane wasn't the only one who could hide behind words.

'Do you share your mother's view that Gillian has just gone off somewhere?' she asked curiously.

'Oh heck, yes. We all think that—you'd have to know my sister to understand why. Believe me, I fully expect her to turn up for Christmas dinner one day, and wonder what all the fuss would be about when we demand to know where she's been for the last few years!'

Hillary nodded. 'I'm sorry, but that still seems to me to be somewhat off-the-wall, even for a so-called "free spirit". I didn't really like to ask your mother this, and I don't want to upset you, but would you say your sister might have some, er, mental issues?'

Rebecca laughed and poured herself a glass of lemonade. 'Do I think our Gilly's a bit doolally, do you mean?' she chuckled.

'Wouldn't be a bit surprised,' she added with total aplomb. 'But not in a needs-a-doctor kind of way. I don't think we're ever going to have to hand her over to the men in white coats or anything. She's always been able to look after herself, and she's totally harmless. She just dances to a slightly different tune to the rest of us, that's all.'

Hillary nodded. 'And you have no idea where she might have gone?'

'No. But I've been thinking about it, ever since Mum called, telling me you'd been to see her.' Rebecca got up and walked to a drawer set in a modern little desk, and withdrew a slip of paper. 'I don't know if this will help, but I've written down all the people Gilly was tight with, just before she upped and left. She always has what I would call fads though, which means that she really gets into something, then gets bored and moves on to something else. So there's no guarantee even if any of these people might have an idea about what she was going to do, that Gilly wouldn't have moved on again.'

'I understand,' Hillary said. 'So what kind of fads did she have?'

'Oh you know. The usual sort of modern-day hippy sort of thing.'

'Like joining up with the travelling community?' Hillary nodded.

'Right. Of course, Gilly's not really much of a gypsy at heart, so that didn't last,' Rebecca said with another gurgling laugh.

'She won't admit it, but she sort of likes being a homebody, like our Mum, but becoming a housewife or doing the whole mother thing is just too scary for her at the moment. She can't seem to grow up properly just yet, you know what I mean?' Hillary nodded and accepted the piece of paper Rebecca handed over. The list of names, a few with addresses or telephone numbers next to them, meant nothing to her.

'And these are?' she prompted.

'Oh, people Gilly was getting in tight with. All of them were into alternative lifestyles and advocating a different way of living or thinking. Some were into healing, laying on of hands, that sort of thing. I was a bit worried about them, in case they belonged to some sort of cult or something. That would be just the sort of thing Gilly might get sucked into. To be honest, that's what's been worrying me more than anything else,' Rebecca admitted reluctantly. 'That she might be living in some sort of weird religious commune and will end up a victim of mass suicide, like those sorts of things that happen in America from time to time.'

Hillary nodded. 'OK. It'll give my young colleagues back at Kidlington something to work on.' She smiled grimly as she imagined Vivienne complaining about having to track down and interview all of the people on the list. No doubt Sam would end up doing most of the work, but that was fine by Hillary.

At least she could trust Sam to do a proper job.

'Well, if you think of anything else, please let me know. I take it Gilly never mentioned her secret admirer to you?' Hillary added casually.

'Oh yeah, she did. But I don't think it came to anything. I mean, Gilly had her share of men friends, and she was a bit lax about that sort of thing. I don't think it bothered her much. He wasn't particularly creepy, I don't think. She never said that he was, anyway.'

Hillary blinked and thought about the wooden cross back at HQ with Gillian's initials burned into it. She swallowed hard, and forced herself to smile. 'OK. Well thanks very much for this,' she said, and waved the list of names in the air.

And then she left Rebecca Frost's cottage with a quick step, and a cold feeling in her heart.

SIX

THE NEXT DAY, Hillary picked up her mail from the pub and headed in to work. Living on a narrowboat could make such things as post problematical, but luckily, she had known the pub landlord for years, and he had no objection to being an unofficial mail drop. Since she was running a little late, she didn't stop to go through the envelopes then and there but drove into work, carrying the few bits and pieces in with her.

Last night's sparring with Steven had been interesting if nothing else, and this time, the fact that she still hadn't slept properly had a lot more to do with a certain superintendent than bad dreams about the man who had left the scars on her neck. Their occasional friction at work was definitely adding spice to their encounters in her tiny bedroom, and she was very much aware that she hadn't felt this good in years.

It worried her. Her disastrous marriage had left her very wary indeed of trusting any man. Nevertheless, she had been awake when Steven had left just after six, and had watched him dress with a certain amount of proprietary pride. He had a neat, elegant way about him that she found very attractive. And his gorgeous good looks didn't hurt, either. Sometimes she worried about the fact that he was a good few years younger than herself. At other times—and this morning had been one of them—she couldn't give a tinker's curse.

Now as she walked into HQ, still clutching her un-
opened mail, she gave the desk sergeant a bright smile
and headed down into the basement rabbit warren where
the CRT hung out.

She noticed in passing that the small communal office
was empty and checked her watch. She assumed Sam
was at uni, and had long since stopped trying to figure
out Vivienne Tyrell's working hours, but wondered what
had kept Jimmy.

She went to her own stationery cupboard, shrugging off
her jacket and settling behind her desk and pulled out her
notes. It was high time she got some sort of grip on this
case. Deliberately, she let her mind range over the three
victims, looking for anything that tugged at her radar.

Meg Vickary had been having an affair with a married man—her boss. So had Judy Yelland, although in
her case, Christopher Deakin had no connection to her
work place. So, was it possible that Gillian had also been
seeing a married man? Was that what set their killer off?
Was he punishing unfaithful women? Had his own marriage been wrecked by an affair? Or had his mummy
cheated on his daddy, thus giving the poor little dinkums
some sort of hang-up?

Hillary picked up the phone and called Rebecca Frost.

'Hello, Mrs Frost, it's Hillary Greene again. Sorry, I for-
got to ask you something about Gillian yesterday. Do you
know if your sister was or had been seeing a married man?'

'Bloody hell no,' Rebecca's voice responded em-
phatically in her ear. 'Gillian really hated cheaters. Our
brother went through hell with his first wife—he's long
since divorced the two-timing cow now, and is happily
married again to someone much better for him. But Gillian was what, fourteen, fifteen, when it happened, and

Gary was always her favourite, and it totally soured her against infidelity. I often think the reason she's leaving it so late to marry herself is because she can't take the risk it might happen to her. She'd rather cut off her own foot and eat it than look twice at a married man.'

'OK, thanks, I just needed to ask,' Hillary said with a sigh, and hung up. So scratch that idea then.

She glanced up as Steven knocked on the door and looked in. He smiled at her and she scowled back. 'Has Geoff Rhumer come up with anything from Deirdre Tinkerton?' she asked smartly.

Steven grinned. 'Good morning to you too, love-bunny.'

'Yeah, yeah, Tinkerton,' Hillary shot back, but her lips were twitching. 'And if you ever call me that in public again, I'll break your arm.'

'Geoff didn't have much luck with getting a photo-fit,' he said, holding up a hand as she swore softly. 'But the encounter happened only the once, and that was nearly three years ago,' he pointed out reasonably. 'But he did get a fair-ish description from the witness. He was about twenty-five, dark-haired, well built—which fits with your thoughts—and he was hovering somewhere near the six-foot mark, or maybe a couple of inches short of that. And there was something else Mrs Tinkerton noticed about him at the time, but can't now quite put her finger on. Something distinctive though.'

'A tattoo? Nose piercing?' Hillary offered abruptly.

'No, neither of those. But Rhumer's team is busy collating photographs of all their top suspects and he's going back to her with them as soon as he can. So maybe she can pick him out.'

'Right,' Hillary said grimly. 'And maybe she can't. Maybe he's not even on the list. We can't even be sure he's still a cop. He could have resigned, transferred or even be a civilian worker, in which case he isn't even on our radar.'

Steven nodded. 'I know.' Did she think that he didn't lay awake at nights as well, worrying about stuff just like that? He knew better than anyone just how much the odds were stacked against them. And it brought him out in a cold sweat whenever he thought that the bastard might try and get at Hillary again. But there was no way he'd let her guess his doubts. 'But we'll get him—nobody's going to give up until he's collared. If he contacted Deirdre, he might have contacted the other family members of his victims, and yes, before you ask, that's what Geoff and the others will be concentrating on today. You'll be the first to know if we get any confirmation or a better ID.' Hillary nodded. Steven glanced over his shoulder at the deserted corridors behind him, and then turned back to her. 'I won't let him hurt you again,' he said softly. 'You're watched day and night, and you'll never be left alone. You know that, right?'

Hillary nodded. She knew that. She also knew that they couldn't watch her day and night forever. If they didn't catch him soon, Donleavy would have to reassign the manpower somewhere else. He'd have no other option. And Hillary wouldn't have it any other way. They needed all the manpower they had to protect the public.

Since the attack, she'd taken a refresher course on self-defence. She also, unbeknownst to Steven, carried a very sharp bladed (and illegal) flick knife in her purse that she'd once taken off a very nasty-minded pimp, back in the days when she'd been walking a beat.

'So how's Donleavy taking it so far? Is he happy with how things are working out?' she asked, and, as she listened to his reply, she reached for the post and began opening it. It was, as she'd suspected, the usual guff and her phone bill.

And a letter from Lol.

Hillary read it, then wordlessly handed it over to Steven, who broke off from what he was saying, read it and swore. 'Right, I'll get this to forensics.' But Hillary knew, as well as he did, that it would be a waste of time. Lol wasn't about to leave either his fingerprints or his DNA on it. Still, every contact he made said something about him, and gave them something else to work with.

'I'll get a copy of this to the profiler Geoff's brought on board. Have you read his thoughts on Lol so far?' Steven asked, not liking the pale, pinched look that had settled on her face.

Hillary nodded, although she wasn't sure that she put much stock in such things. It was all right if you had a suspect to compare it to, and might be useful to academics when collating data, but what use it was in real police-work, when it came down to actually helping catching the bad guys, she wasn't so sure.

'Yeah, yeah. Probably never had a real relationship with a woman, probably still lives with his parents, won't have risen very high in the ranks, has a problem with authority/and/or female figures. Yada, yada, yada.'

Steven laughed. 'You're a real Renaissance girl, ain't yah? Good thing I still love you,' he added lightly. 'Look, I've got to go. Budget meeting.' He grimaced. 'What are you going to be doing today?'

Hillary glanced at her watch. 'If Jimmy's in, I thought I'd go and interview Marcus Kane's wife.'

'Kane—this is Meg Vickary's boss, right? The one

she was having an affair with? The one Meg's flatmate thinks had something to do with her disappearance?'

'That's the one. Although Georgia Biggs couldn't really come up with any reason for that belief. It was sort of odd that, now that I come to think about it. At the initial interview with her, I had the feeling that it was the way Meg spoke about Kane that gave her that impression. Anyway, I've already spoken to him.' Hillary's lips twisted. 'Didn't like him at all. He couldn't give a tinker's cuss that she's missing, and the only thing he *was* anxious about was that the little woman didn't find out about it.'

Steven smiled widely. 'So because you didn't like him you're going to drop him in it with the trouble and strife? Nice.'

Hillary tut-tutted. 'Now you know I wouldn't be that petty,' she admonished him. Then thought about it for a second, and added, 'Well, not unless he *really* pissed me off. No, it was just that he was so sure that she didn't know about it, that it made me wonder.'

Steven nodded, instantly following her line of reasoning. And Hillary wasn't sure just how she felt about him being able to read her so well, this quickly. 'But the wife, even if she did know about hubby's affair and objected to it, can't possibly have had anything to do with Meg's disappearance. And we know she's not the stalker.'

Hillary grinned. 'Not unless she's a big, buff lass who likes to work out and has a deep gravelly voice and gender issues. The Kanes don't have any kids, so you never know—Marcus may be married to a tranny.'

Steven laughed, but then began to look more pensive. His eyes sharpened on her thoughtfully. 'You look pale and tired. And, please don't take this the wrong way, but you seem to be approaching this case as if you were starting a murder inquiry from scratch. It's not that I'm questioning your methods, but....'

Hillary sighed. 'You're questioning my methods,' she echoed him ironically. 'I know. I know. But I just....' She sighed and leaned back in her chair. 'I don't really know how to explain it. It's not just that I've got Geoff Rhumer doing the job that I really want to be doing, nor is it the fact that we haven't come into this case from the beginning, but like we've been dumped into it half-way through.'

'Rather like coming into the theatre in the middle of the play you mean, and are constantly trying to play catch-up?' he put in.

'Yeah, that doesn't help,' she admitted. 'But it's something more than that. I keep feeling we're not getting the right angle on it. Or we can't see the woods for the trees. Oh hell, I can't really put it into words. When I was a rookie, I had this case with my old mentor, DI Brackley. I'd worked with him before on three or four cases, all of which had followed more or less the usual pattern. But this one case—nothing seemed to fit. Interviews didn't pan out. Coincidences that seemed too much to swallow, turned out to be just that—coincidences. The clues seemed to point one way, the evidence the other. We just couldn't make it gel, you know? And he said that sometimes, not often I'm glad to say, but sometimes, you get a case like that. It just won't play ball with you. He called them the dogs'-breakfast cases. I've never had one happen to me when I was lead before.'

'But now you think you have?' Steven asked, both curiosity and concern evident in his voice.

Hillary shot him a sour look. 'I know what you're thinking: that I'm a bit off my game. I'm not sleeping properly and still feeling a bit wrong-footed after the attack. And all of that might be true. But I still can't get this case to behave.'

Steven nodded. 'We all have cases like it. They're a bugger. The only thing you can do is plough on and don't give up.'

'Oh I'm not giving up,' Hillary said grimly. And although her hand itched in her lap, she didn't let it wander up to her neck to feel the fading scars there.

Steven grinned at her. 'Attagirl. I'll see you tonight and you can tell me if Marcus Kane is married to a cross-dressing Amazon who could be our killer.' Hillary threw a pen at him, but he was too fast and it bounced harmlessly off the door closing behind him.

For a moment she sat there, thinking.

Had he really said, "It's a good job that I love you" in any way that could be taken seriously?

Then she shook her head. Out of all that they'd just discussed, was that the only thing that she could think about? She really was going to have to get a grip!

PRICILLA KANE LIVED in a big white mansion in North Oxford—the kind that only multi-millionaires could dream of. As Hillary and Jimmy pulled into the gravelled forecourt, Jimmy gave a long, low whistle. 'And who says crime doesn't pay?' he muttered grumpily.

Jimmy's views on solicitors and barristers who represented the criminals that he worked so hard to nail were well known, and Hillary grinned as she climbed out of the car, but wondered why she was getting such a sense of *déjà vu*.

Then it hit her: Christopher Deakin, Judy Yelland's married lover, had a rich wife called Portia. Pricilla and

Portia. Were there baby name books published only for the seriously well-off? Still amused over that thought, she pulled the old-fashioned iron bell pull and wasn't surprised when a foreign-looking maid opened the door. She spoke excellent English however, and left them briefly in an impressive hallway, before reappearing and showing them through a large lounge in dazzling white, and on through to an even larger conservatory that looked like something from Kew Gardens.

It was humid and hot, and rife with huge flowering things that reminded Hillary uneasily of the classic Wyndham sci-fi novel, *The Day of the Triffids*.

'Hello, I'm over here by the orchids. Please, mind the wet floor,' a Sloaney voice called out from behind a water-feature that had what looked like dead branches from huge trees crisscrossing a small pond. On them, plumes of weird-looking, tortured-shaped flowers sprouted. The woman who was tending them was dressed in a pair of white slacks and an emerald-green silk blouse. Her dark-brown hair was held up in one of those elegant chignons that Hillary was sure must take hours to arrange. It was held in place by a hair slide that glinted with what could only be real diamonds and emeralds. She was wearing a matching emerald and diamond drop pendant, and a diamond-encrusted wristwatch. Incongruously, her fingers were stained brown with earth. 'Police, Marta said?' Pricilla Kane said peremptorily, looking at them from a pair of level, hazel-green eyes. The eyebrows above them were perfectly plucked, naturally.

She looked a very well-preserved twenty, which meant she was probably already well into her forties, Hillary gauged. Her make-up was light, but applied with an expert and experienced hand.

'Yes.' Hillary held out her ID, did her usual spiel about who she was and what the CRT did, and ended, 'We're currently looking into a missing persons case.'

'Ah. I take it that you're talking about that tart who used to work for Marcus, my husband?' the lady said, turning her attention, and a pair of secateurs, back to a wilting peach-tinted bloom. With a quick, vicious snip, the flower was beheaded, and fell to the wet floor.

Beside her, she felt Jimmy stir nervously. No doubt he was picking up on the subtext too, because Hillary had no doubts herself that the thing the lady was actually snipping off had more—subliminally—to do with her husband's dangly bits, than it had to do with good horticultural practice.

'It's about Margaret Vickary, yes,' Hillary confirmed cautiously. 'You referred to her as a tart, Mrs Kane. Did you have any specific reason for doing so?'

'Apart from her sleeping with my husband, you mean? After having divorced whatever poor slob she was married to before? No, not really.' The other woman gave a nonchalant shrug, then frowned at something on a stem that needed a spritz of something chemical from a spray bottle.

Hillary watched this studied performance of indifference, and nodded. So much for Marcus Kane wanting to keep the truth from the little woman. But the fact that he was unaware that his wife already knew about his fling with Meg meant that Pricilla had been careful to keep her knowledge to herself. Which was interesting. Most women liked to confront cheating spouses and were perpetually throwing the truth in their faces.

Obviously, Mrs Kane had a different approach. Was

it one she had learned to use over many years of his infidelity, or was it a one-off tactic though?

'Does your husband often, er, play away?' she asked
curiously.

Pricilla Kane eyed a black-spotted leaf and moved in
with the clippers again. 'Not often, no. And never with
someone from the office before. That's just so tacky.' She
gave a grim little smile and a fake shiver. 'To be honest,
I was surprised that he dared try it on, being right under
Daddy's nose and all that.'

Hillary gave a small sigh. Ah. 'You were worried
that Meg Vickary might be serious competition, then?'
she asked, and was instantly the centre of Mrs Kane's
attention once more. 'I mean, if he was prepared to take
such a risk, perhaps Mrs Vickary was someone special?
Not like all the others, but an actual threat to your marriage?' she baited gently.

Pricilla Kane smiled. 'Hardly. Marcus understands
who wields the power at the firm.'

'Daddy,' Hillary said flatly.

'Exactly. And he knows what would happen if he
should step out of line too far.'

Again Hillary nodded. 'I'm curious. Tell me, how did
you feel when Meg disappeared? Didn't it make you wonder what had happened to her and where she'd gone?'
And, she added silently, did you not wonder if your husband might not just up and disappear to join her one
fine day?

Pricilla shrugged one thin, green-clad silk shoulder.
'When she ceased to be a problem, I ceased to think
about her.'

'You weren't worried at all?'

'Why should I be worried?'

'That something might have happened to her? After all, if a woman disappears, that has to be cause for some concern, surely?' Hillary kept her voice level. 'Didn't you even think that perhaps your husband might have done something to her?' Once again, Pricilla's laser-like gaze fastened on hers.

'Why on earth should Marcus have "done something" to her?' she demanded sharply.

'As you said—he knew who had the real power in your relationship. And at his place of work. What if Meg Vickary became a problem for him: demanding things— maybe insisting that he leave you and marry her. That would put Marcus in a very precarious position indeed, wouldn't it?' Hillary pointed out, careful to keep her voice calm and purely logical.

Pricilla's eyes narrowed for a moment, and then she gave another of her now trademark, uninterested shrugs. 'Marcus is a clever man. And he'd think of using the law, first and foremost, to solve his problems. That's his forte after all, and he likes to stick to his comfort zones.' Pricilla gave a mean little smile.

'He'd probably sue her for libel, or who knows, maybe at a pinch, get one of those gangster louts he likes to represent to warn her off.' Suddenly, the other woman laughed sourly. 'Not that he'd have much luck with that, I think. From what I heard on the grapevine—Daddy's secretaries do so like to gossip—Mrs Vickary had a penchant for the bad boys, and had most of them wrapped around her little finger.' She slowly put down the secateurs and looked at Hillary thoughtfully. 'You don't really think Marcus had anything to do with her going off, do you? Seriously, I mean?'

Hillary gave a small shrug of her own. 'The thought

obviously didn't occur to you,' she said. 'Did *you* have anything to do with her disappearance, Mrs Kane?' she asked casually.

Pricilla Kane blinked, then gave a slow, wide smile. 'Do I need to call Daddy to come over and represent me, do you think?' She laughed, a braying sound of seemingly genuine amusement.

'For all the years that Daddy's been practising criminal law, I've never had to call upon him professionally. Wouldn't it be amusing if the first time I had to do so, it was because I was a murder suspect?'

Hillary cocked her head slightly to one side. 'I never mentioned murder, Mrs Kane.'

'Oh please! All these dark hints you've been dropping about "something happening to her" and "her disappearance" and what have you. You said you were a former DI, before you became a civilian consultant, so you're obviously not an average flatfoot. It's obvious that you think something dire has happened to the tart. Why else have you come here with all these questions?'

Hillary nodded. 'Well, thank you for your time, Mrs Kane,' she said pleasantly, and saw that she had managed to surprise the other woman at last. 'If you should happen to think of anything that might help us locate or find out what happened to Mrs Vickary, perhaps you could call me?' She handed over her card, gave the orchids a final, unimpressed look and left.

Jimmy, who hadn't said a word throughout, waited until they were back in the gravel forecourt before taking a long deep breath. 'I pity the poor sod married to her, guv,' he said with a grin.

'Don't bother—it's a wasted effort,' Hillary said shortly. 'Believe me, that pair deserve each other.' On the way back to HQ Hillary pondered on what she'd learned. It wasn't all that much really. Except that there was definitely no chance of the waspish Pricilla being their stalker in drag!

THE LUNCHTIME, TOM WARRINGTON sat in the HQ's local pub and waited for Vivienne Tyrell. He was still replaying that wonderful moment in the works' car-park when he'd watched Hillary walk by him, pretending not to notice him.

He loved it when she teased him like that. But it also made his blood boil. Having found 'the one' at last, he'd always known that she was going to be a handful—someone of Hillary's calibre needed to test him to make sure he was a real man after all—so being her lover would always represent something of a challenge. But she had to learn that, play delicious games together as they might, he was still the alpha male. It would never do to let her think that she had the upper hand.

He wondered what she'd thought about his letter. She would have had to show it to the others eventually, but she must have kept it to herself for a little while. Smiled over the words, hugged to herself that wonderful feeling of— 'Hi. Bloody hell, it's getting hot out there. They say we're in for another heatwave.' The cheerful voice, crashing as it did through his pleasant daydreams, made him want to explode out of the padded booth and throttle her.

Instead he forced himself to smile. 'Hello, beautiful. What are you having to drink?' After she'd taken an age to make up her mind, he went to the bar and returned with the drinks, having ordered salads for them both. 'I've ordered you the Parmesan and cress. All right?'

Vivienne nodded. In truth, she'd rather have had the

pizza, but she wasn't about to say so. 'So, when are we going to go somewhere for the weekend then?' she asked, taking a sip of her drink and giving him her best, pansy brown-eyed come-hither smile.

She knew that Tom still lived with his parents, and sympathized, up to a point. She too had to share a flat with two others, and knew just how impossible it was on a copper's wages to get a mortgage for a place of your own. She'd already decided that she wouldn't be applying to join the police force once her stint at the CRT was over. But she was getting impatient to move things along. It was ridiculous: having no place they could get together seriously was beginning to get on her nerves.

She moved closer and pressed her thigh against his, loving the hard clenching of his muscles against hers. He was so damned fit and buff, and yet they hadn't done the horizontal tango yet, and it wasn't as if she hadn't put out enough signals, she thought angrily.

His excuse that he couldn't take her home, that her place was too crowded was wearing a bit thin now. In fact, she was beginning to wonder if he might be in the closet. Didn't all her friends say that really good-looking guys into body-building were nearly all gay?

Yet she didn't really get that vibe off him. She put her hand on his knee and squeezed, and heard him catch his breath, and gave a small mental crow of triumph. Yes! No way was he gay.

Tom, still thinking of Hillary, tried to pretend that it was her hand touching him, under the table, out of sight, deliberately tormenting him. It worked for a moment, but then he had to turn his head and look at her, and it was Vivienne's stupid, vapid face looking back at him.

He swallowed back the bile and reached down to

squeeze her hand, surreptitiously lifting it away from him as he did so. 'I'll have to see about booking us in somewhere nice, then, won't I? How about the Cotswolds, or do you fancy somewhere in the Chilterns? Nowhere too far away at any rate—we don't want to waste our time travelling.' As her pretty face lit up, he took a sip of his half of shandy. He had no intention of spending money on a hotel. 'I've been thinking about getting a caravan. I know a farmer who lets me use a part of his field, in a nice quiet little spot out of the way.'

Vivienne screwed up her face. 'A caravan? A bit naff, isn't it?'

'It'll be a nice one,' Tom said. 'It'll be all right in the summer. At least it'll be somewhere we can go in private.' And the more he talked about it, the more he realized that it might actually be quite a good idea. A little caravan, hidden away in the trees and off the radar could come in very useful indeed. He needn't tell anybody and he could always buy it for cash, on the QT. Give a false name and fake details, and nobody would ever know about it, or be able to trace it. Only the farmer would know, and who was he going to tell? So long as he gave the old sod no cause for complaint, there shouldn't be any problem. And the farmer rarely came near the little copse. Yes, it might be just what he needed.

'I suppose so,' Vivienne said, then cheered up suddenly, and nudged closer. At least if he was making plans for a shag-pad, she reasoned, things had to be looking up.

Tom Warrington smelt her cheap perfume and felt the snake of rage in his belly tighten and twist. She disgusted him. She had no class and no quality. The one time he'd been close enough to smell Hillary's perfume—his heart thudded at the memory of holding her close, his arm around her collarbone, a knife to her throat—he could tell at once it was one of those expensive, designer French fragrances. Something light and citrus-based, but with an undercurrent of sensual power. He could still smell it now whenever he closed his eyes and thought back to that day in the car-park.

He had to have that again soon. To actually feel her, to have her talking to him, to feel the adrenaline rush as he wondered exactly what she was thinking and planning. How she would react.

He was going mad. He just had to have that again—he couldn't stand this dull, boring, void without her.

'Just hurry up and get that caravan, yeah?' Vivienne's voice and her coarse words once again cut ruthlessly across his delicious thoughts.

Tom's patience snapped. It was no good. Whether she was his eyes and ears on Hillary's team or not, he was going to have to kill her.

And perhaps it was time that he made a spectacular move anyway. Hillary would be waiting for him to do something outrageous, and this would certainly fit the bill. She'd be furious with him! And that would teach her to pretend to ignore him, the little minx.

He smiled across at Vivienne and pulled her closer. 'Don't worry. I'll get onto it the moment I've got some spare time. I can't wait either.' Vivienne sighed happily and reached for her drink. At last. As she began to contemplate the upswing in her love life, Tom began to fantasize about Hillary's reaction on hearing that he'd taken one of her own.

SEVEN

VIVIENNE RETURNED TO the rabbit warren in the basement of Kidlington's HQ with a spring in her step and a sparkle in her eye that was short-lived, mainly because when she went into the tiny cramped, shared office where she had to work, the first person she saw, talking to her number one crony, was Hillary Greene.

Try as she might, Vivienne couldn't see why everyone seemed to be such a Hillary Greene fan. Right now, the old geezer Jimmy Jessop was hanging on to her every word as if it had been carved in stone, and Sam was listening and nodding like a frenzied muppet. Anyone would think she was a queen bee deigning to notice a few drones in her colony. Not that either of those two losers counted for much, of course, Vivienne thought with a sniff. One was too old to tie his own shoe laces, and Sam Pickles was just a kid barely out of nappies.

But how had she managed to snare the scrumptious Steven Crayle? He outranked her, was younger, gorgeous and clever. Why did he want to get hooked up with a wrinkly like Hillary? It was not only Crayle who seemed to rate her, but people like Marcus Donleavy too. OK, so she had a medal for bravery—big whoop-dee-do— but she also had bad marks against her too, right? Being married to a crooked cop, and being investigated herself by internal complaints just for starters. And everyone knew something iffy had happened with one of her old sergeants. Everyone suspected Hillary had covered up for her, or done something dodgy. Something that had made her quit being a DI, anyhow. So why hadn't she just gone and stayed away for good? Why the hell had she had to come back?

Vivienne gave a mental shrug, and hung up her bag behind her chair. She'd been well on the way to reeling in the sexy superintendent for herself, before Hillary Greene arrived and stuck her big fat nose in. Still, Steven had lost his chance, so it was his loss. Besides, she had Tom now—he was almost as good looking, younger and had more muscle than Steven. Although he didn't have that certain something that Steven— 'Ah, you're back. Vivienne, I want you and Sam to do some background research for me.' The queen bee's voice broke into her thoughts and Vivienne rolled her eyes. More boring paperwork. It's all they ever seemed to do, her and Sam. And this case was turning out to be even worse than the others—at least those had been murder cases, and Hillary had let them do some of the field work and the interviews.

But this was just missing persons, and for some reason it made no sense to her, she was beginning to feel as if she and Sam were being deliberately kept out of the loop. Why was an active DI like Geoff Rhumer involved? It didn't add up to Vivienne, but no one bothered about what she thought.

'Don't worry—you'll find this interesting,' Hillary said with a smile, not having missed the theatricals and correctly guessing the reason behind the latest display of discontent. 'I want you to go through the client base of Marcus Kane's company and pick out all the costa villains from the usual run-of-the-mill. You know the sort—

professional gangsters, the kind who never get arrested for anything unless it's income tax fraud. I want you to start nosing around, perhaps chat to some of them if you can reach them through the barrage of solicitors they hide behind, and see if you can find out if Meg Vickary was ever…shall we say, over-friendly with any of them.' Vivienne, as expected, perked up on hearing this. Talking to real criminals was more like it. At least it would be a bit of excitement; something interesting for a change.

'Guv?' Sam said, uncertainly. 'You think she might have been knocked off by one of them?'

'No, I don't,' Hillary said shortly. If she had, she'd hardly have sent these two youngsters to sniff out what they could. 'I want you to start with the law firm's other admin staff. See if you can glean the gossip about Meg with regard to these specific clients. Was she flirtatious with any of them in particular; did she seem cosy with any of them, maybe have asked favours of them, or did the odd favour in return?'

'I get it, guv,' Vivienne said smugly. 'You want to know if she was a groupie for costa villains, right? Like, some women get off on getting together with men in uniform, or some silly cows like writing to prisoners and starting relationships with them behind bars. That sort of mad stuff, right?'

'Something along those lines,' Hillary agreed slowly. 'But be careful. If you do find any of them still living in this country willing to talk to you, be polite, and stick to questions strictly about their dealings with Meg. You'll find a lot of the men, especially the fat, middle-aged ones, will want to boast about any hot totty they can still attract. But they might turn nasty if they think you're sticking your nose into their financial business.

So don't. There are whole squads whose job it is to do that, so don't go standing on their toes, either.' The last thing she wanted was for the CRT to get raked over the coals because they'd inadvertently jeopardized someone else's undercover operation.

Sam looked a little happier. Like Vivienne, he found doing nothing but paperwork boring, and this sounded exciting, but he was far more sensible than his female colleague, and had a more innate caution. So he was relieved to find that what Hillary was asking for wasn't too risky. When all was said and done, professional criminals were hardly likely to bother putting the boot in with the likes of himself and Vivienne: they were far too insignificant on the pecking order to bother with.

Besides, Hillary had already taught him that men such as these liked to think of themselves as businessmen. And it was bad business to rile the cops and bring themselves to their attention when they didn't have to.

After the two excited youngsters had left to start nosing around the solicitor's office in Summertown, Jimmy looked at Hillary with a raised eyebrow.

'What was all that about?' he asked curiously.

'They've got to start getting their hands dirty sometime,' Hillary said philosophically. 'Besides, most of the costa villains are under constant surveillance by either one of our lot or the Customs people anyway. They're not likely to get themselves into any dangerous territory.'

'No, I know that,' Jimmy said. 'I mean, why do you want to know if Meg Vickary *was* a wannabe gangster's moll? It can't be relevant, can it?'

Hillary shrugged helplessly. The truth was, she couldn't really have said why she wanted to know. 'Let's just say, we can't have too much information about these three women, and leave it at that.'

'You think our stalker might be bent, as well as warped?' Jimmy mused. 'That he might be on the payroll of one of the villains, and is, or was, passing on information to them, and that's how he came across Meg Vickary in the first place?' Jimmy's tone of voice said that he thought that it was a bit of a stretch. On the other hand, something had to connect these three women. Something they had done, or people they had in common, had somehow brought them to the attention of their stalker and killer. Who was to say that Marcas Kane's office didn't hold the key to that common factor somehow?

Again, Hillary shrugged. 'I'm just making sure that we don't leave any stone unturned,' she said, somewhat lamely. In the back of her mind, she was beginning to get that feeling that she'd caught the scent of something, but she was damned if she could yet figure out what it was. So she was operating almost entirely on gut instinct, something that was never a good idea at the best of times, as any copper worth their salt could have told her.

Perhaps it was just as well that she had Geoff Rhumer working the case as well. The way things were going, it was looking far more likely that he would be the one to solve it anyway.

She told herself off for being so negative and forced herself free from a growing sense of inertia. 'OK, what's next on the to-do list.' She reached for her notebook and checked her notes. Nothing stood out as being any more important than anything else. She heaved a sigh. 'It's all so damned nebulous.' She considered the three victims again and wondered why she kept going back to Judy Yelland. Was it because she was the first to go missing? Or had she somehow seemed more like a victim to Hillary than the others?

That thought made her scowl.

From what they knew about Meg Vickary, she was probably the most thick-skinned and tough of the three missing women. She had been a beautiful woman who hadn't been above using her looks to get her way, was ambitious and probably had more than her fair share of savvy. Did that make any difference? It didn't to Hillary, but had it annoyed her stalker?

But then, why wasn't she more concerned about Gilly Tinkerton? She was obviously a gentle soul, restless, and seeking some way of life that would suit her. To think that she'd had all that curiosity and potential snuffed out of her by some selfish bastard to suit his own hideous needs was appalling.

And yet it was still Judy Yelland, for some reason, that Hillary found herself thinking about first whenever her mind went to the missing girls. Why was that? Did she just feel more sorry for her than the others? Having met her parents, and the sterile home in which she had grown up, did it just feel as if her case was somehow more pathetic than the others? Did she matter more than the others?

Hillary gave a mental head shake. No, that wasn't it. She never made distinctions between victims of crime. It was one of the staples that she'd drummed into all of the young officers whom she'd mentored over the years. You stood for the victim—always and only. It didn't matter if that victim was a young helpless child, or a six foot, twenty stone man. It didn't matter whether the victim was sympathetic or got your back up. It made no difference.

And with the dead, it made less difference than ever—

because a dead victim only had you to fight their side—
and it wasn't your place to judge them.

So why did Judy Yelland seem to be calling to her in
a way the others didn't? Or maybe she was just losing it.
Perhaps the attack on her had actually severed some vital
part of her that let her be a cop. Maybe she'd become a
victim herself in some way and now couldn't do her job.

'Guv?'

She heard Jimmy's sharp voice and gave herself a
mental shake. 'Sorry, Jimmy—just wool gathering.' To
cover up her slip, and the sudden sense of panic she felt
at where her thoughts were leading her, she wandered
over to Sam's desk and went through his in-tray.

'He's been going through Rebecca Frost's list of Gilly
Tinkerton's friends,' she said with forced casualness.
'We might as well interview some of them—if I can find
someone still local.' She ran through the boy's notes,
and nodded. 'OK, this looks promising. Grab your coat,
Jimmy.' At least action was better than contemplating
the fluff in her navel.

NAOMI CLARKSON LIVED in a caravan site in the former
RAF village of Upper Heyford. The place turned out to
be a park with the kind of mobile homes that looked like
miniature houses built in one big but attractive unit, and
set down on breeze blocks in a semi-permanent state.
Laid out in neat rows, they had something pleasantly
nostalgic about them.

The park was on the very outskirts of the village,
facing a small fallow field which ran downwards to a
brook running through one boundary. The lower area
was free of homes, and it had a slightly boggy look to it,
and Hillary sensed that it might be prone to flooding in

the winter. As Jimmy parked up beside a row of homes painted in various pastel shades, Hillary thought how charming it all looked. Most of the homes were pristine, clean, and surrounded by flowers. It had a sort of olde worlde look to it—like an archetypal village you might have found back in the fifties—the sort of place where Agatha Christie had liked to set her novels. There was even a shack of a 'village' post office-cum-grocery store.

As she climbed out of the car, she half-expected to see a postman bicycle past, or some rustic farmer chewing a blade of grass, lean across a gate into the field and ask them if they were lost.

Then she noticed all the satellite dishes, and the parked cars, and wondered what the place looked like in the dead of a wet winter. She shook her head at her own whimsy, and glanced around, setting out to find Crooked Spindle Cottage.

It turned out to be one that was painted a pale mint green with large tubs of scarlet geraniums standing sentinel beside a white-painted front door. She went up the three wooden steps that led to it and knocked. Inside, a frenzied yelping chorus started up, and Jimmy glanced down automatically at his ankles. They looked rather vulnerable under his trouser legs.

The door opened, and a young, plump woman stood there. Around her, three Yorkshire terriers danced and yelped, but more in excitement than in any apparent zeal to guard their pack leader.

'Miss Clarkson? Naomi Clarkson?' Hillary asked.

'Yes?' The woman had long, slightly curly mouse-brown hair and rather muddy-looking greyish eyes. She looked nervously from Hillary to Jimmy. 'You're not tax people, are you? I thought I got all that sorted out last year.'

Hillary smiled and held out her ID. 'No cause for alarm, Miss Clarkson. We were given your name by Gillian Tinkerton's sister. She said you were a friend of Gillian's? As you know, she's listed as a missing person, and we were wondering if you might be able to help us.'

'Oh, Gilly! Yes, of course, come on in.' She opened the door, and the Yorkies bounded ahead, ushering them through with a waggy-tailed escort to a small but neat front room, overlooking the field and brook.

'Please sit down. The last time I saw Gilly was, what, must have been three years ago. Maybe more. So I don't know if I can help, but I'll do what I can. Drink?' A few minutes later, they were all sitting in comfortable chairs, a dog on each lap, and a mug of tea in hand.

Hillary stroked her own canine friend's silky ginger head and looked across at their hostess. 'Gilly's mother is sure that her daughter has found some temporary place of refuge where she's probably trying out some alternative lifestyle and will show up eventually. Her sister thinks much the same. How about you?'

'Oh sure.' Naomi waved a plump hand in the air, and fed the dog on her lap a piece of biscuit. 'The last time I spoke to her, she was asking me where she could take night classes for arts and crafts courses. You know—how to make stained-glass windows, that sort of thing. I think she wanted to design modern pieces for modern houses, rather than the traditional pieces for churches or whatever. She said that nowadays, what with all those telly shows on restoring old homes and doing up houses and what-not, there'd be a market for one-off original pieces of stained glass for front doors and windows in barn conversions and that sort of thing.' She finally paused for air and a bite of biscuit.

Hillary nodded. 'Sounds like a sensible plan. Her mother said that Gilly, for all her hippy ways, had a good head on her shoulders.'

'Yeah, that's true. In a sort of way. I could imagine her learning the trade and doing OK at it,' Naomi agreed, then grinned. 'Though perhaps not sticking to it for long. That's always been the real trouble with Gilly—she's easily bored. I'll bet, whatever she's doing now, it won't still be stained glass, but something else. Something she can make money at, and all that, but something different. She likes learning how to do stuff, more than actually knuckling down and doing it as a steady job like. Oh, and she'll have moved on. She doesn't like staying in one place too long.'

'Itchy feet,' Jimmy said, feeding the dog on his own lap a piece of his own biscuit. The dog on her lap gave Hillary a big brown-eyed look, but Hillary merely smiled down at it. Hard luck, mutt, she thought. You drew the short straw—she'd declined Naomi's offer of the biscuit barrel.

'Did Gilly ever talk about her secret admirer?' Hillary asked casually.

'The man who sent her flowers and stuff? Yeah, she did. But I don't think anything ever came of it. She never said anything about him getting in real contact with her.'

Hillary nodded. 'You never noticed anyone following her, mooning over her, that sort of thing?'

'No. Why? You think something bad has happened to her?' Naomi's muddy eyes widened suddenly in alarm, and the dog on her lap yipped suddenly, as if sensing her distress.

'We have no reason to think so at this time, Miss Clarkson,' Hillary lied smoothly. 'We're simply trying to trace her. Do you have any idea where she might have gone?'

'Not really. Well, I can tell you where she *won't* have gone, if that's any help at all. She won't have gone to a city, or even a town. I know that's traditionally where most people who "run away from home" go to, isn't it? The bright lights and glamour and all that. But Gilly hates cities and all that hustle and bustle—she's a real country gal. So wherever it is, it'll be some bucolic dream she's living—a bit like this, really, I suppose,' Naomi said with a grin, indicating the view outside. 'I design and make my own jewellery. I have a stall on Banbury market, and some of the boutiques take my stuff and sell it for a commission. I get by.'

'And you think Gilly, wherever she is, will be doing something along the same lines.' Hillary nodded. 'I don't suppose she ever got in touch with you?'

'Oh, no. But then she wouldn't. Gilly never was much for that sort of thing. She lives in the moment, out of sight, out of mind. That's Gilly.'

'All right. Well, thank you, Miss Clarkson.' Hillary gently lifted her lap-warmer to the floor. 'You've been very helpful,' she added, again not particularly truthfully.

Jimmy hastily swallowed the last of his biscuit, and drained his mug. Outside, they stood for a while, watching the spring butterflies on the buttercups in the field.

'Not that I object to getting out of the office, especially on a day like this, guv, but aren't we just spinning our wheels questioning the friends and family of our vics like this? Nobody seems to know anything.' Hillary nodded absently. But even as her head nodded, the mind inside it was paradoxically moving in the other direction, because that something nagging away at the back of her mind was telling her that the visit to Naomi hadn't been a waste of time—if only she would pull her head out of a very different part of her anatomy and do some proper thinking.

Her hand started to wander up to the scar on her neck and she ruthlessly caught it in mid-motion. To hell with that. And to hell with Lol. She had to get her priorities straight and start doing some serious work, damn it.

Either that, or just hand in her notice, cruise off in the *Mollern*, and turn her back on all of this once and for all. She was no damned use to either herself or the three missing girls, floundering around like this, that was for sure.

She shook her head. 'Let's get back,' she said flatly. Not that she wanted to return to the office particularly, but because she couldn't at the moment, think of anything else to do.

And that thought, perhaps more than any other, was shameful.

But as if fate or whatever passed for it had decided to give her a bit a break, she found something to do the moment she returned to her office.

She had a visitor: and a not particularly pleased visitor at that.

RUTH COOMBS LOOKED up from her chair in the lobby, and got to her feet the moment she saw Hillary. The desk sergeant had the grace to drop his pen and disappear behind his desk. It was his job to deal with members of the public, and the HQ was not exactly the local bobby shop, where people wandered in off the streets.

But Hillary let the incident pass without even a sarcastic comment, as Ruth bore down on her.

'Detective Greene. I need to speak to you,' Ruth said, grim-lipped and obviously in no mood to be denied.

But Hillary smiled at her and nodded. 'Of course, Miss Coombs. Please, follow me down to the office. It's not the best location in the house,' she carried on, as they went downstairs, and installed Judy Yelland's best friend into one of the chairs in the empty office. 'Would you like a cup of coffee?'

'No, thanks.' The big-boned brunette settled herself into Vivienne's chair and fixed her gaze on Hillary. 'Have you found out anything more?' she demanded.

Hillary smiled briefly. 'I'm afraid I can't discuss that with you, Miss Coombs. Even family isn't always given access to official information, and you're not, technically, even that.'

'Oh those people,' Ruth said dismissively. 'Judy never cared about them or they about her. She only had me. And Christopher, of course,' she added, reluctantly. 'It's about Christopher that I'm here, actually.'

Hillary nodded, not surprised. 'You seem to find Mr Deakin fascinating, Miss Coombs.' She decided, abruptly to go on the offensive. Nothing else had worked so far, so perhaps it was time to rattle some cages. 'Did Judy know that you fancied her boyfriend?' She sensed Jimmy perk up and reach for his notebook, immediately cottoning on to her line of thought.

Ruth flushed. 'He wasn't her boyfriend—he was her married lover,' she snapped. 'And no, she didn't know I fancied him, because I don't. And if I appear to be fascinated by him, it's because I know he did something to my best friend and got away with it. And you police don't seem to want to do a damned thing about it. I thought you were different!' Ruth was breathing hard now and Hillary watched her closely. She looked and sounded indignantly outraged, and Hillary had no reason to doubt the sincerity of either of those emotions. But that, she was sure, wasn't the whole story.

'And why do you believe that Christopher is responsible, Ruth?' she asked calmly.

Ruth took a few deep breaths, and some of her high colour leeched away. 'Because I've been watching him, that's why. Ever since you first talked to me, I knew that for some reason you were working Judy's case again. So despite what you say, something new must have happened. You don't just reinvestigate old cases on a whim. Something must have triggered it off. So I decided to watch Christopher really closely.' Hillary said nothing but made a mental note to herself: Ruth was both clever and resolute.

'If you've talked to me, you must have talked to Christopher,' Ruth said, her chin angling up and almost challenging Hillary to deny it.

Hillary didn't oblige her, but merely nodded again. 'Go on,' she said, neither confirming nor denying it.

'So it follows that he must be rattled now,' Ruth concluded triumphantly. 'Just think about it! After all this time he thought he'd got away with killing Judy, but now the police come sniffing around. So he'll be worried. I hoped that he would be worried enough to give something away. I don't know—maybe even check up on Judy.'

Hillary blinked. 'Check up on her?'

'Yes. Go and check wherever it was he buried her. Make sure no wild animals had disturbed her grave, or whatever. He must have buried her somewhere, right? And I've read up on the subject—it's not easy finding a place to bury a body where nobody can see you transport it or dig a hole. And even digging a grave is hard—much harder than you might think. People see it happen all the time on television dramas and think it's easy, but it isn't. You have to find a place that's totally hidden, and that usually means woods. But you can't dig a deep hole in a wood, because of all the roots. And besides, it's hard, physical work to dig a proper grave—six feet deep and all that. Even most grave-diggers nowadays do it with one of those yellow digger machines. And although Christopher is fit enough, I suppose, he's always worked behind a desk. So the most he would have been able to dig was a shallow grave somewhere.' She paused and looked at Hillary defiantly. 'As I said, I read up about it. Serial killers and true-crime stories and all that sort of thing. And a lot of them went on about how hard disposing of a body is.'

Hillary nodded. She was impressed. Disposing of a body was by far and away one of the hardest things to do, and it was usually bungling this—and being grassed up by those in the know—which led to the majority of killers being caught and convicted.

'You've done your homework,' she acknowledged briefly.

'Right. So ever since you came to me, I've been driving over to Chris's place and watching him.'

'And did he drive to any remote woods?' Hillary asked gently.

Ruth flushed. 'Don't be so bloody superior! If he had, I'd have called you straight away and told you to bring some cadaver dogs.'

Hillary had to smile—just a little twitch of the lips. 'Yes, Miss Coombs, I'm sure you would. So, Mr Deakin hasn't *checked up* on Judy. What has he done?'

'Nothing much. The first night he went to one of his lock-up facilities, but that's only where he stores some filming equipment and the expensive cameras and stuff. It has good security. He's been working long hours,' she added reluctantly. 'But he's acting oddly,' she insisted defiantly. 'I can tell. He's upset and worried.' Hillary looked at Ruth for a long moment. Just what did this strange, obsessed woman regard as acting oddly? she wondered.

'Oh?'

'He's losing weight. I mean, visibly, I can tell. And it's only been a few days. You don't lose weight that fast unless you're really stressing, do you?' Ruth said flatly.

Hillary blinked. Just how closely was this woman watching Christopher Deakin that she noticed if he'd lost a few pounds?

'Is Mr Deakin aware of your, er, activities, Miss Coombs?'

Ruth's eyes flashed. 'Of course not! Give me some credit. I keep my distance.' But have a good pair of binoculars, I'll bet, Hillary added silently.

'I'm telling you, he's the one you want. You need to speak to him again,' she said stubbornly.

Hillary nodded. 'Very well, Miss Coombs, I'll be sure to do that.'

'When?' Ruth asked aggressively, and for once, looked surprised, but then satisfied, as Hillary got to her feet.

'Right now in fact, Miss Coombs. Let's walk you out. I dare say you can tell me, is Mr Deakin at work now, or at home?'

'Oh he'll be at work,' Ruth said at once. 'He never

knocks off early, even though it's a Friday afternoon.' Hillary, Jimmy and Ruth Coombs, walked back through the CRT rabbit warren and back up the stairs into the warm May afternoon and out to the car-park. There they saw her safely off and then headed for Hillary's old car.

'I'm glad that woman hasn't got her sights on me, guv,' Jimmy said with feeling, as they drove out into the gathering rush-hour traffic. Unlike Mr Deakin, apparently, a lot of other less conscientious workers had left work early, and they had to endure the usual stop-start-stop fiasco of traffic jams all the way into the city. Since they should have been going in the opposite direction from the main flow Hillary couldn't understand it for a moment, until she realized that most of the traffic was due to the school runs.

She idled behind an old Volvo that had a faulty exhaust and rubbed the back of her neck tiredly. She hoped Steven was going to come over tonight. She liked lying next to his long, comforting length in bed; to have him there, to touch when it got to be three o'clock in the morning, and everything seemed that much darker.

'You think Deakin knows what she's been doing, guv?' Jimmy asked, coughing a bit on the Volvo's exhaust fumes, and rolling up his window.

'Well, there's only one way to find out,' Hillary said laconically.

CHRISTOPHER DEAKIN WELCOMED them into the same office they'd visited previously, and did indeed look a little more gaunt than he had before. Hillary could almost imagine the I-told-you-so look on Ruth Coombs's face as she took the seat the television producer offered her.

'So, this is still about Judy, yes?' he asked, looking

from Hillary to Jimmy. 'Have you found out anything new?' Hillary caught the uncertainty behind the question, and felt her hackles rise. Ruth Coombs might be a woman obsessed, but that didn't mean she couldn't be right about certain things, and something in the way that Christopher Deakin's hazel eyes moved restlessly from her to Jimmy, told her that this man was indeed feeling very uncomfortable.

'We're always finding out new things, sir,' Hillary said sweetly. 'We investigate. That's what tends to happen when you investigate—you find out things. Like if someone's been telling you lies. Or, shall we say, not being as totally forthcoming as they might have been.' She allowed her voice to rise slightly at the end of the sentence, thus turning it into a query.

It was an old trick, and she had used it often in the past. When dealing with someone who was trying to hide something, but you had no idea what, sometimes it paid off to simply bluff. If you hinted that you knew all about it, a suspect's dodgy conscience would often do the rest. That, plus the fact that most people had the subconscious desire to confess, simply because the relief when they did so was so great.

So she gazed calmly across at the other man, and saw Deakin's skinny frame slowly collapse, like air going out of a balloon.

'All right. So I didn't tell you about the money I loaned her,' Christopher said with a credible stab at embarrassed nonchalance. 'I just didn't want you to get the wrong impression of Judy, that's all.' Hillary nodded. What money?

'We know how much it was, sir,' she said smoothly.

'Financial records, in a serious criminal inquiry, are never as private as the general public seem to think.'

Christopher nodded gloomily. 'Like I said, I didn't want you to run away with the idea that Judy was some sort of gold-digger, or that she was the money-grubbing sort. She wasn't. I was happy to loan her the ten thousand.'

Ten thousand, Hillary thought. An interesting sum, that. Not huge, by today's standards. But not peanuts either. She glanced around the room, taking in the ergonomically designed chairs, the limited edition prints on the walls bearing famous names in the world of modern art, the arrangement of fresh lilies in a cut crystal vase on a good-quality nineteenth-century mahogany sideboard.

Yes, he could well afford it. Probably. On the other hand, people didn't get rich and successful giving money away. But Judy hadn't been just anyone, had she? Hillary mused? She'd been his lover. So—was it blackmail or genuine affection? She tilted her head and looked at Christopher Deakin thoughtfully.

'You appear to have lost weight, sir,' Hillary said, and saw him shoot her a totally flummoxed look. 'You're very lean anyway, which is why I noticed. Since it's hardly likely that you're on a diet, I wondered if it might be due to stress. Have you been feeling particularly under pressure recently?' she asked innocently.

Christopher swallowed hard. No wonder Ruth Coombs thought he was acting strangely. Right here and now he was acting the classic guilty man, found out.

'Oh, just work,' he said, his voice slightly hoarse. 'Working in television is always very time-orientated you see. The pressure is always on to get things done on schedule because productions over-running are so expensive. And filming on one of our documentaries has hit a snag. Unforeseen circumstances and all that—and we haven't budgeted for it. That sort of thing.' And then, as if aware he was rambling, he abruptly stopped talking.

Hillary looked at the good-looking, blond man, and felt uneasy. She also experienced an odd little frisson of *déjà vu*.

'Let's get back to the money you *loaned* Judy. I take it you never got it back?' When in doubt, follow the money trail. How often had she heard that from her old sergeant, back in the days when she'd still been in uniform?

'No. Well, she, er…left, and so, of course, she could… didn't repay it. Not that I really expected her to,' he added quickly. 'I mean, we called it a loan, between ourselves, but we both knew that really it was, well, a gift I suppose.'

Hillary nodded. 'Did she say why she needed it?'

Deakin hesitated, and then again, just as he had before in their previous interview, quite obviously—to Hillary at least—lied. 'No,' he said firmly, his eyes briefly flickering. 'She didn't. And I didn't like to ask.' Hillary nodded. And wondered.

Had Judy become truly afraid of her stalker by then? Had she asked her lover for money so that she could run away and hide? To disappear for a bit, to maybe just shake off the man who was harassing her, long enough anyway, for him to get bored and find someone else to torment? And if she had, wouldn't she have told him? So was Deakin so freaked out because he thought that Judy was alive and well somewhere and in hiding from her stalker, and that cops stumbling around might put a spoke in the wheel? But then, that would mean she'd spent four years in hiding, or so he thought. And if he was still holding a torch, waiting for her, then he was a better man than she'd have given him credit for.

If any of this was true, or he thought it was, then why didn't he come clean about it now? Obviously, Judy herself might have asked him not to.

Hillary mentally shook her head. No. It was all too farfetched. It was far more likely that their affair had run its natural course and he hadn't given her a thought since. He had probably even been relieved, since it meant the risk of his wife finding out would finally be over. Deakin might simply have seen the money as a good investment if he knew that Judy was going to take it and go out of his life for good.

And now, years later, here it all came back to potentially bite him in the backside.

Yes, that might be it.

Then again, it might not. No. It might not.

Hillary nodded. 'Well, thank you for your time, Mr Deakin. And please don't lie to us again. If you think of anything, anything at all, that you think we should know, please give me a call. You still have my card?'

'Oh yes,' Deakin said, smiling with visible relief, and stood up when they did.

Hillary nodded, turned and walked to the door, then stopped halfway and turned back. 'Oh, and, Mr Deakin, if you want to file a complaint against Ruth Coombs, you can also do that through me, if you like.'

Christopher smiled shakily. 'Oh, no. Ruth's fine. I mean, she's just a little…no, it's fine.' Hillary nodded. At that point she would have bet money on him saying just that.

Once back outside, they hit the rush hour proper and

sat for nearly half an hour in stalled traffic on the Banbury Road.

Hillary said nothing, although once or twice she saw
Jimmy glance across at her curiously. But by now Jimmy
knew enough about his guv'nor to know when to talk
and when not to interrupt her when she was thinking.

And Hillary *was* thinking, at last. For what felt like
the first time since taking this dog's dinner of a case, she
felt as if she was beginning to properly function again.
Act like the cop she was, and always had been.

The only trouble was—what she was thinking was
insane. Indeed, it was so insane that she had no intention of voicing her theories out loud. Apart from anything else, Steven would yank her off the case before she
could complete so much as a full sentence.

No. She needed to gather evidence, and the rock-solid,
incontrovertible kind of evidence at that. If what she was
beginning to suspect was even remotely true, then it was
so far off the wall, that only an air-tight argument would
do. Otherwise they really would be sending for the men
in white coats to come and take her away.

But where the hell did she start?

EIGHT

THAT FRIDAY NIGHT, Tom checked his appearance in the mirror. He was wearing tight-fitting, good quality denim jeans that showed off his powerful thigh muscles to perfection, and a plain white T-shirt, again, stretched tight to show off his pecs. He slung a fashionably beaten-up leather jacket over his shoulders and smoothed back his hair.

He was taking Vivienne to a pub-cum-restaurant in the nearby village of Hampton Poyle and he was feeling rather flat. Why couldn't it be Hillary that he was dressing to impress? He scowled at his image in the mirror, then smiled slowly as he turned and reached for the three envelopes on his desk.

They were all brown padded envelopes, with computer-printed address labels on the front. They all had self-seal tabs on them, and he'd used water to paste down the stamps. Each was addressed to Hillary Greene and each had a small item inside that he'd been almost loath to part with. He'd enjoyed gloating over them over the years, imagining delicious scenarios concerning their original owners. It would be a shame to give them away.

Still, it was in a good cause. He needed to up the game. Since he'd discovered she was being guarded and watched day and night by that bastard Steven Crayle's lackeys, he hadn't been able to do much. She might be wondering if he'd forgotten about her or given up on their game, and he couldn't have that.

He smiled when he thought of her getting his latest gift via the services of Her Majesty's Royal Mail, and what her reaction would be. She'd be intrigued, and surely relieved to hear from him.

He picked up the envelopes with a tuneless whistle and pocketed his car keys and then, still whistling, checked his mobile. He'd been left one text message, but he recognized the number and ignored it. He was due to meet a guy who had a caravan for sale, but it could wait. He probably only wanted to change the time when they'd agreed to meet so he could look it over, and he had more important things on his mind just now.

Running down the stairs into the hall, he called a vague 'goodbye' to his parents, who he could hear listening to the telly in the living room, and went out to his car. He drove to the small village and decided to use the post box there to mail his letters. He took a quick look around and on finding the village lanes deserted, he mimed kissing the back of each envelope, imagining it was his Hillary's lovely lips he was kissing, popped them into the iconic red box and then took off his driving gloves and walked into the pub.

Vivienne was late. But then, she nearly always was.

Tom used the spare time to buy the drinks, and think about how he was going to kill her. When she finally arrived, she was dressed in one of those flowery summery print dresses that reminded you of your granny, but were now back in fashion. With her curled long dark hair and expertly made-up pretty face, she instantly attracted the attention of every man in the room, but Tom took one look at the frilly Laura Ashley confection and knew that Hillary wouldn't be caught dead wearing it.

He forced a smile. 'I was beginning to wonder if you'd stood me up.'

'Nah, just busy. You wouldn't believe what the mad cow has got us doing now,' Vivienne said, missing the sudden tightening of his smile and the way his cat-green eyes glittered angrily.

'She's only got us sorting through any costa cons that one of our missing girls might have got mixed up with.' Tom, fighting the urge to slap her silly face and warn her to watch her foul mouth when talking about Hillary, felt himself suddenly stiffen.

'What do you mean?' he asked sharply. 'What costa cons?' Then, realizing that she was surprised by the tone of his voice, quickly forced the smile back. 'I mean, it sounds dangerous. You shouldn't be talking to real villains; it's not as if you're a real copper yet.'

'Oh that's sweet! You're worried about me,' Vivienne teased, taking a sip of her drink.

Tom smiled. He couldn't care less what trouble the silly bitch got herself into, but he needed to get to the bottom of this. It didn't make sense, and that worried him.

'Which missing girl we talking about then?' he asked casually, looping one leather-clad arm around her shoulders and splaying his fingers tantalizingly across the top of her arms. He gently rubbed her skin with one thumb, and took a sip of his own pint.

'The one who worked in the posh solicitor's office,' Vivienne said, putting a hand on his thigh under the table. Bloody hell, it felt as if it were made of iron! 'Apparently, the outfit she worked for did a lot of the defence work for a load of ex-pat villains. It's how they make a lot of their money, apparently.'

'Why does she want to know about them for?' Tom asked, genuinely curious.

Vivienne sighed and shrugged. 'Dunno. Who knows how her mind works? Still, I'm not complaining, not really. It gets me and the ginger minger out of the office and doing something a bit more interesting. Mind you, all we've been doing this afternoon is chatting to her workmates at the office and trying to find out who she was close to. We've got some names, and we're going to try and interview them on Monday morning, so that'll be a bit of excitement. I've never met a career criminal before. I'll bet you have,' she said, flatteringly, nudging up a bit closer and digging her fingers suggestively into his flesh.

Tom smiled enigmatically. The only criminals he knew were the boozed up tossers who cut each other in knife fights every weekend, or vandalized bus shelters. 'Course. They're all right, some of them. Just you be careful though,' he added, realizing that she was expecting him to say something like that. 'But what's she thinking of? Has she said why she wants you to find out about them?' It worried him when Hillary did stuff that he couldn't figure out. What had she got hold of that he hadn't? The more he thought about it, the more likely it seemed that she had thought of something that he'd missed, and that thought left him breathless in equal parts of admiration and unease.

But what could it be? It made no sense. Unless... 'Meg Vickary,' he said casually. 'You've been talking to her workmates you say. So, *was* she close to any of them? Any of the costa villains, that is?'

Vivienne sighed. To be honest, Sam had done most of the chatting, since all the secretaries were women, and they seemed to take to him; the stuck-up cows hadn't wanted to give *her* the time of day. And she hadn't liked to ask Sam what he'd found out, because then she'd have to admit that she hadn't come up with much herself.

But she wasn't about to admit any of this to Tom, so instead she sighed again. 'Come on, lover boy, you know I can't talk about it,' she cajoled. 'Hillary Greene would have my hide. She's always going on about our need for discretion and keeping our mouths shut. Anyone would think we were working for the Secret bloody Service or something. I tell you, that woman's unhinged.'

Tom nodded understandingly, but his hand, curled around his pint glass, tightened until his knuckles showed white. What the stupid cow meant was that Hillary Greene was a professional, through and through. Being forced to work with sub-standard dregs like Vivienne, the old geezer and Sam Pickles must really rankle. It made him want to go up and shake the top brass by their silly bloody necks and ask them what the hell they thought they were playing at, treating their star player like this.

He forced himself to push the anger away and concentrate, knowing he could be in serious trouble here. He'd always known that Hillary, his wonderful Hillary, was clever. Tenacious; the best bloody cop at HQ, but he didn't like the way her mind seemed to be working.

He didn't like it one little bit.

He only hoped the three envelopes would distract her. Otherwise…well, otherwise, he'd have to speed things up before it all got spoilt. And he couldn't let it get spoilt.

'Have I told you I'm seeing a man about a caravan this weekend?' he said softly, turning to nibble on Vivienne's earlobe. 'Me and you are gonna have to make plans to start spending some quality time alone together. All alone, in the woods somewhere…'—he let his voice lower softly—'where no one can hear you scream,' he added with a twinkle in his green eyes.

Vivienne smiled smugly. '*Now* you're talking!'

THE WEEKEND WAS one of those golden ones that mark the end of spring and the beginning of summer. The sun showed its true strength, and on the *Mollern*, Hillary and Steven threw open all the windows and took to the outdoors. The ducklings were growing apace, and the swallows, all now arrived, were busy swooping along the khaki-coloured water of the Oxford canal, scooping up beaks full of liquid to help them to construct their mud nests.

Lying on top of the roof on fluffy beach towels, they spent the days sipping chilled wine, reading, talking, and sunbathing before going below to fix light meals.

Steven had taken the whole weekend off, and Hillary appreciated the pampering. At night, they wandered to The Boat for their evening meal, then spent the nights together in her small bed. Sunday morning, they went for a long walk northwards, passing the village of Kirtlington's Three Pigeons Lock, the hamlet of Northbrook, and as far as the villages of Lower and Upper Heyford, before turning back. She taught him what cuckoo flowers looked like, and the difference between buttercups and celandines. He told her about his past marriage, his ambitions for the future, and how he loved the minuscule proportions of her ridiculous bed.

It was one of those moments in life that should never have to come to an end, but when it did, and she followed him into work the following Monday morning, she knew that something fundamental had changed in her life.

And she wasn't sure that she knew what to do about it.

On the plus side, she'd not thought about the fading scar on her neck once.

BEFORE VIVIENNE AND Sam set off for the Smoke, where they were due to talk to three fairly low-level and now fully retired criminals about Meg Vickary, she gave them another task.

Vivienne, who was impatient, stood restlessly beside her desk, glancing tellingly at her watch and sighing elaborately. Hillary ignored her.

Sam, however, listened carefully.

'When you get back from London, I want you to check out any rural artistic-type retreats you can find,' she told him. 'Go country-wide, but they have to be set in the countryside—converted farms, barns, mills, anything of that sort, and they have to be artisan-based,' Hillary explained. 'No religious overtones, or anything political. I don't think either of those are Gillian Tinkerton's thing at all.'

Sam nodded. 'You think she might have run off to some place to paint butterflies or something, guv,' he said, grinning.

Jimmy, who knew damned well that Gillian was dead, looked up curiously, wondering why Hillary was giving them this particular task now. Even if Gillian had gone off to join some sort of artist's colony to escape her stalker, it was clear she hadn't made it. But perhaps the guv thought that he might have followed her to wherever she'd gone and then snatched her from there? In which case, the youngsters might just uncover a witness. But it was a hell of a long shot, in his opinion.

Hillary smiled briefly at Sam, giving nothing away.

'Something like that. Concentrate on those that provide live-in accommodation or provide solid business links with the local community. I can't see Gillian being taken in by any outfit where the artists end up paying the management for the privilege of staying there. And she's canny enough to want to be sure to make a living out of what she's doing. So any fly-by-night or dodgy set ups is out. I think she's canny enough to have checked them out beforehand, so concentrate on those that have been going for some years and have a solid rep. You can do most of it on the net I expect, or by phone. I want a list of possibles on my desk as soon as you can.'

'Right, guv.'

'Can we get going now?' Vivienne whined. Hillary smiled patiently, and waved them away.

Jimmy watched her leave the office and go on through down to her own small space. He didn't know how she could stand it in there—it would drive him mad. Still, she lived on a narrowboat, so obviously claustrophobia wasn't one of her problems.

He frowned, wondering what she was up to. Usually he could follow her thinking and get some idea of where she thought the case was going, but not this time. So far, she'd solved both of the cold case murders that the super had given her, and his confidence in her was only growing. But this case was obviously giving her trouble, and Jimmy wasn't so sure that being stalked could account for all of it. He didn't believe she'd lost her nerve, but her confidence wasn't as strong as it should have been. Her mind though, he would have bet his last pay packet, was as razor-sharp as ever.

But for the life of him he couldn't figure out her strategy. Was her mind really not on the job? Being attacked and nearly knifed to death had to affect you, no matter how tough you were. Was she still feeling so distracted by the thought of being the next target of a serial killer that she really couldn't think straight?

Jimmy didn't think so. He believed he had the measure of Hillary Greene by now and, when it came down to it, he'd place his bets on her any day of the week. If her stalker thought he'd got the better of her, he'd better think again.

Besides, so far, between the super, himself and his old pals, they'd been keeping her covered every moment of every day, and she knew it. And, needless to say, chummy hadn't made a move on her. Knowing they had her covered had to help her feel secure.

He knew that the super had spent the entire weekend with her, and not just because he wanted to keep her safe either, but Jimmy didn't let himself speculate about that. It was none of his damned business. But she did look more relaxed and happy than he'd seen her in a while, which said it all, really.

He shook his head, and reminded himself again that the private lives of his bosses was no place for a canny retired sergeant to stick his big fat nose, and reached instead for DI Rhumer's latest report. But the DI's team had had no joy so far on whittling out a name or face from the long suspect list. Well, that was always going to be a long job, wasn't it? And they couldn't even be sure, a hundred per cent sure, that chummy was on the job. Anyone could buy a police uniform from a costume shop and buy fake police ID on the Internet.

He was just closing the folder when Hillary came back into the office. She had three opened padded brown envelopes in her hand. Her face was perfectly expressionless.

'Can you call the super in?' she said flatly. 'And tell him we're going to need forensics, and DI Rhumer.' She waved the envelopes in the air, and Jimmy tensed.

'Been in contact, has he?' Jimmy said flatly.

'Yes,' Hillary said. 'He just can't seem to resist it, can he?' she added, with grim little smile.

GEOFF RHUMER, STEVEN, Hillary and Jimmy crowded around Steven's desk. All of them were wearing gloves.

'Obviously, as soon as I saw them in the mail, I put mine on,' Hillary said, indicating her white, cotton-clad hands. 'I knew I wasn't due any mail like this, and besides...' She shrugged and just let the sentence slide. She'd just known that they had been sent by Lol. You get an instinct about this sort of thing, and she could see by the way the others in the group were either nodding their heads or giving a rueful smile, that they understood without needing to be told.

She met Steven's solemn, questioning brown eyes, and gave a small smile in return, silently telling him that she was fine. But whether he believed her or not, she couldn't tell. She reached for the first envelope, which she had carefully unsealed, causing the least possible amount of interference for the forensics people to moan about later, and tipped out the contents.

On to the table fell an ugly, fluffy pink key ring with a troll's face. It was both comical and grotesque. The second envelope was thicker and she carefully pulled out a striped, multi-coloured pair of leg warmers. The third envelope produced a necklace consisting of what looked like good quality pearls, with the biggest and fattest in the middle, graduating to smaller ones the closer they got to the clasp, which was made of gold.

For a moment, they studied the items in question, none of them venturing the obvious observation, until Steven obliged.

'You think these come from the victims?'

Hillary nodded. 'I think the troll key ring is probably Gilly's. It's the kind of whimsical, funky thing she'd use. The strand of pearls, I'm guessing, would be Meg's, simply because she was a class act and somewhat vain about her looks, and I can't see her covering up her legs at all, let alone with something like these.' She nodded at the jaunty leg warmers. 'Which, by process of elimination, I'm guessing, belonged to Judy.'

'No note with any of the items?' Geoff Rhumer asked without much hope. If there had been, they'd have been studying it by now.

Hillary shook her head. 'But then, there doesn't need to be, does there?' she asked flatly, and for a while they stared down at the three items on the table. Each unique to their owners, their forlorn eloquence had no need of the written word.

Steven briskly shook off the gloom. 'OK. Geoff, get these to forensics and see if you can find any trace of your man on them. I doubt you'll be lucky, but you never can tell. Hillary—'

'I know—I'll get on to the witnesses and see if we can confirm the ownership of the items. For that, I'll need first-class photos of the items.'

'I'll get that done first, and get them to you,' Geoff Rhumer said briskly.

RUTH COOMBS VERY quickly identified the leg warmers as being Judy's. In the office at the back of the large shop, she looked at the photographs intently. 'Of course,

I can't swear they're hers,' she added cautiously, determined to be scrupulously fair. 'I dare say a lot of them were sold to a lot of people. But I remember Judy buying a pair just like these from Bicester market. When we had one of those really cold winters, you know? She liked the colours.'

Hillary nodded. 'We were wondering if you might have kept anything of Judy's that might still have traces of her DNA on it? A hairbrush maybe? Otherwise, we'll have to take a DNA sample from her parents, to compare it to any traces we might find on the leg warmers.'

But Ruth shrugged helplessly. 'Sorry, I can't help you. I packed up all her stuff after a year or so, and asked her parents if they wanted it. I didn't particularly like doing it—I knew Judy never gave them the time of day any more, and probably wouldn't have wanted me to either. But…well, I didn't really have any right to hold on to them, you see.' Ruth held out her hands helplessly. 'And when push comes to shove, family is family, right? In the end they took it, not because they wanted it, but because it was the "done thing". It would have looked odd if they'd refused, and that's all they cared about. Too busy worrying about what the neighbours might say, but not caring a damn about what might have happened to their own daughter,' she added bitterly.

Hillary said nothing to that, but thanked her quietly and left. Geoff Rhumer had already confirmed that a lone uniformed PC had talked to Ruth shortly after Judy had been reported missing, and that Ruth had confirmed that he had been left alone for a short time. Which meant that he certainly could, therefore, have done a quick search of his victim's room, had he been of a mind to do so.

And lifted more items than just the leg warmers? Hillary thought, on balance, that he probably had.

Unfortunately, Ruth's description of him had been even more vague than that provided by Mrs Tinkerton.

GEORGIA BIGGS LOOKED at the photograph of the graduated strand of pearls thoughtfully, and then smiled somewhat ruefully. They were once again crowded into her small dental office, with the smell of antiseptic sharp in the air, and posters of gum disease rampant.

Unlike Ruth Coombs, Georgia Biggs hadn't been at the flat when the man in a police uniform had shown up making inquiries about the missing woman, but he had talked the landlord of the premises into letting him 'take a look around'. Unfortunately for Geoff Rhumer and his team, the landlord was now deceased, leaving them with, quite literally, a dead end, when it came to getting another independent description of the man they were looking for.

'I know Meg had a necklace quite like this,' Georgia told them, then laughed softly. 'She was furious about it.'

'Oh?' Hillary asked, tensing just a little. Could they have been a gift from the stalker? She could quite see why Meg Vickary wouldn't have wanted anything to do with them, if they had been. But if they had been one of his original gifts, why had he stolen them back?

'It turned out they weren't real. Oh, they were very good quality, cultured, or whatever it is they are when they're not really natural. Worth a few hundred quid, or so the jeweller told her, but not the thousands they would have been if they'd been the genuine article,' Georgia explained, then sighed. 'I quite liked them personally. I would have worn them and been happy to—they had this pretty pinkish quality to them. But Meg just tossed them into the back of her jewellery case and never wore them. She gave the man who gave them to her the push as well. Well, that was Meg, really. She didn't like being messed about.'

'He was an old boyfriend, was he?' Hillary asked quickly, then felt her hopes drop as Georgia nodded.

'Yeah, she went out with him for a while. He was a company rep for some pharmaceutical company or something. Can't remember his name now.'

'Can you remember what he looked like?' Hillary persisted. It was possible the stalker had made contact, after all, and maybe even persuaded Meg to date him a few times.

'Really tall beanpole of a bloke,' Georgia said. 'Really fair hair and pale skin. Almost an albino, you know?'

Hillary nodded glumly. 'Do you still have them, or know what happened to them? The pearls, I mean?'

Georgia thought about it for a second, and then frowned thoughtfully. 'I don't know. They're probably still with her stuff. It's all in storage. You can look if you like.' She gave them the details of the lock-up where Meg Vickary's worldly possessions were still kept. 'I keep paying the rental on the space, thinking that one day she'll turn up for them.' Georgia shook her head and looked Hillary straight in the eye.

'But she won't, will she?' Hillary smiled gently. 'If you'll just give us written permission to access the storage?' Georgia obligingly wrote down the address and handed it over.

They drove to the lock-up, which turned out to be in one of Swindon's suburbs, but although they eventually found Meg Vickary's jewellery box, they found no string of pearls—fake or otherwise.

Hillary was interested to note that all the jewellery in the box was of the costume variety. But she was sure that a woman of Meg's tenacity and ambition must have been given plenty of the genuine article by her many admirers.

So where was it?

It was possible that Georgia Biggs had 'redirected' it to her own jewellery box, and she knew that many of her colleagues would automatically assume that that had been the case. And they might be right.

But there was another explanation for it being missing, and Hillary was beginning to think she might have a damned good idea what that was.

DEIRDRE TINKERTON TOOK one look at the photograph of the fluffy troll key ring and abruptly and rather heavily sat down on a chair. 'Oh, that ugly thing. Yes, Gilly had one just like it, but...' She looked up at them, her pleasant round face slowly turning pale. 'Why are you showing me a photograph of it now? Is there something you're not telling me? Is my Gilly...?' Her voice suddenly seemed to lose its strength, and she cleared her throat noisily. 'Is my little girl dead?' she asked in a small voice.

Hillary cursed herself for having to bring this to the poor woman's door, and cursed the stalker even more. It seemed heartlessly cruel to rattle Deirdre Tinkerton's comforting belief that her daughter was alive and well somewhere, and just thoughtlessly remaining out of touch, especially if what Hillary was coming to believe might be true, was indeed actually the case.

'We have no reason to believe that at this time, Mrs Tinkerton,' she said firmly, carefully avoiding Jimmy

Jessop's eyes. 'I imagine these little fluffy troll things were sold in their millions anyway,' she added.

Deirdre Tinkerton visibly forced herself to rally. 'Yes. Yes, you're right about that. They were a bit of a craze, weren't they? There's nothing to say this was my Gilly's, is there?'

'Nothing at all. We simply wanted to know if it might be,' Hillary said, then went still as Mrs Tinkerton laid a hand on her arm and said quietly, 'You would tell me if you found a body, wouldn't you, love? One that had a key ring on it like this?'

'Mrs Tinkerton, I swear to you, we haven't found any bodies,' Hillary said, perfectly truthfully.

She fought back the ridiculous urge to say something totally inane, such as 'Try not to worry about it' or something equally stupid, and patted her hand instead. 'We'll be in touch if we have any more questions. Remember, we're still just trying to figure out what, if anything, has happened.' Deirdre smiled, but her eyes were beginning to look haunted. Outside, Jimmy let out his breath in a long, slow exhale.

'Sometimes I hate this job,' he muttered grimly.

Hillary knew exactly what he meant.

BACK AT HQ, Hillary checked her voice mail and found that a long message from Sam had been left for her.

Their very first interview with one of the retired gangsters had come up trumps. Whilst Mike Pratt had claimed not to have taken much interest in Meg himself—he was in to very young, leggy blondes, apparently—he did know for a fact that a 'colleague' of his had very much taken a shine to her. A man by the name of Liam Hardwicke, who'd specialized in smuggling of all kinds—from booze, to fags to female sex slaves—had 'fancied her rotten'. And had let her know it.

Apparently, Meg had been suitably flattered and, by all accounts, the interest had been mutual.

She and Jimmy listened to his report and then grabbed their coats. It was time to talk to Marcus Kane again.

KANE PRETENDED TO be wearily annoyed but painstakingly patient to see the police in his office again.

'Yes, hello again, Mrs Greene, and just what can I do for you this time?' Hillary settled herself comfortably in the chair in front of his desk and smiled cordially. She'd teach the bastard to call her *Mrs Greene*.

'Liam Hardwicke,' she said briskly. 'He was a sex slave trafficker and general all-round nasty piece of work. Your firm represented him and acquired Queen's Counsel for him on a number of occasions during the past ten years. Is that correct?'

Marcus Kane didn't even blink. 'All our clients are entitled to legal representation, Mrs Greene, as I'm sure you know,' he said smoothly.

'I do know,' Hillary said shortly. 'I also know that Mr Hardwicke seemed to be very impressed with Meg Vickary. And that she didn't, shall we say, exactly discourage him in his interest either. I'm sure that a smart man like you couldn't have failed to notice.'

Marcus shifted slightly on his seat. 'Liam was a bit of a ladies' man, yes. He'd been married and divorced, I think, three or maybe even four times,' he agreed cautiously.

'Was he between wives when Meg Vickary did the paperwork on his case?' She shot the questions at him rapidly, allowing him little time to think up lies.

'I believe he was.'

'Where is he now?' she demanded.

'I have no idea. As you'll be aware, if you've done your homework, Mr Hardwicke was found Not Guilty in his last court appearance,' Marcus returned fire smoothly.

'Were you jealous of him? You and Meg were, after all, involved in an affair of your own.'

'Of course I wasn't jealous of him!'

'A good-looking man, is he? I have to say, I haven't seen a photograph of him, but I can imagine the type.' Hillary smiled knowingly. 'Middle aged, but in good physical shape, I imagine. Something of the bad boy about him—women always seem attracted to those sort, don't they, Mr Kane?'

Marcus flushed slightly. 'If you like the bluff, somewhat bucolic look, I suppose he wasn't that bad looking,' he agreed thinly.

'Did Meg flirt with him?' Hillary asked crisply.

'Meg liked to keep the clients happy,' Marcus said, his voice becoming more and more clipped.

Jimmy, his pen flying across his notebook as he took notes, was careful to repress a smile. The guv'nor was getting under his skin all right.

'Was that one of the things you paid her for, Mr Kane?' Hillary asked softly.

'I'm not a pimp!' Marcus said sharply, then suddenly let loose with a shark-like smile. 'And really, I can't see where all this can possibly be going. As far as I can remember, Liam Hardwicke retired to Spain somewhere months before Meg went missing.'

Hillary nodded. 'Well, thank you, Mr Kane,' she said, abruptly dismissing him. 'That will be all for now.' Then she appeared to change her mind and added very casually, 'Oh, by the way, you wouldn't happen to have a contact phone number for Mr Hardwicke, would you?'

Marcus Kane rose and smiled beatifically at her. 'I'll ask my secretary to make sure you get it on your way out, Mrs Greene.'

LIAM HARDWICKE CAME to the telephone the moment Hillary Greene identified herself to his Spanish house-keeper. According to Kane's records, he was living on the south coast in one of the lesser-known resorts, but almost certainly in a sumptuous villa with a view of the Med.

It made Hillary sick to think about it.

But back at HQ, with Jimmy listening in to her end of the conversation, she forced herself to concentrate on the task in hand.

She identified herself, and her work at the CRT. 'Mr Hardwicke, we're currently trying to trace the where-abouts of a missing person by the name of Margaret Vickary. She was a secretary working for your solici-tors, back here in Oxford. I'm sure you remember her?'

The voice on the other end of the line was understand-ably cautious, but he agreed that he did. 'Sure, a good-looking woman. Charming too. I'm sorry to hear she's gone AWOL.' Hillary could trace the last vestiges of a lingering cockney accent in Hardwicke's voice.

'From all accounts, you seem to have got on very well with her. You wouldn't have happened to invite her over to Spain at any time, would you, Mr Hardwicke?'

There was a moment of silence. Then, 'Like I said, I got on fine with her. She had a good sense of humour and was a lovely lady and charming with it. But why should that mean that I would invite her over to Spain with me?' Hillary didn't fail to notice that he wasn't giving her any yes or no answers, but was forming the habit of answering her with a question of his own. She found the equivocation interesting.

'Just trying to tie up any loose ends, sir,' she said brightly. 'After all, we don't want to waste our valuable time and resources trying to find her, if she's simply relocated to Spain, do we?'

'Has anyone told you she's over here?' Liam Hardwicke asked jovially.

'No, sir,' Hillary said. 'Like I said, we're just checking.'

'No 'arm in that, as my old man always said. Sorry I can't help you, luv.' Yeah, I just bet you are, Hillary thought, as she put the phone down.

'Well?' Jimmy asked curiously.

'Slippery as an eel,' Hillary said flatly.

Jimmy shrugged. 'I can't really see that it matters one way or the other, guv, does it? Meg disappeared over here in Blighty, and we already know the who and the why of it, after all.' Hillary nodded slowly.

'Yes,' she said thoughtfully. 'I believe we very well might.' Jimmy shot her a quick, puzzled look, then shrugged.

She continued to stare out of the window, her mind carefully and methodically looking for flaws in the growing intricacies of her theory.

And not finding all that many.

NINE

At NOON THE next day, Tom Warrington was walking slowly around a fully road-worthy and quite spacious white camper van. It was in fairly good nick with perhaps just a hint of rust around the wheel arches, and was about ten years old but came with a full service record and tax. Although it looked rather pedestrian inside—being more leatherette and fake pine veneer than IKEA—it was clean and serviceable.

The price wasn't too bad, but on principle, he spent half an hour haggling it down with the seller, a middle-aged turf accountant who was getting divorced, and wanted to stash as much cash away on the q.t. as he could before his soon-to-be ex-wife's solicitor came sniffing around.

Finally, they shook hands on the deal and Tom left, telling the gloomy old sod that he'd be around later that evening sometime to pick it up, with the first instalment in cash, and more bone fides to ensure that he'd get the rest of his money, though Tom rather thought that his police uniform was doing him more favours than his solid credit rating. It was rather touching how some members of the public still trusted the police.

He was back late from lunch, and the dragon guarding the records office sniffed at him and looked at her watch with a significant roll of her watery eyes, but she at least had the good sense not to say anything. Tom gave her his best green-eyed toothsome smile and turned to his computer.

He played with the idea of calling up Hillary's personnel file, just so that he could feast on her past glories and moon over her ID photograph, but with the dragon already miffed and keeping an eye on him, he knew it wasn't a good idea. He contented himself with sending Vivienne a text message instead.

Then, with a sigh, he got down to work.

VIVIENNE READ THE text message in the office, a big smile lighting up her face. Sam was with her, and they were just finishing up the latest boring stuff Hillary had given them to do whilst talking over their exciting day yesterday, when they'd actually got to talk to real-life gangsters.

Needless to say, she'd been more impressed than he was by the big houses, the bling, and the glamour of the wives, although none of the men had looked much like Ronnie Biggs or even Ray Winstone for that matter, which was a bit disappointing.

But Tom's text cheered her up no end. He was picking up their little love nest later on, and he was anxious for her to come and try it out with him. Finally, Vivienne thought smugly, saving the text and putting the mobile back into her bag. It was about time she got him between the sheets! And wasn't playing hard to get supposed to be a woman's prerogative, anyway?

The printer was just printing off the last round of artistic colonies that she'd been able to find on the Internet, when Hillary Greene finally deigned to grace them with her presence. Vivienne listened with genuine interest, however, as her boss updated them on her latest inter-

view with Marcus Kane, but knew that she'd only bothered to do so because it was their information and hard
work that had turned up the lead for her in the first place.

If 'lead' was the right word. For the life of her, Vivienne couldn't see where all this was supposed to be
going. Then again, it was clear that she and Sam were
still being kept out of the loop on the investigation. She
had no idea what Hillary had been doing all morning,
for example, except that she'd been closeted in Steven's
office with DI Rhumer.

She'd have loved to have been a fly on the wall in
there and find out what it was that was really going on.
But she'd bet her wage packet that it wouldn't be long
before they were back to doing more of the boring stuff
and, sure enough, once Hillary had finished telling them
about Meg Vickary's exploits, her next words made Vivienne's heart sink.

'Now,' Hillary said, glancing down at her notebook.
'I need a thorough background check run on Christopher
Deakin's financial status. He admitted to lending Judy
Yelland a substantial sum of money just before she disappeared and I want to know how much it would have
hurt him, if at all, to do it. I know he's obviously doing
well today, but I have a feeling that might not have been
so much the case four years ago. The company was still
relatively new. As it was started mainly with his wife's
dosh, I want to know if she was the type to keep her eye
on it, or if she simply trusted to her husband's business
acumen.' Hillary thought that it might tell her a lot about
Christopher Deakin to know the answer to that particular question.

Vivienne grimaced at the thought of trying to translate

spreadsheets and accountant's gobbledegook. Luckily, Hillary's eyes went straight from hers to the ginger minger.

'Sam, that can be a job for you. If the banks give you trouble, start with the Inland Revenue and stuff in the public domain. I'm sure his company is a public limited one, so there'll be records. His personal finances might be harder to trace, but it'll be good practice for you.'

'Guv.'

'And then you can come with me to interview the wife,' Hillary added, with a small smile.

'Guv,' Sam said, with far more enthusiasm.

'Vivienne, do you have that list of artist colonies I asked you for?' She turned to look at the young girl, who was dressed in what looked like hot pants. Good grief, were they back in fashion now? Or was she just expressing her much-vaunted 'individualism'? Hillary didn't know, and couldn't have cared less.

'Just printing off the last of them now, guv,' Vivienne said smugly, and handed over a sheaf of papers. 'I haven't had a chance to go through them yet though.'

'I've highlighted in yellow some of the more promising ones we did earlier, guv,' Sam said, with an apologetic glance at Vivienne. 'The ones at the bottom of the pile. I was working on them while Vivienne was doing the last of it.' Vivienne shot him a knowing smile. He was so anxious to earn brownie points it was pathetic.

'Thanks, Sam. Right, you can get on with Deakin then. Vivienne...you can type up the report on the costa cons.'

Vivienne grimaced. 'Right, guv,' she said listlessly. Did she look like a bloody typist? Or a secretary?

'Or you can always help Sam with the financial search,' Hillary said archly.

'No, that's OK, guv,' Vivienne said quickly, scooting back behind her computer screen. Over in his chair, Jimmy Jessop coughed tellingly into his cupped hands. Hillary gave him a wink as she sauntered out.

Back in her office, she began to sort through the list of possible retreats that Gillian Tinkerton might have been interested in.

There were, surprisingly, quite a few. Even though it was hardly the Age of Aquarius anymore, alternative lifestyle options were obviously just as popular as in the hippies' heyday. The choice was surprisingly cosmopolitan. They ranged from learning how to become a crofter in the far flung Scottish Highlands, to becoming an eel-catcher in the Norfolk Broads, to learning how to weave baskets and other traditional wares in osier, or green willow. And not all were work-based or profession-related either. A lot of places offered would-be Picassos tutorials whilst being catered to in country-house type residences, whilst yet others offered more leisure-based activities. Musicians offered to give flute lessons, and several places promised to give 'degrees' in alternative healing therapies. Hillary read one on-line brochure on how she too could be taught to place warm stones on 'healing' centres on middle-aged flabby bodies in country spas, and shuddered.

She put all Vivienne's most recent offerings to one side and turned to Sam's highlighted list.

And nodded in approval.

Yes, these were more what she wanted, and she began to compile them in geographical order, with those nearest to Kidlington at the top.

Seven in particular, looked like the kind of thing that

she might be interested in, and she settled herself comfortably in her chair and reached for the phone.

Two hours later, she had a short-list of four.

The owner-managers (or in two cases, the representative of the co-ops) of the facilities had varied in the limit of their desire to help the police with their inquiries, but she hadn't picked up any really bad vibes from any of them.

Due to modern technology, she'd been able to wing a photograph of a young-looking Gillian Tinkerton to all seven places, but none of them had immediately acknowledged knowing her. But then, that in itself meant nothing, she knew.

For a start, Hillary knew from experience, that people could change and physically alter drastically over the years, and the photograph Deirdre Tinkerton had given her of her daughter was in itself a few years old to begin with. People, and women in particular, could look vastly different in just a few years: weight lost, weight gained; hair styled or cut differently and probably, in gypsy-like Gillian's case, dyed; eyeglasses discarded for contact lenses, or failing eyesight meaning the need for glasses on a woman previously unencumbered with them could all radically alter the look of a person's face. So it was easily possible that people genuinely wouldn't recognize someone else from a photograph if they were sitting just a few feet away.

Then again, artistic communes were probably as good a place as any, if you needed a reason to 'hide' from society. Women keeping out of the way of abusive partners, for instance, would probably find refuge there. Or men trying to avoid paying child maintenance. Hillary could well imagine that if you had a tight-knit community, especially one where some members had been together for a long time, that nobody would be anxious to discuss your business with strangers on the telephone.

Wearily, she made herself a cup of coffee and leaned back in her chair, tapping the paperwork in front of her thoughtfully, mulling over the scant details she'd been able to glean from speaking to the organizers.

Greensleeves Artisans, based in Wiltshire, had been going for nearly twenty years. The founder member had been a farmer's son, already disillusioned with the way the farming industry was going, and had seen some ramshackle barns on his property as a way of supplementing his income. He'd employed local stone-masons, carpenters and other skilled workers to convert the barns to accommodation and studios, mainly pottery and artists' studios, with a woodcarver's workshop tacked on. Cannily, he'd had several of the renovators work part-time for him, training others in their particular disciplines, as well as renting out the accommodation to other people more interested in pure art.

Leyline Literati were based on the Berkshire border, and boasted an old rambling rectory as their main place of residence, in a small village that still mostly belonged to a vast estate. As its name implied, it gave room and board and 'vanity publishing advice' to writers who were interested in the more esoterically minded disciplines. If you wanted to write about interesting hauntings, the possibility of alien visitations, the uncanny, otherworldly knowledge supposedly possessed by ancient tribes, or any other whimsy from psychics with ESP, to cats that could predict the future, they could help guide and advise. The small print assured you that they only took a small percentage of any royalties you might earn. It was,

Hillary supposed, a small price to pay for any budding author, desperate to see their name in print.

Hillary could well see that Gillian might be attracted to the idea of being a published author. Hadn't her friend said that she never stayed with one discipline for long? And didn't everyone believe that they had at least one book in them?

Hillary had to smile at herself there. She herself had written a book last year, a fictional piece based on one of her old cases, and sent it off to a publisher.

Naturally, she'd heard nothing back since.

The third of the outfits she was interested in was based just over the Welsh border, and specialized in glass, teaching people to blow glass, make stained-glass windows, small collectable animals, paperweights with those intricate designs and even glass jewellery. Through a Glass Brightly also offered live-in accommodation and promised 'gifted' glass artists a show-case for their work and the chance of a regular income via a number of local shops that would display and sell their items on a commission basis.

The last of the four was set on Dartmoor in Devon, and was mostly based on painted art, with live-in tutors willing to give lessons to professional artists who wanted to expand their repertoire. But they did offer a side-line for those who wanted to become illustrators for children's books, or become graphic artists. Or, Hillary interpreted cynically, grown men who wanted to stay little boys by creating comic-book characters. Baskerville Artist's Colony might appeal to Gillian if she had any drawing skills.

Hillary sighed, and looked up as a tap came on the door. Quickly, she stuffed the paperwork into a folder as

Steven, without waiting for an invitation to enter, pushed open the door and looked in.

He watched, with interest, the way she casually closed the folder and smiled. 'Everything OK?'

'Fine,' Hillary said.

'Geoff and his team are making progress you know, even if it is only in ruling people out.' Hillary nodded. They'd spent all morning with Geoff Rhumer, who'd filled them in on his team's progress to date. So far, as Steven had said, they'd eliminated, for various reasons, nearly half the people on his list.

'Don't worry—I'm not getting impatient,' Hillary said truthfully. 'I always knew it was going to be painstaking work, and would take time. And I'm not getting disheartened. You don't have to mollycoddle me.' Steven grinned at her, and Hillary felt her heart give a little flip. Damn, he was too good-looking for her own peace of mind.

'Perish the thought,' Steven said, leaning negligently against the door post. 'Why don't you come to my place tonight? I'll cook.'

'You can cook?'

'Well, I wouldn't go that far,' he admitted. 'Let's just say that I can produce food that's reasonably edible.'

'Deal.' He grinned, turned and left her, but as he passed the communal office, he caught Jimmy Jessop's eye and gave a quick 'follow me' gesture with his head.

Jimmy sauntered out after him, but Vivienne, who was always aware of Steven Crayle's proximity, watched him leave with a jaundiced eye. Whatever it was that she and Sam were being kept out of the loop about, it was clear that the old duffer was in on it.

Jimmy followed the super into his office, then closed

the door behind him. Steven sat down behind his desk and looked at him levelly.

'Do you know what she's up to?' he asked flatly. Jimmy hesitated visibly.

'Come on, Jimmy, she's hiding something from me, I can tell. What's she got up her sleeve?' Jimmy shrugged, but gave him an accurate rundown on their activities so far. On the one hand, it felt vaguely disloyal to do so, but on the other, he knew that now was not the time to take sides.

Steven listened in silence and then frowned. 'I don't get it. I don't understand what she's thinking.'

'No,' Jimmy said grimly. 'I don't either. I can't get a handle on her logic, somehow.'

Steven nodded. 'But she's definitely on to something. I can just feel it.'

'Yeah, me too. And she's good, guv,' Jimmy said thoughtfully.

'You know she is. So whatever it is, it'll be gold, you'll see,' he predicted confidently.

'I agree. I thought, at first, that Donleavy might have been over-egging her skills, but now I know he wasn't. She's one of the best all right.' Jimmy smiled. But he didn't say what they were both thinking. Yes, Hillary Greene was good, but was she working at the top of her game on this particular case?

'Well, just keep an eye on her,' Steven said at last. 'And, Jimmy, you will tell me if…if you start to get worried about her. About anything to do with the case, I mean.'

Jimmy nodded. 'Yeah, guv. I know what you mean,' he said heavily.

IN HER OFFICE, Hillary ringed the four names of the artists' colonies and knew she'd have to visit them. But

Jimmy would wonder why and so would Steven. And she couldn't, yet, give them a reasonable explanation.

She sighed and massaged the back of her neck which felt knotted and stiff with tension. Tomorrow, she'd have to call in sick, and visit the two nearest colonies in person. Perhaps then she'd have a better idea of whether or not she was on a wild goose chase.

Or seriously losing her marbles.

Her hand began to wander up to the scar on her neck and once more she caught the movement before it could finish its task. She glanced at her watch, and knew that if she called it a day, nobody would say anything about her leaving early.

And she did feel tired.

On the other hand… 'Sod that,' Hillary said, and reached for the phone. There was one last thing she could do before she headed back to the *Mollern* and gave a nod to whoever it was that was parked in the pub car-park and assigned to watch over her.

HILLARY CHECKED HER ORGANIZER, opening the page at the letter T. She knew she should have an electronic version of the big notebook by now, but somehow had never managed to get around to it.

She found the name of Richard Torridge and noted the address and phone number, pleased to see that her memory hadn't let her down. She only hoped he was still living in the same area of Spain.

She rang the number, wondering if she'd get lucky and find it still current. 'The Brit Bar,' a female voice sang cheerfully into her ear.

'Hello. Can I speak to Dick, please?'

'Whossis then?' the voice asked at once. It had a slight

Geordie accent to it, and Hillary suddenly remembered that former sergeant Richard Torridge had married for a third time to some lass from Newcastle way, shortly before retiring and heading to Spain to run that perennial ex-copper's dream—a pub.

'I'm DI Hillary Greene,' Hillary said, purloining her old title in an attempt to head off the suspicion that she could hear bristling in the other woman's voice. Mind you, from what she remembered of 'Dirty Dicky's' reputation with women, she wouldn't be surprised if the poor woman had good reason to be perpetually jealous. 'I was an old guv'nor of his. I just need him to do a quick favour for me.'

'Oh aye? Better call him then, hadn't I, pet?' Hillary heard her squawk her husband's name and the clattering noise as she put the telephone down onto a hard surface. Over the line came the sound of glasses clinking, games machines pinging, and a babble of voices, mostly in English, but with some Spanish thrown in.

But then, with a name as unoriginal as The Brit Bar, Hillary suspected that Dirty Dick had probably cashed in on the expat's need for proper British beer and that most of his customers came from the homeland. She heard his wife mutter something dire at him a moment before he came on the line.

'Hillary, is that really you? Bloody hell, Hillary Greene, after all these years, as I love and bloody breathe. You still on the force then?'

'Yes,' Hillary said, not wanting to go in to her retirement, and her subsequent return to CRT. 'How are you doing, Sergeant?' In the old days, she'd been responsible for the feckless git on many a case. She remembered him as being big, humorous, and surprisingly canny. At first he hadn't liked having a female boss, but once she'd knocked that out of him they'd got on surprisingly well, and had put away a goodly amount of villains between them. She had tried to talk him out of going off to Spain, knowing that the force could ill afford to lose such a useful thief-taker, but he'd been adamant that he'd had enough. And ultimately, there was no arguing with that.

'Can't complain, guv. Business is good, the women are gorgeous.' He lowered his voice as he said the last bit so that the Geordie woman who was no doubt hovering within earshot wouldn't catch it. Hillary grinned, picturing him in her mind's eye. Never sartorially blessed, he was probably sitting at his bar dressed in baggy shorts and a colourful shirt, probably red as a beet and sweating, but bright-eyed and alert. 'So, what can I do for you, guv?' he asked next, confirming her memory of him as being sharp as a tack.

'You in a mood to do an old mate a favour?' she asked cautiously.

'For you, guv, always. What's up?'

'A con by the name of Liam Hardwicke. Heard of him?'

'Yeah, of course I bloody well have. He's got a villa not far away from…. Oh ah! And what's he done to appear on your radar then, guv? The scuttlebutt here is that he's definitely retired. Made his fortune and scarpered, and is now happy to leave all the wheeling and dealing to his competitors. Don't tell me he's got tired of all that sun and sangria and gone all nostalgic for the bad old days?'

'I've got no reason to think so, Dick,' Hillary said honestly enough. 'But do you see him around? He's pretty local to where you are, right?'

'I don't see him around the same town as where I've

got the bar, if that's what you mean—it's too down market for the likes of him. But the next big place just up the coast a few miles is a bit more classy like. Me and the missus go there sometimes to kick up our heels and have a good time. He's mostly to be found in the top night clubs, or the fancy eateries mind, which is out of our bracket. But you can see him driving around in his Roller sometimes, or occasionally walking around the designer shops.'

'Right, so you'd know him if you saw him,' Hillary said gratefully. 'Do you still have your cameras with you?' she asked. Photography, along with skirt-chasing, had always been Dirty Dick's main passion, and he'd even had a few prints exhibited at the local galleries in Oxford and Woodstock in his day. More proof, if it were needed, that there was far more to DS Torridge than his bluff, outwardly loutish behaviour would indicate.

'Sure I do. Mind you I mostly take pictures of the sunset or sunrise over the ocean nowadays for the tourist shops. Atmospheric shots of seagulls or the mists on the distant mountains, that kind of tat. I managed to wangle a deal with a postcard company for a few of them that provides me with a nice little earner. Why?' he asked warily, but Hillary smiled. She could hear the catch of interest and excitement in his voice that told her that she had him hooked.

'Fancy doing a little surveillance for me? On the q.t. like,' she added scrupulously.

She heard the silence on the other end of the line and could guess what he was thinking. A phone call from an old guv'nor asking for work on the q.t. meant that, whatever it was she was working on, was probably being done without the brass knowing about it. Not that that in itself would worry Dirty Dicky much—he'd circumnavigated the top brass often enough himself back in the old days.

'Normally I'd say yes like a shot, guv,' Dick said cautiously.

'But I've got the missus to think about now. And I ain't got no back-up out here; I'm a long way from home and me mates. Getting on the wrong side of someone like Hardwicke wouldn't be no picnic. If I'm rumbled he's not going to be happy about me nosing around taking pictures of dodgy geezers doing business with him, and I'll likely end up with broken legs—if I'm lucky.'

But Hillary was already way ahead of him. 'Quite right too, Dick, and you should know me well enough by now to know that I wouldn't ask it of you. So relax. I'm not interested in any likely looking men visiting his villa in the early hours of the morning, or whose hand is in whose sticky little pockets. Like I said, I've no reason to suppose that anything like that would still be going on.' Over the line, she heard a faint sigh of relief.

'No, this is much more right up your street,' she said with a grin. 'I want you to get on film any of the birds he's hanging out with. And you can do that in broad daylight, whilst pretending to be doing your usual stuff, if you like. Follow them to the beach, or when they go shopping. I'm not asking you to stake out his villa and risk catching the eye of any muscle he's still got working for him.'

'Now that sounds more like it,' Dirty Dick said, with glee. 'A man like that is bound to have some really glamorous types hanging around, I'll bet.'

'His villa is probably a Hugh Hefner pad by any other name,' Hillary agreed with a laugh. 'Then again, he may just have the one permanent one in residence. If so, I especially want photos of her—as clear and as close-up as you can get.'

'With the zoom lenses I've got, you'll think she was sitting in your lap, guv. Trust me, you'll be able to count the pores on her nose. I'll get on to it right away. Give me a day to suss out the lie of the land, and I should be able to email you something within the week.' He paused, then sighed. 'Mind you, I don't know what I'm gonna tell the missus,' he added mournfully.

Hillary thought of the woman behind that suspicious Geordie voice and laughed. 'Me neither, Dick. But that's your problem, mate.'

Dirty Dick snorted. 'Here I was forgetting—you're all heart.' Hillary was still laughing when she hung up.

TOM FELT VIVIENNE slip her hand around his waist, and forced a smile to his face. Beside him, the old reprobate selling the camper van beamed at him enviously. 'You like it then?' Tom asked her, discreetly handing over a rolled-up wad of cash to the other man, that the turf accountant quickly made disappear, as if by magic.

'She's great. She is roadworthy, isn't she?' Vivienne asked uncertainly.

Tom, with a raised eyebrow look, passed the question over to the former owner, who nodded reassuringly. 'Passed her MOT with flying colours. Got half a tank of petrol. She's hot to trot.' He made a great ceremony of handing over the keys, which Tom accepted, before gallantly helping Vivienne to climb up into the passenger seat.

After collecting the documentation, he got in beside her and headed out of the drive. 'For now, I'm going to park it at Mum and Dad's place,' Tom said, as he drove carefully into the traffic, trying to get the hang of the way the large, cumbersome vehicle moved. 'But I've got a nice rural spot out in the woods already lined up.'

Vivienne nodded enthusiastically. 'I can't wait. But let's go to the pub, yeah? After the day I've had, I need a drink.'

'What, more gangsters?' he mocked, trying to judge the clearance of a tight corner.

'Nah—I wish. It's just more of the same—more bloody computer scut-work,' Vivienne moaned. 'If I have to read any more guff about creating beautiful calligraphy—whatever the hell that is—or how to design your own jewellery from dried beans, or how to make fabulous works of art from "found items" or sweet wrappers I'll go barmy.'

'You what?' he asked, with half a laugh.

'I'm serious. I've only been looking up all these weird artist colony places that Gillian Tinkerton might have visited. For some reason, the mad cow thinks it's relevant.' Gillian Tinkerton. Art colonies. Tom felt a cold prickle on the back of his neck, and feverishly, his mind began to work. It didn't take him long to see the way Hillary's own mind had to be working.

Could she be right? The thought of it brought him out in a cold sweat.

He wouldn't want to bet on her being wrong.

Oh, Hillary, he thought, with a rush of pride and painful despair. You're just too damned good, sweetheart. You're going too fast.

He glanced across at Vivienne, his mouth going dry with excitement. OK, so he was just going to have to match her pace and move faster himself. He couldn't let her down after all. Especially not now, when she might just be beginning to doubt him.

Besides, it meant that finally, after all he'd had to put up with from this stupid, sarcastic, ungrateful bitch, he could shut her foul mouth once and for all. And he wouldn't have to put up with her pawing him all the time either.

'So, what say we christen the van as soon as we can?' he said softly. 'And, by the way, we've got to give the old girl a name. Why don't you choose.' Vivienne patted the leatherette dashboard thoughtfully.

'Hmm. I'll have to think about it,' she said coyly.

'You do that,' Tom Warrington said quietly.

THE NEXT DAY Hillary got up early, dressed and walked down the towpath to the pub car-park where her car waited for her. In passing, she nodded casually at one of Jimmy's retired mates who was sitting in an old van, and drinking from a thermos. She gave him a cheerful wave and a toot as she passed, and watched in her rearview mirror just to make sure that he wasn't going to shadow her all the way into HQ.

He didn't and, with a sigh of relief, she watched him turn off in the opposite direction to town. Once out of sight, she pulled over and called in sick, being careful not to speak to Steven directly, but leaving a message to be given to him by the main switchboard.

That done, she turned off her mobile, which she knew would probably incense him, but which couldn't be helped. She didn't want him offering to come over and mop her fevered brow or anything.

She smiled at the thought and set off for the Berkshire Downs, where Leyline Literati hung its hat. It was a nice enough day and the hour or so it took to drive down there passed pleasantly. The rolling green fields kept her company on either side, and the gradual proliferation of horses told her that she was definitely heading towards the muddy green wellington set.

She found the village easily, an anachronism in this day and age, given that it still belonged to one titled individual. It meant that there were no out-of-keeping council houses, and the village pub and shop remained adamantly and defiantly open. Both, Hillary guessed, were run by a local village co-op.

The vicarage where dedicated scribblers could pen their masterpieces turned out to be a gem of a Georgian building, exquisitely square and elegantly proportioned.

Unfortunately, although the manager, when confronted by the constabulary in person, became far more helpful than he had been on the telephone, her journey turned out to be a waste of petrol. There were eight writers in residence, and none of them recognized either Gillian Tinkerton's name or photograph.

With a sigh, Hillary thanked her host and set off for the Wiltshire border.

She was just passing the Uffington white horse, cut into the chalk over 3,000 or so years ago, and was glancing appreciatively out of her window at it, when she glanced at the clock and realized that she really should call in and talk to Steven, if only to reassure him that she wasn't up to something or doing anything silly.

Like wandering about on her own out in the wilds, chasing down elusive theories.

She pulled over and rang his number, her heart beating just a little faster in anticipation of hearing his voice. She knew he was going to be mad, and that only made her blood tingle that little bit more. She looked at her reflection in the mirror, noted the brightly sparkling eyes, and gave herself a little warning shake of the head. 'You're riding for a fall, my girl,' she told herself, then jumped as Steven's voice sounded in her ear.

'Hillary? What's up? What's wrong?' She felt a pleasant little warm wave wash over her that he sounded so concerned, then sighed.

'Nothing. I'm just a bit under the weather that's all,' she said, banking on her guardian angel not having called in with the information that she should now be safely at work. 'I'm just feeling a bit iffy, so I decided to stay on the boat. I think I might be coming down with a summer cold—and you know what a bugger they are. They say you're most contagious in the first few days, so I don't want to pass it on to everyone else.'

'Oh, OK. Do you want me to come over tonight?'

'What, and get the sniffles yourself? Don't be daft. If it comes to anything I'll let you know. If it turns out to be nothing, I'll be back into the office tomorrow.'

'OK, sweetheart. See you soon.' Hillary agreed, and hung up, feeling guilty. Yep, feeling guilty about lying to a man was definitely the first step on a slippery slope all right.

She wondered how long it would be before Steven or Jimmy thought to check in and see if her minder needed relieving, and thus realize that she'd gone AWOL. Probably not all that long, if she knew Steven.

Hey-ho, she thought wearily, as she pulled away and continued past the ancient white horse deeper into Wiltshire, and on to Greensleeves Artisans. She'd just have to cross that bridge when she came to it.

Which, as it turned out, was to be pretty damned soon.

GREENSLEEVES ARTISANS NESTLED in a truly lovely little valley, the converted barns now surrounded by both vegetable patches and flower gardens. As she parked beside a large open barn, the smell of sawdust hit her the moment she opened the car door.

From another smaller brick building she could see some complicated chimneys, and guessed that it was the pottery kiln. A young man sat out on a bench in the sunshine, his shirt off, and assiduously chipping away at a sizeable chunk of wood with a chisel.

As Hillary approached, she could see that he was carving a magnificent-looking eagle. It looked both ferocious and beautiful, and she wouldn't have minded buying the finished article for herself. Except that it would probably be far too big and heavy to fit comfortably on a narrow boat.

The young man looked up with a smile as she approached.

He had buck teeth and freckles, but there was something so open and honestly friendly in his smile, that Hillary felt her belief in humanity briefly flare up.

She quickly squashed it back down again, where it belonged.

'Hello. I was wondering if you could help me out. I'm looking for this woman,' Hillary said, handing over a picture of Gillian Tinkerton. 'Her mother's worried about her. She hasn't called in for a while, and she just wants to know that she's OK.' The man grinned and pointed wordlessly to the brick shed before turning back to his carving of a set of wickedly sharp-looking talons. Hillary blinked, then wondered if he was a deaf mute, or simply preferred not to speak much.

She thanked him and walked to the pottery kilns, wondering why he thought that anyone inside might be more able to help her. Perhaps the boss was in here, or someone who dealt with the admin or members of the public.

She pushed her way into the shed, and saw that it was occupied by a solitary figure, sitting at a potter's wheel. The thick-set woman was bowed over a lump of clay, her feet pumping an old-fashioned treadle, and Hillary approached silently, watching as the woman wet her hands and seemed to miraculously shape the lump of grey clay up into an elegantly-shaped vase.

Then the woman sensed her presence and looked up.

Hillary felt her heart do a quick, confused but satisfied and joyous flip.

Yes! She was right. She was not ready for the scrap heap just yet.

Hillary Greene smiled and said softly, 'Hello, Gilly. I'm really glad to see you.'

Gillian Tinkerton looked up at her, and half-frowned in puzzlement. 'Sorry, do I know you?' she asked.

TEN

HILLARY SMILED SOMEWHAT IRONICALLY. 'No, Gillian, you don't know me, but I feel as if I've come to know you—quite well. My name's Hillary Greene, I work for the Crime Review Team out of Thames Valley.'

'Police?' Gillian asked, wide eyed, then quickly looked down at the wet clay between her hands. 'Just a mo, let me get this finished, and then we can chat.' Hillary watched, her mind racing, as the younger woman finished shaping the pot, then used what looked like a large cheese wire and scraped it across the base, to remove it from the wheel. 'I just need to put this in the drying room,' Gillian explained over her shoulder, as she transferred the still wet clay vessel onto a thin wooden platter. She then walked with it into a little room at the back of the shed, which radiated warmth when she opened the door.

She came back a moment later and went to a sink where she thoroughly washed her hands. She had gained a lot of weight since she'd left home, and her hair was now much longer, and dyed a vivid black. She was wearing ragged jeans and a large, warm-looking sweatshirt with the name of a football team emblazoned across it. Or was it a rugby team? Hillary wasn't much of a sports fan.

Hillary felt as if she had to keep watching her just to make sure that she was actually there. She was still feeling slightly shell-shocked by her discovery of the younger woman, even though she'd been half-expecting it.

'OK, so what's it all about?' Gillian finally asked, and Hillary realized that all the activity Gillian had indulged in since Hillary had introduced herself had just been a way of putting off asking the question, and there was probably only one reason for that.

'No, don't worry—your mum and dad are fine. All your family are,' Hillary was quick to reassure her. 'I'm not here to deliver bad news.'

Gillian slowly let out a long, relieved sigh. 'Bloody hell, you had me worried.'

Hillary, on hearing those words, snapped her fingers and reached for her phone. 'That reminds me, before we do anything else.' She called up the memory list and keyed up Deirdre Tinkerton's home phone number. 'Gillian, you really need to speak to your mother.'

'It's Gilly,' Gilly corrected absently, then frowned. 'Why? Is she in trouble? You haven't arrested her for anything, have you?' Her voice rose to a disconcerted, disbelieving squawk.

'Of course not,' Hillary said, beginning to feel faintly annoyed now. Things already seemed to be getting out of hand with this interview, and she wondered if Gilly's scatterbrained approach to life could be catching. Right now she had a million and one questions for her and here she was, playing the role of fairy godmother. Then she heard the ring-tone on the other end, and said angrily, 'When was the last time you called home, do you think?'

Gilly blinked. 'Er, I dunno. A couple of months ago.' Hillary glared at her.

Gilly shuffled her large frame from one foot to the

other. 'Or maybe a bit longer,' she admitted reluctantly. 'It's a funny thing, isn't it. Time?'

'Yeah, hilarious,' Hillary said, then held up a finger as she heard another voice in her ear.

'Hello?' Deirdre Tinkerton said.

'Mrs Tinkerton? This is Hillary Greene. I have someone here who wants to speak to you,' and with that she thrust the mobile at Gilly, who had the grace to look shame-faced.

'Hello, Mum?' she said into it tentatively.

Hillary distinctly heard the squeal of delight come from the other end of the line and with a smile, moved a little way away, to give the two women privacy. Even so, she could just picture Deirdre in her cheerful kitchen, sinking down on a chair with relief, whatever domestic chore she'd been doing now forgotten, washed away by joy and relief.

Sometimes Hillary loved her job.

Over by the open barn, the silent man was still carving his eagle. Hillary found herself grinning at him like an idiot. Because she'd been right. All along, she'd felt as if this pig's ear of a case had been leading her up the garden path, and all around the mulberry bushes for good measure. And it had only been by taking a step back, and starting totally anew, and making no assumptions at all, and taking nothing for granted, that she'd finally been able to see some sort of path through the maze.

Even so, the theory she'd been left with had seemed almost too bizarre to be real. Coincidences that defied logic, had mated with a sick mind to produce a case so convoluted that it became almost surreal. And yet....

She turned around and watched Gilly Tinkerton talking to her mother, at first apologizing and then beginning to sob a little as she realized just how much her thought-lessness had cost her family, and Hillary realized that, bizarre or not, she had got it right at last.

Or maybe not quite all the way right, just yet. The thought of Judy Yelland still worried her. It was all well and good giving herself a massive pat on the back and for feeling chuffed to bits at herself for finding Gillian Tinkerton. But there was still a long way to go.

'Here, she wants to speak to you.' Gilly suddenly appearing at her side cut off her somewhat sombre train of thought and she took the phone back absently.

'Hello? Mrs Tinkerton?'

'Bless you. You found her. I was getting scared. I can't thank you enough. What can I say?' Hillary smiled as the breathless, delighted short sentences overflowed into her ear.

'I'm just glad that you can stop worrying now,' Hillary said, and finally began to put the case first, instead of getting caught up in the Tinkterton family saga. 'I'm going to ask Gilly to come back to HQ with me. We're going to need a statement from her, so I expect you'll be seeing her later on today.'

'That's fine. Oh my, I've got to bake some coconut sponges. They're her favourite. Would you like some too?' Hillary, smiling, agreed that she would, gently disengaged herself from Deirdre's renewed and effusive thanks, and shut the mobile down.

'OK, Gilly, you and I need to talk,' she said determinedly.

Gilly nodded. 'OK. There's a bench just over in the flower garden. Let's sit there.' She led Hillary past the woodcarver, who looked up and waved at them, but again never said a word, and on towards the flower garden.

There they found an obviously hand-made bench made out of silvering beech, set amid a sea of lupins and peonies.

'So, Mum tells me the police thought that I was a missing person,' Gilly said, resting her considerable bulk on the far right side of the bench. 'How come?'

'Do you recall being stalked, Gilly?' Hillary had had enough of indulging her, and ignored the irrelevant question.

'What? Oh, you mean the cards and flowers and silly text messages,' Gilly said, and shook her head. 'Good grief, is that what this is all about? I never met the guy—he was all bark and no trousers.'

'You never saw him?'

'Nope. It was around then that I was beginning to get fed up with home, and wanted to try something different. I told Mum I was off to see what I could find. I don't know why everyone's making such a fuss now,' she added, a shade petulantly.

Hillary bit back a sharp retort and smiled instead. Instinct told her that she might as well bang her head against a wall as try to explain the realities of life to this self-obsessed young woman. 'No, I can see that. When you left, you didn't take your phone with you?'

'Nah. Like I said, this bloke obviously knew the number, so I just tossed it and bought a pay-as-you-go.'

'And money? According to our records, your bank account became dormant around then. Why was that?'

'What? Oh, that's just the set up here. When I found this place, it had a central banking account. All the bills are paid for out of it, and everyone puts a percentage of their income into it to pay for joint costs. At the time, I still had pieces of some stained glass to sell, but then I really became interested in throwing pots. So I sold the glass and put the money in the pot. The pottery classes were free here, and when I got my first commission for one, that went into the central bank as well, and I realized I could live without touching my own capital. So I just let it sit and build up a little nest egg for myself.' Hillary listened to this somewhat rambling account with an ever-growing ironical smile.

So it had been as simple as that. Gilly had bought a new phone, and found herself such a comfortable billet that she hadn't even needed to spend any of her own cash to set herself up. Her mother had been so right when she said that her daughter had a knack of landing on her feet.

As a result it had looked, to all intents and purposes as if she'd just fallen off the edge of the planet. Or, to be more precise, as if she'd been killed and her body buried in some secret, shallow grave somewhere, leaving the likes of silly sods such as herself, to presume the worst. It was just one more way this bloody case had tripped her up and wrong-footed her, right from the beginning.

With a lot of help from a sick, twisted bastard, of course.

'OK.' She shook her head, trying to shake off the demoralizing feeling that she'd been played for a sucker, and concentrate on one thing at a time. 'So, after you fetched up here, you never had contact with the stalker again?' She needed to get things perfectly clear now.

'Well, no.' Gilly frowned. 'I mean, he wouldn't have known where I'd gone, would he?'

The simplicity of that made Hillary catch her breath for a moment, before she found herself unable to do anything but laugh. 'No, I suppose not,' she finally admitted. And the same would hold true if Meg Vickary had indeed run off to the Costa Del Sol with Hardwicke.

Although there still remained some questions: such as why had Meg deliberately made it look so suspicious by not telling anyone her plans? And why hadn't she accessed her accounts? True, there hadn't been much money to leave behind, since she tended to live right up to her income, but even so. She seemed to have gone out of her way to make her disappearance look iffy. Why not hand in and work out her notice? Why not do things properly?

But Hillary had a theory about that, too. But it could wait.

'So, are we going back to Oxford then?' Gilly again interrupted her train of thought. 'Only I need to pack a few things if we are.'

'Yes. You go and do that. I'll wait by the car. It's the disreputable Volkswagen Golf, I'm afraid.'

'Oh, that's OK—I'll drive my own, thanks. You can get going if you like, and I'll meet you there.' Hillary was about to object to the two-car idea, but realized that she wasn't being reasonable. Gilly would need her own transport to get back again once she'd been ticked off and treated to the fatted calf by her relieved family. Still, having gone to all this trouble of finding her, she was reluctant to let the young madam out of her sight.

'I'll wait. You can follow me back to Kidlington. I need you to make and sign a statement,' she added firmly, as Gilly Tinkerton opened her mouth to object. 'You have been officially on the Missing Persons List for some time, and that means paperwork. Besides, is your car legal? We have no recent record of you applying for a driver's licence.'

Gillian flushed guiltily, and said that perhaps her friend Greg would drive her. 'We won't be long then,' she said hastily.

And she wasn't. She moved off towards one of the converted barns, and came back a scant five minutes later, toting a heavy-looking backpack, and a curious, pony-tailed friend.

Hillary glanced at her watch. It was nearly three. Say an hour to get back, if they didn't run into too much traffic. Yeah, there'd be time for a good debriefing.

She nodded to Gilly and her friend and followed them part way to another large barn where a row of various vehicles, some of them in an even worse state than Puff, were lined up. Gilly made her way to a sporty little Mini, that had to be twenty years old, but still looked good.

'Jimbo's our resident mechanic and car buff. He loves waxing the old girl and treating her,' Gilly said, patting the hood of the car affectionately. 'He says he gonna give her a racing stripe one day.' Hillary nodded, marvelling yet again at how the Gillians of the world seemed to get all the luck and watched her and her friend climb in. She called curtly, 'Follow me closely all the way back, yeah? I'll fix a parking space for you at HQ if need be.' Gilly nodded dutifully, and her friend, though clearly puzzled, grinned good-naturedly in response.

Hillary walked back to the Volkswagen, and sighed at it in passing. 'Don't suppose you fancy a racing stripe, do you?' she asked sardonically.

The car started at the very first attempt, as if wanting to court her favour. Perhaps it really did fancy a racing stripe at that.

Dream on, rustbucket, Hillary thought, but was wise enough not to say it out loud.

On the way back, she was careful to wait until she was stuck in a line of traffic before using her mobile. The last thing she needed was to get done by a conscientious traffic cop.

She called Steven's office direct. 'Hello, look it's me,' she said, the moment he answered. 'I need you to find and round up Geoff wherever he is and get him into the office. I've just caught a massive break in the case, and I'm bringing in a crucial witness,' she said, her eyes on the car ahead, which luckily still showed no sign of moving. 'And you're never going to guess who it is,' she couldn't resist crowing, just a little bit.

There was a moment of ominous silence on the other end of the line, and then Superintendent Steven Crayle said coldly, 'You managed to break the case and find a witness, huh? Many of them about, are there, in your sickbed, back on the boat?' Ah, Hillary thought. Oh yeah.

Shit.

'Uh, I suddenly felt better?' she offered.

SHE BRACED HERSELF as she knocked on Steven's door and walked in at his curt summons. Seated opposite his desk was DI Geoff Rhumer and in a corner, trying to look invisible, Jimmy Jessop, who shot her a boy-are-you-for-it look in warning.

Hillary smiled brightly, stepped to one side, and ushered in Gilly. Out in the car-park, whilst her pony-tailed friend settled down to wait patiently, Hillary had asked her if she had a hat or a cap that she could wear. Though clearly puzzled by the request, Gilly had obligingly rummaged about in her backpack and found a bright green golfing cap and put it on. This she now took off as she walked past Hillary and glanced around.

Hillary could tell at a glance that none of the men in the room had recognized her. 'Gilly, this is Superintendent Crayle, DI Rhumer, and former Sergeant Jessop. Gentlemen, meet Gillian Tinkerton.' There was a moment of profound silence.

'Hello,' Gilly said nervously, sensing the odd atmosphere.

'Gosh, are all you important people really here because of me?' she asked, again with a decidedly nervous laugh.

Jimmy Jessop, suddenly aware that he was doing a stunned mullet impersonation of great breadth and scope, abruptly snapped shut his gaping jaw. Geoff Rhumer half rose, then subsided again. Steven Crayle studied Hillary with those dark, damned sexy eyes of his. They promised retribution later, and the thought made her shiver.

She held his gaze with a bland smile of her own. 'I found Gilly living at one of the artists' communities that Sammy and Vivienne found for me, sir. We just need to get her statement about where she's been which shouldn't take us long. Perhaps we can get a WPC in to take it?' Steven, still keeping his smouldering eyes on Hillary, reached for his intercom and summoned a WPC, who took a slightly bewildered Gilly away, after Hillary had fully briefed her on what was needed. 'And don't enter her name just yet into the system,' Hillary told the WPC as she was leaving. 'For the moment this is strictly hush hush. When you've done the paperwork, don't file it anywhere, but bring everything back down here to me. Oh, and, Constable, you don't talk about this to anyone. Not even your guv'nor. Got it?' The WPC nodded, obviously impressed by the seriousness of Hillary's voice, and left.

When the door closed behind her, Geoff Rhumer said, helplessly, 'I don't get it.' And that, he thought, as far as understatements went, was up there with the best.

'What the hell's going on, guv?' Jimmy agreed.

Hillary slowly took the seat next to Geoff, and looked across at Steven. 'First of all, sorry about going off on my own. I just had an off-the-wall hunch that probably wouldn't pan out, and if it hadn't, I didn't want any witnesses to it, that's all.'

Steven nodded slowly. 'We'll discuss that later,' he said, with a slight twist to his lips that had Hillary's eyes briefly flaring in response. 'Right now, let's just have it. From the beginning.' Hillary nodded.

'OK. Here goes. Right from the start, when I began looking in to these three girls' disappearances, things didn't seem to fit quite right. Little things didn't make sense or add up. I couldn't seem to get a purchase, a grip on anything solid. And I finally realized that it was because I already had the solution—or thought I did—and that I was just trying to find the facts to fit the theory, namely, that a stalker had killed all three girls, when, normally what I would have been doing at the start of a case is trying to find the facts first, and then see what theory fitted them.

'So I decided to put aside everything we thought we knew, and approach it as I would any other cold case— or any other potential murder case, come to that—and the more I investigated, the odder it became.' She paused and tried to marshal her sometimes chaotic thoughts into a coherent whole.

'Let's take Gilly first. She didn't fit in with the other two girls, because (a) she'd told her family she was going, and (b) she'd packed some things. So, taking Lol out of the picture, what would I normally have thought would be the most likely thing to have happened to her?' Hillary turned to Jimmy here and raised an eyebrow. 'The obvious, right? That she'd simply gone off somewhere, like her family all thought.'

Jimmy nodded. 'Right, guv.' If those were the only facts that they'd had, that would have been just what was assumed.

'OK. Now let's move on to Meg Vickary,' Hillary said. 'She was a totally different kettle of fish from Gilly. She was vain about her looks, and was known to use men to get what she wanted from life. She liked money, and the good life, and she had an affair with her married boss that went sour. When I began to look into her case, lo and behold, we come across a costa con. A man loaded with money, who'd been known to be interested in Meg. Now, what would you think, Jimmy, if Meg suddenly up and left?'

'That's she'd run off and shacked up with the con, and was living *la dolce vita* somewhere warm, guv,' Jimmy said at once, nodding.

'Wait a minute though,' Geoff Rhumer put in. 'She didn't just give her married lover the heave-ho and go though, did she? *She disappeared.* She didn't pack any clothes, didn't clear out her bank accounts, nor did she work out her notice or tell anyone where she was going.'

'Quite right,' Hillary agreed promptly. 'No, for Meg, everything seemed to point to her being the victim of foul play,' Hillary agreed, making both Geoff and Jimmy frown.

This time it was Jimmy who said simply, 'I don't get it, guv.'

'No, neither did I, Jimmy,' Hillary said. 'Not at first. At least, not until I began to think about Meg Vickary's personality. Right from the start, do you remember, Georgia Biggs seemed sure that Marcus Kane had had something to do with her disappearance?'

'Yes, she did,' Jimmy agreed.

'But why? Unlike Ruth Coombs, she had no interest in Kane. She hadn't even met the man. And she wasn't an obsessive personality type like Ruth either. She might have been friendly with her flatmate, sure, but I never got the feeling that they were bosom buddies. So where was the only place that Georgia could have got that impression from?' It was Steven who answered of course. Of all the men in the room, Hillary knew that he was the brightest and quickest.

'From Meg herself,' he said, and when Hillary turned to nod at him, he smiled. 'I get it. You think that Meg *wanted* people to worry about her, to report her missing, to…' He nodded slowly.

'Of course. In order to give Marcus Kane a hard time.'

'Yes,' Hillary said. 'Remember, Meg Vickary was used to twisting men around her little finger. She married her first husband for money and, when his business crashed, got rid of him quickly enough. And she soon found Marcus to be husband number two.'

'Only he wasn't playing ball,' Jimmy put in.

'No. He was too comfortably married to a rich woman of his own. Moreover, one with a powerful daddy. When Meg finally realized that he wasn't going to divorce her, she looked around for another meal ticket. And found him. But Meg is vain and spiteful, and she wanted to stir up trouble for her ex-lover. She definitely wasn't the forgive-and-forget kind. So when she left, she made damned sure that she was leaving a giant headache for him behind her—and she succeeded. I bet, right now, Kane is ruing the day he ever hired her! Anyway, she carefully planted seeds of doubt in Georgia Biggs's mind about her relationship with Kane, so that when she vanished, Georgia would report her missing. She carefully packed no clothes, and told no one that she was going. It probably irked her to have to leave her money behind, but then again, she didn't really have that much in her accounts, and besides, Hardwicke was loaded. He'd be taking care of all the bills from now on and showering her with baubles and the best champagne anyway. All she needed was to get abroad without the use of her passport. She'd guess that the police would run a routine check to make sure that it wasn't used. But then to a man like Hardwicke, setting her up with a fake passport would be a cinch. I've got a friend over in Spain now who's taking some photos of Hardwicke and his household. Until they come in, we can't be one hundred per cent sure, but'—she shrugged graphically—'I'm willing to bet a year's wages that when they do, we'll have some good snapshots of Meg Vickary alive and well and sunning herself by the pool.' Geoff Rhumer shifted in his seat, shaking his head.

'Bloody hell. If I hadn't seen Gillian Tinkerton with my own eyes—'

'You'd be thinking I was going off my rocker,' Hillary finished for him without rancour. 'Yes, and I wouldn't blame you. I've been wondering the same thing myself lately. When I first thought all this out, I kept thinking I must have got it wrong somehow. It just seemed so *unbelievable*. So you can see why I couldn't bring any of you in on what I was after, until I had some solid proof.'

Jimmy's lips twisted. 'They don't come more solid than Gillian, guv.'

Hillary laughed. 'No.'

'She is a big lass,' Geoff Rhumer said, with a chortle of his own.

'And Judy Yelland,' Steven said, breaking in to the slightly hysterical atmosphere with a sharp question.

Instantly, Hillary's smile fled. 'Yes,' she said quietly. And met Steven's eyes levelly. 'Judy.'

'You think she's dead, don't you?' Steven said, instantly catching her mood.

Hillary sighed. 'Yes, I do. Right from the start, the atmosphere around Judy felt different from the others. She had no reason to disappear. No reason to lie to her family, who didn't care about her anyway, or just drop out of life without a word to anyone.'

'What? You think the stalker killed her?' Geoff Rhumer asked sharply.

'No,' Hillary said at once. 'There are only two candidates for who might have killed Judy. Jimmy?' She turned to the old ex-sergeant who nodded slowly.

'Ruth Coombs and Christopher Deakin,' he agreed.

'And of those, who's the obvious suspect?' Hillary pressed. 'If we take out all the distractions, and bearing in mind Occam's Razor?'

'Occam's what?' Rhumer asked, puzzled.

'Sorry,' Hillary said. 'It's a theory that says the most obvious solution is usually the right one. In cases of murdered women, who is most usually the culprit?'

'The man in her life,' Jimmy said flatly.

'Right. Christopher Deakin,' Hillary agreed. And looked at Steven. 'Starting tomorrow, sir, we need to work on Deakin properly, with a search warrant for his premises for a start.' Steven nodded.

'I can get that ball rolling now.'

'Hang on just a minute, what about the man who attacked you?' Geoff Rhumer demanded. 'The man me and my team have been working our arses off the last few days trying to track down? Are you really saying that he's had nothing to do with any of this?'

Hillary smiled grimly. 'Oh, I wouldn't say that. He's one sick puppy. He definitely stalked all three women, and he tried to slit my throat, don't forget. Don't worry, I haven't forgotten about Lol,' she said grimly.

She took a long, deep breath. 'But this is where things are really twisted around. It's why it was so complicated and so messed up. Why I couldn't see my way clearly for quite some time.'

'Guv, I'm with DI Rhumer here,' Jimmy felt compelled to interrupt her. After Hillary had produced a rabbit such Gillian Tinkerton out of her hat, he'd been following her reasoning and logic closely, and was perfectly willing to place his bets on her being right. When the recon photos from Spain came through for instance, he'd be more surprised than not, if Meg Vickary wasn't in them. And he'd always felt something was off about the way Deakin had been acting whenever they'd talked to him. Squirrelly, was the word that had sprung to his mind, and he didn't really doubt at all that Hillary Greene would bring the murder of Judy Yelland home to him. And yet.... What about the bloody stalker? Where did he fit in? It still made no sense.

'He *was* the one who stalked the girls, right?' Jimmy asked, trying to grapple his way through carefully.

'Yes,' Hillary confirmed.

'And sent you all the messages, the gifts, the cards, the crosses, for Pete's sake?' Jimmy pressed.

'Right.'

'And he attacked you?'

'Right.'

'But still, he had nothing to do with any of the girls going missing?' His voice rose incredulously. 'I just don't see how that can be, guv.'

'No. I know how you feel,' Hillary said, with genuine sympathy. 'It shouldn't have happened that way, but it did. It must have.' Hillary looked from the scowling, somewhat sceptical Rhumer to Steven's thoughtful face.

'Just lay it all out for us, Hillary,' he advised quietly. 'How do you think it played out?'

Hillary nodded. 'OK. Let's try and get into Lol's sick little mind for a while,' she said, with genuine distaste. 'We know from the vague descriptions we have of him that he's youngish, well built and probably good-looking. We think he's in the job, too, so he's in uniform—which I'm reliably informed some people find sexy and irresistible.' All the men smiled but wisely made no comment.

'So, women should be a doddle for him—attracting them, sleeping with them, forming some sort of bond. But we know that it isn't. According to the shrink, he's almost certainly a loner, and women probably instinctively avoid him or mistrust him. So he starts watching them, stalking them, getting more and more enraged and alienated.'

'I'm with you so far,' Steven agreed.

Hillary nodded. 'He fantasises about women. Starts following them, sending them presents and making a, generally, mild nuisance of himself. And if that was all, then it wouldn't much matter, not in the grand scheme of things, but fate, or bad luck, or the Devil or whatever you want to call it, plays a hand, and something drastically alters for our Lol.' Hillary sighed heavily.

'Judy Yelland, the first of them, disappears. Worse

still, a while later, so does Meg, and then, lo and behold, so does Gilly.'

'That's just too much of a coincidence to swallow,' Geoff said agitatedly. 'Sorry, Hillary, but I just can't see that. The three women he chooses to stalk, all disappear? No way.' He shook his head vehemently.

Hillary sighed patiently and said quietly, 'Who says there were only three, Geoff?'

Steven slowly leaned forward in his chair. 'You're right. There must have been more. Maybe a lot more. Look at his MO: text messages, cards, flowers, gifts. Worshipping from afar. He could have been fixated on any number of women—dozens of them over the years. And probably more than one at a time.'

'I think there were. Gillian said of him that he was all bark and no trousers,' Hillary agreed. 'Up to a point, she was right. I think Lol probably fantasized and stalked lots of women without any major incident, before Judy Yelland came on the scene. But when Judy went missing, I think everything changed for him,' Hillary said, her voice becoming grim now.

'Just think about it for a while. Reason it out. Here we have an inadequate man, obsessed with body-building and women. Women who rejected him. Women who were making his life miserable. And then, Judy Yelland, his latest infatuation, is reported as a Missing Person. What does he think?'

'That she's scarpered to avoid him,' Jimmy said flatly.

'Yes. Maybe at first, that's all it was,' Hillary agreed. 'And it would have made him feel good, right? Here she was, a woman at last showing him the proper respect, giving him the kudos he deserved, by being afraid enough of him to run away. It would have given his ego a tremendous boost. But then, less than two years later, another of the many woman he'd singled out for his special attention also goes missing. Meg Vickary. Now what does he think?'

Steven frowned. 'I'm not sure I like where this is going,' he said quietly.

Hillary smiled faintly. 'Welcome to my world. He's a sick fantasist remember? A woman hater. An inadequate nobody who yearns to be a somebody. Someone to be feared and respected. Just think what it did to his psyche to have another young woman, and a beautiful, young, kick-ass, aggressive woman like Meg Vickary no less, suddenly to go missing as well. What does he start to imagine is happening? What fantasy can he start to build up with the evidence at hand?'

'Oh bloody hell,' Jimmy Jessop said, finally catching on.

'What?' Geoff Rhumer barked, realizing he was the only one still not in the loop and not liking it.

'He begins to fantasize that he really has killed them. Judy and Meg?' Steven said, his wondering voice making it both a question and a statement.

'Right,' Hillary said firmly. 'You get wannabe pop stars who, to fulfil their dreams, try to get onto television talent programmes and make it that way. You get wannabe football players who play for a local five-a-side and dream of Wembley. You can get wannabes who are anything you care to mention. Steam-train drivers. Plastic surgeons. So why not a wannabe serial killer?' Hillary asked.

'Whoah!' Geoff Rhumer yelped. 'Isn't that taking it a bit far?'

Hillary nodded. 'Yes, that's exactly what I was thinking a few days ago. But the more I thought about it, the more it made sense. Don't forget, Lol is on the job. He's a policeman. He's fascinated by crime, but since he doesn't have the guts or the brains to be a criminal, he decides to make a sideways move into the area that fascinates him. He's on the periphery, so to speak, never in the spotlight. He's had a taste of the giddy heights when two of the girls he's been stalking go missing, and then Gilly makes it three. Now, to you and me, who are all pretty sane, and have our feet rooted firmly on the ground, that makes for one hell of a coincidence. Out of the scores of women he's had in his sights, no less than three of them go missing. But we all know that in real life coincidences are as real as anything else. Gilly simply told her family that she was going to go off, and did so. Judy fell foul of the man in her life. Lots of women do. And Meg was a girl with an eye on the main chance. Individually, there was nothing remarkable in what happened to any of them— and I don't mean to demean what happened to Judy. But the point is, to you or me, with our rational, sound minds, we can accept that stranger things have happened. But to a diseased, excitable mind, it must have seemed like… I don't know, some sort of a sign.' Hillary paused. 'And then, as if to underline it in gold, as it were, there was one more thing that happened that pushed him well and truly over the edge.'

'What?' Steven asked.

'Me,' Hillary said flatly. 'There he is, fantasizing about having killed three women. He even goes to the families of the missing girls so that he can steal some sort of keepsake from his 'victims'. He'll have read all the material on serial killers, remember. He'll know how they like to keep sick mementos. And he'll want to fit the profile perfectly. The more real he can make the role playing, the more easy it will be to convince himself that it's all true. Hell, I wouldn't even be surprised if hasn't even got himself some fantasy burial spot as well, somewhere that he can go and imagine the three girls lying under the earth, where he put them.' Over in his corner, Jimmy shuddered.

'But the game's getting a bit sour, a bit old. It's not so much fun as it once was. No more girls have gone missing. Somewhere buried in the back of his sick head, he knows that it's all make believe,' Hillary went on. 'But then he spots his next victim. And everything changes, as Lol decides that his next girl is going to be me.' Steven drew in a long slow breath.

'It sort of makes sense,' he agreed slowly. 'You're more exciting. More dangerous, and more of a challenge. You're on the job yourself, with a reputation as a detective, and a solverate second to none. You're more *worthy* of his attention.'

'Right. In choosing me, he's playing with fire, getting his rocks off, and ramping up the stakes. Which is why he has to go all out to impress me. To intrigue me. To suck me in.'

'The crosses with the three girls' missing initials on them,' Jimmy said, snapping his fingers.

'Yes. He can't resist boasting, trying to impress me.'

'Wait a minute, isn't that just asking for trouble though, guv?' Jimmy said. 'What if you actually figure it all out? His whole crazy fantasy world comes crashing down around his ears.'

'I know,' Hillary said sombrely. 'That's why I had Gilly wear a cap before she got out of her car, and why I told the WPC taking her statement to keep Gilly's presence a secret.'

'Because if Lol finds out, he's going to know that you're on to him,' Steven said.

'That's one reason yes. Also, I don't want him alerted, because now I think we have a way of tracking him down at last,' Hillary agreed.

'How?' Geoff asked. He still wasn't at all convinced by Hillary's arguments, although the presence of Gillian Tinkerton, alive and well, was a bit of a facer. He was a simple, straightforward sort of copper, and the things that Hillary Greene had been saying still made little sense to him. But one thing he was sure of. Lol existed, Lol had attacked a fellow police officer, and whatever the truth about the three missing girls turned out to be, Lol was one sick stalker, and Geoff and his team had been getting eyestrain trying to find him. Tedious, painstaking, boring work it had been too. If Hillary thought she had a way of tracking him down—now *that* was definitely something he could get his brain around.

'If you were Lol, and you wanted to keep an eye on your "girls" what would you do?' Hillary asked. 'Remember in his fantasy, he's this terrible and notorious serial killer of women. And he's "fallen in love" with the detective assigned to find out what happened to them. You're on the job. You've been stalking women for years. What would you want to have access to?'

'Bloody hell.' Jimmy made everyone jump by suddenly yelling. 'Records. You'd want to have access to records.'

'Absolutely. From time to time, I think he must have volunteered to work in admin,' Hillary agreed. 'It would be the only way he could get access to stuff.'

Geoff stood up. 'I'll get cracking on the list.' He glanced at his watch and grimaced. 'Damn, the day shift has gone by now. I don't know how many of the men on our radar have had secondments to records and admin, but it can't be that many. If we get on it right now it won't take us long to find them, and then we can have them all in first thing in the morning.'

'I suggest you make a clean sweep of it,' Steven warned. 'If Lol is on that list, then we don't want him to twig what's happening. If you don't have enough men on your team to bring them all in for questioning simultaneously, let me know, and I can get you all you need. It needs to be meticulously co-ordinated.'

'Good idea,' Geoff said, and left quite happily. Even so, he shot Hillary a slightly troubled and thoughtful gaze, as he left. Jimmy caught it and grinned.

'I reckon our DI's still half convinced you're off your rocker, guv.'

Hillary shrugged. 'Can't say as I blame him. Just as long as he gets Lol tomorrow.'

Steven looked up at the tone in her voice. 'What's up? Why the urgency?'

Again she shrugged. 'I just feel as if things are coming to a head that's all. Remember, he's been living it high for these last few weeks. His attack on me has given him confidence. It's given him a taste of real blood, not to put too fine a point on it. All along he's been a wannabe killer. By now, the urge to actually do it, to become the genuine article, must be almost unbearable. He's been dreaming of being the killer of women for so long, what's to stop him from making it a reality at last?'

'You think he's going to have another run at you?' Steven said sharply. 'That does it. I'm coming back to the boat with you. I'm not letting you out of my sight.' He smiled across the desk at her. 'And apart from anything else, I've still got a bone to pick with you, remember?' Hillary shot him a oh-yeah smile.

'And don't worry,' Steven said softly, 'if you're right, and I'm beginning to think that you always are, Geoff and his team will have Lol in the bag tomorrow. There won't be that many who would have volunteered to work in admin—most coppers are sick of paperwork as it is, without volunteering to have it all day, every day. I doubt there'll be half a dozen, if that. Once we've narrowed the gene pool to that extent, it won't take you long to pick him out. He'll probably start drooling the minute you walk into the interview room.' Hillary nodded, ignoring the unsavoury imagery his words provoked.

'I suppose you're right,' she agreed.

So why didn't she feel quite as sanguine as she should?

THAT EVENING, VIVIENNE Tyrell had just got in from work when she received Tom's latest text, and she grinned as she read the message.

TAKEN TOMORROW OFF. FOUND JUST THE RIGHT ROMANTIC SPOT FOR THE VAN, AND AM PARKED UNDER THE STARS AND AWAY FROM PRYING EYES. FANCY ME COMING OVER AND PICKING YOU UP? I'VE GOT THE WINE ON ICE, BUT EVERYTHING ELSE IS WARM!

Quickly, happily, Vivienne texted back: COME AND GET ME LOVER.

ELEVEN

THE NEXT DAY, when it was only just beginning to get light, Hillary drove into work, checking every now and then in her rearview mirror to make sure that Steven was still behind her in his car. Naturally, he was. He had spent the night, as promised, on the *Mollern*, and she'd begun to feel as if his presence there was becoming definitely significant.

Not only were some of his clothes beginning to take up a little of her limited wardrobe space, and his spare razor to sit on the shelf of her tiny bathroom, but he seemed to be moving into her world in ways far less demonstrable, and yet no less real. She knew at some point that they were going to have to address the issue head on, but now hardly seemed the right time to start discussing where their relationship was heading.

Down in CRT, she went first to her own office to check her messages and was surprised to find, so soon, an email with an attachment from Dirty Dick over in Spain. He'd obviously worked quickly, and she was grateful as she quickly printed off the attachments and took them through to Steven's office.

There, Geoff Rhumer and Jimmy were already waiting.

'Before we start, these are through,' she began, and handed Steven the photographs from Spain, and then Meg Vickary's case file. All three men crowded around

for a look, but it was obvious that the woman photo-
graphed, variously, lounging around the pool at Hardwicke's villa, shopping at a Gucci store in town, and
lunching al fresco at a restaurant, were all Meg Vickary.
A little older, maybe, but still with a perfect figure and
immaculate make-up and clothes.

'Well, that's one thing ticked off the list,' Steven said,
leaning back. 'Not that there was much doubt. OK, we
all set for this morning?' He checked his watch. It still
wasn't yet six o'clock.

Geoff Rhumer nodded. 'As I was just saying, there
were five men on the list who fit the bill. We've got the
manpower to bring them all in at seven-fifteen exactly.
You want to come in on it, sir?' he asked, with more po-
liteness than enthusiasm, it had to be said.

Steven thought about it and then shook his head. He
knew that to have a superintendent in on one of the col-
lars would be unsettling for men already uptight at having to bring in one of their own. 'No, I'll stay here and
co-ordinate the interviews. We have any that look more
promising than the others?'

'Two,' Geoff confirmed at once. 'Of the five, one is
forty-two years old, which is a little long in the tooth to
be described as youngish, I would say. Two others are
nearly bald, or have those shaved-head haircuts that seem
so popular nowadays. Mind you, both of them were, or
have been, dark-haired, so they could still be our man,
if he's had a bit of a hair-loss problem since he last spoke
to Mrs Tinkerton.'

Steven nodded. 'But?'

'But there're two others—a PC called Tom Warrington, and an acting-sergeant Faulkner who both stand
out. Faulkner's a hulking rugby player, and Warrington

works out. Both are dark, could be described as good-looking, and have the reputations of being loners. And all five, as I said, have worked admin or records.'

'OK. Well, I'll let you get on with it then, Geoff,' Steven said, and then held up a hand as Hillary opened her mouth to speak.

'And before you ask, no, you can't go along. This is strictly Geoff's pigeon, remember? If we have trouble identifying our man from the interviews then we might have to bring you in to try and get him to react. But that's strictly a last-ditch resort. Think what his defence barrister will say if they find out you were allowed to sit in on the arrest and initial interviews.' Hillary closed her mouth with a snap, and nodded reluctantly. He was right, damn him. He usually was.

'Besides,' Steven said, understanding her frustration, and sympathizing with it. 'You have your own agenda. I'm going to get straight on to the search warrants for Christopher Deakin's house and places of work. Your priority right now is Judy Yelland. Right?'

Hillary nodded. Again, he was right, damn him. 'Yes, sir,' she said.

Steven shot her a don't-you-bloody-yes-sir-me look, and then deliberately smiled at her dazzlingly. She scowled back at him. As she got up and walked to the door, however, Hillary's lip's twitched. She was definitely going to have sort out Steven Crayle before long. The man was getting too damned big for his boots.

Jimmy followed her out and to the general office. Sam looked up hopefully as they came in, and Hillary nodded at him.

'Right, Sam, as soon as the super has the warrants,

we're going to turn Christopher Deakin's life upside down. You ever conducted a fingertip search before?'

'No, guv,' Sam said eagerly.

'Well, there's a first time for everything. I doubt there's nothing that Jimmy here can't teach you about it, right, Jimmy?'

'Guv.' Jimmy rolled his eyes. 'If I had a tenner for every time I tossed a gaff....' Hillary nodded, her eyes going to Vivienne's empty chair.

'Is Vivienne not coming in today?' she asked absently.

Sam, who knew that she *was* due in, and was just running late again, coughed. 'Er, not sure, guv,' he prevaricated. He didn't want to drop her in it. He didn't think even Hillary's patience with her could last forever.

Hillary, amused by the lad's inability to meet her eyes, smiled. She was going to have to teach him how to lie much better than that!

'Right,' she said flatly. 'Well, update the case files while we're waiting. I'll be in the office if anybody wants me,' she added, glancing at her watch. Right now, Rhumer and his teams should be gearing up and heading out in five different locations to nab their suspects.

It was, she felt instinctively, going to be a long, long day.

GEOFF RHUMER AND a PC on loan from Juvenile Crimes had been allocated Phil Faulkner. He'd chosen Faulkner personally, because he and Tom Warrington had to be prime contenders for being their stalker, and he wanted at least a fifty-fifty chance of being the one to bring him in. Although Rhumer and his team had the job that had been the least rewarding, in that it had consisted mainly of computer work, interpreting statistics, and using a painstaking process of elimination, the pay off came in moments like this. And he wouldn't have been human if he had not wanted to nab one of the plum roles for himself.

Feeling a little buzz of adrenaline-induced excitement, he made sure his voice was calm as he directed Robert White to Faulkner's address on the outskirts of Kidlington. White, Geoff was glad to see, was a beefy young lad, and he made sure that they were both equipped with pepper spray and a taser when they walked up to Faulkner's door. He was well aware that the stalker was known to be young, fit and muscular, and if it was indeed Faulkner, and he did try and make a fight or a run for it when he realized the game was up, Geoff had no intention of being caught unprepared.

Besides, he was too damned old and too damned wily to get a fist in the gut or any of his precious remaining teeth knocked out.

He checked his watch, made sure it was 7.15 exactly, and then let PC White take the lead and knock on the door.

Faulkner lived in a typical council-house semi, painted a pale cream, in a pleasant enough cul-de-sac.

Geoff was fairly sure that it would be Faulkner himself who answered. It always made for complications when it was the wife, or even worse, one of the kids, who opened the door when you came to nab someone, but in this case, Faulkner had neither. He was, Geoff knew, divorced and currently living alone.

The door opened abruptly. 'Yeah?' Faulkner was still half-undressed, and had obviously been caught in the act of shaving. He looked surprised at finding a uniformed copper on his door, but his eyes went straight to Rhumer, being the man in civvies. He frowned, clearly not liking what he was seeing.

'What's up then?' he demanded.

'Acting-Sergeant Faulkner?' Geoff asked pleasantly, fingering the pepper spray in his pocket.

'Yes.'

'I'm DI Rhumer, this is PC White,' Geoff said, using his left hand to show his ID. 'We just have a few things that need clearing up back at the station. Could we come in? You need to finish shaving and get dressed.' Faulkner's dark eyes narrowed slightly, then he shrugged. Like all coppers, he didn't feel comfortable being on the receiving end of having his collar felt, and was clearly unhappy about it. But he stepped back from the door and let them inside. Geoff was careful to keep himself out of arm's length, but Faulkner merely turned and headed back upstairs.

Geoff nodded at White, who followed him up. He waited in the hall, tensed and ready to act should there be any sound of a scuffle or a dull ominous thud. But barely five minutes later, Faulkner came back down and followed them outside and got into the back of the car with Rhumer without a word.

He hadn't asked what it was all about, which intrigued Geoff slightly. Then again, it was becoming clear to him that Faulkner belonged to the strong, silent group. Either that, or he just knew enough not to volunteer any information, and to hold his fire until he was sure in which direction the battle lay, and *then* scream for the representation to which he was entitled.

As White drove them back into HQ, Geoff glanced at his watch. So far there'd been no calls either on his mobile or over the radio to indicate that any of the others had had any trouble.

So at least, that was something.

HILLARY GREENE, SAM and Jimmy were just pulling out of the HQ car-park lot as Rhumer drove in. They didn't quite pass, and Hillary was too busy looking for a break in the traffic to notice them. The search warrants had come in, and she was headed for Summertown.

'So what exactly are we going to be looking for, guv?' Sam asked from the back seat, clearly excited.

'Now that's the question, son,' Jimmy responded for her.

'And the knack to conducting a successful blind search.'

'Blind search?'

'Yes. There's three kind of searches,' Jimmy explained patiently. 'You have a suspect you think knifed someone in a bar-room brawl. So you're looking for a specific item—a switch blade or whatever. That's one of the most common ones, and straightforward enough. Then you have a suspect, say a suspected rapist, and a victim, and you're searching his house for any signs that the rape took place there, or signs of the victim's presence—like her ripped panties, or torn-out ear-ring, or what have you. A bit wider in scope, but still fairly straightforward. Then you get something like this—where you don't really know what you're looking for, but just hope like hell that you'll recognize it when you find it.'

'Oh,' Sam said. Behind her, Hillary heard the lad gulp.

She smiled. 'Don't worry, Sam. We're looking for anything that can help us find out what might have happened to Judy Yelland. When I've got a better idea of how the land lies, I'll direct you to look for something specific—

maybe a diary, or women's clothing, something specific anyway. Jimmy and I will do the *blind* bit.'

Sam sighed. 'I don't know if I'm ever going to be good enough for this job, guv,' he said quietly.

Hillary smiled again. 'Don't worry. We all thought the same thing, at some point. You can only do so much studying and training. The rest is just experience and time served. You'll do fine,' she reassured him. Which was more than could be said for the still absent Vivienne.

She was going to have do something about Miss Tyrell, Hillary realized with an inner sigh. It was clear she had no place in the police, and she'd have to make her feelings clear to Steven.

Not that she liked ensuring that anyone got the push, but in Vivienne's case the writing was on the wall.

BACK AT HQ, Geoff Rhumer and Steven Crayle had a problem. All the teams had returned to HQ, only one of them had come back empty-handed.

The team assigned to pick up PC Tom Warrington from his parents' house had to report that Warrington had not returned to the family home the night before. His parents, however, weren't either worried or particularly surprised, since their son had recently purchased a caravan, and had left last night to set up a site for it.

Unfortunately, they had no idea where that might be.

HILLARY PAUSED AT the Summertown roundabout and tapped her fingers on the steering wheel. 'You remember what Ruth Coombs said, Jimmy, about her following Christopher the day that she knew the case had been reopened?'

'Yeah.'

'Didn't she mention him going to one of his storage places, or something?' Jimmy grunted and twisted around to get the file off the backseat. Sam quickly passed it over. Jimmy rustled through the pages for his notes. Behind her, an impatient git in a flash BMW blared his horn and Hillary shot him the finger in her mirror.

'Right, guv. To a storage place in Headington. Apparently, television equipment can be bulky and costly, so a lot of TV production outfits rent space like it.'

'But do you remember how Deakin made a point of saying how he was running into scheduling problems recently?' she asked, ignoring the BMW driver as he made a point of manoeuvring around her and roaring away up the Banbury Road.

'So?' Jimmy asked.

'If you were a busy and harassed television exec, would you take time out to go and check on camera equipment in storage?' Jimmy shrugged.

'You want to start with the lock-up?' He wasn't much fussed where they began, and if the guv had a hunch, he was more than happy to follow her lead. Though it seemed a bit thin to him.

Hillary shrugged. 'We've got to start somewhere. And I really can't see that he'd keep anything incriminating in his office, do you?'

Jimmy nodded. 'Fine by me.' Hillary indicated to take the next left and headed towards the Oxford suburb of Headington, high up on the hill.

It turned out to be an inspired choice.

The storage facility was manned, but the security guard checked their ID and read the search warrant carefully and then let them straight in without a fuss. Unit 48,

when he opened it with the pass key, was indeed large
and full of equipment. Jimmy found the switch for the
overhead strip lighting, thanked and dismissed the guard,
then stood peering into the cavernous space gloomily.

'OK then, Sam,' he said, eyeing a huge television camera that was set on wheels. 'Ever taken apart one of these
babies?'

'No, guv.'

'Me neither.' Jimmy grinned.

But Hillary had already spotted something else. 'Hold
it.' She beckoned them to follow her and led the way to
the back of the unit. Against the back wall, and humming
faintly to show that it was plugged in and working, was
a large, white chest freezer.

Hillary stopped and looked down at it thoughtfully.
'Do you suppose there can be much fancy electronic
equipment that needs to be kept frozen?' Jimmy tensed,
then frowned uncertainly.

'I dunno, guv, I'm no technological wizard. Maybe
film, developing equipment, or acids, or something like
that needs to be frozen to stop it deteriorating?'

Hillary sighed. 'Could be. I'm no expert on stuff like
that either. But I'd have thought that nowadays, it's all
digital stuff and computers, isn't it? I'd have thought actual film and chemicals were miles out of date. But I
could be wrong.' She smiled grimly. 'There's only one
way to find out.' She reached out, took a breath, and lifted
the lid of the freezer. Inside were lots of smallish-to-
mid-sized packages, wrapped in what looked like black
plastic bin liners. She and Jimmy took one each, both
instinctively keeping the lad away from them, as they'd
had identical thoughts as to what just might be inside. As
they'd been talking, they'd donned rubber gloves, so they

had no worries about contamination. But the first package to be opened, the one Jimmy had, revealed nothing more ominous than spools of some sort of film.

Hillary let out a long slow breath. It had probably been too much to hope that the search would be as short-lived and as easy as all that. Now she was sure that they weren't dealing with chopped-up body parts, she stood aside and nodded to Sam to take over, and began to wander around the shed.

Why had Deakin come here? Surely if something had needed retrieving, he would have sent a gopher. Or perhaps Ruth had had it wrong, and— 'Guv,' Jimmy said sharply, and Hillary felt her heart thump as she turned and quickly walked back to the freezer. She peered inside to see what had caused the hint of anxiety in Jimmy's voice and quickly understood.

Jimmy and Sam had removed all the smaller packages, to reveal one very long, very large, black-wrapped bundle folded at the bottom. Even to Sam's untrained eyes, it looked like a human form, with knees bent, and head tucked around, to fit into the confined space at the bottom of the freezer.

'Do we peel back the plastic?' Jimmy asked uncertainly. Hillary took one look and shook her head.

'No. Let's get forensics in here first. And if it turns out to be a very oddly-shaped piece of filming equipment, we'll never live it down.' But it wasn't.

Half an hour later, the ME arrived, and half an hour after that, Hillary, Sam and Jimmy drove to Christopher Deakin's office and arrested him for the murder of Judith Yelland.

At HQ, a curious Geoff Rhumer, Sam and Jimmy stood in the observation room as Hillary and Steven Crayle sat at the table opposite Deakin in interview room eight.

The television executive was pale and shaking. A solicitor sat, impassive-faced, beside him.

Jimmy took one look at the handsome, fair-haired man and shook his head. 'He's gonna crack open like a hazelnut,' he predicted, and glanced at his watch. 'The guv'nor will have it all wrapped up in time for afternoon tea, you watch.' Sam grinned uncertainly. Geoff nodded in agreement.

In the interview room, Steven quickly ran through the procedure and made sure that the tape recorders were working. But he left the questioning to Hillary. They had discussed it before, and had agreed that Deakin, who clearly had all the backbone of a jellyfish, would respond better to a woman with a softly-softly approach, than a man going in hard, simply because, if he crumbled too much, his barrister and their tame hired shrinks might try to get any confession excluded on the grounds of mental health issues, or bullying by the police.

Well aware of this, Hillary smiled gently. 'Mr Deakin, do you understand why you're here?' Christopher nodded.

'For the tape please, Mr Deakin, I need you to verbalize your responses,' Hillary said patiently.

Deakin leaned slightly forward and whispered, 'Yes.' Hillary nodded. She'd prefer it if he spoke up a bit, but she was unwilling to jeopardize the rapport she was trying to build with him by making yet another demand. 'Mr Deakin, I have to tell you that earlier this morning, acting on a search warrant, we searched a storage facility registered to your company in Headington. Do you know the one I mean?' She read out the address.

The solicitor sitting next to him, a small, middle-aged woman with a sharp foxy face and weary eyes, whispered something to him. Deakin shrugged, then turned and looked at Hillary.

'I'm not sure. I don't really have much to do with the nuts-and-bolts of production you understand. I'm more in admin.' Hillary nodded. She could, of course, hit him with the fact that Ruth Coombs had followed him to that very lock up not a week before, but decided to hold back. Not only would it raise doubts about Ruth Coomb's suitability as a witness, and possibly blur the issues, Hillary preferred to hold a little ammo in reserve.

'I see. I'm sorry to have to inform you, Mr Deakin, that in unit forty-eight of that facility, the one you personally set up, signed for, and paid for from the company accounts,' she let the implications of that bit of information sink in for a moment, before remorselessly continuing, 'we found the remains of a young woman.' Deakin swallowed hard but said nothing.

'At this moment, she's being taken for scientific examination, but we have no doubt, at this point, that the victim is Judith Yelland. Apart from being frozen, there's been very little decomposition, and her facial features are quite recognizable. And I have no doubt that DNA will prove her identity beyond any doubt.' The solicitor looked about to speak, then obviously decided not to.

Deakin paled ever more.

Hillary leaned forward slightly. 'I have to say that she looked a bit like an angel, Christopher, when we saw her, frozen like that. Like a princess in a fairy-tale. She was very beautiful, wasn't she?'

'You don't have to answer that,' the solicitor said flatly.

'I can see why you fell in love with her,' Hillary continued, as if she hadn't spoken.

'She was lovely,' Christopher agreed hoarsely. His

hands shook as he poured himself a glass of water and took a noisy gulp.

'What I don't understand is why you killed her,' Hillary said.

'Don't answer that,' the solicitor told him sharply. Then she turned to Hillary. 'If you have any specific questions for my client, please ask them.'

'Why did you lend her the money?' Hillary obliged.

Deakin looked surprised by the sudden shift, and then shrugged. 'I don't know. She asked me for it. She needed it, she said.'

Hillary sighed. 'Ah. She was blackmailing you.'

'No!' Deakin said, at the same time as his solicitor said, 'You don't have to answer that.' Hillary sighed.

'Come on, Christopher. We know you had an affair with her. We found her body in a freezer in a unit that you rented. Haven't you lived with this on your conscience long enough? A man like you—a sensitive, decent man, it must have been torture all these years. Just tell us how it happened. Was it an accident?'

'Yes! That's what it was.' Deakin, as she half-expected, reached for the life-line she'd just offered with eager, desperate fingers.

But Hillary remembered a time back in Unit 48 when the ME pointed out the possible finger-marks on the neck that suggested Judy had been strangled. Hillary sighed but nodded gently.

Just how did you 'accidentally' strangle her, Christopher, she wanted to ask. Instead, she kept her voice steady and gentle as the solicitor beside the fair-haired young man frowned heavily. 'I'm sure it was. You didn't mean to kill her, right?' she prompted softly.

'No, I didn't. But we argued. She wanted money, and

I was scared she was going to tell my wife. She said she needed to get away for a little while, but I don't know how it happened. I accused her of not loving me anymore, and she said that was rich, and that it was *me* who didn't love *her* because I wouldn't leave my wife and…and somehow my hands were around her neck and… I don't know how it happened. I just don't know.' He leaned forward suddenly, resting his face against his arms, which were lying flat on the table and began to cry.

Hillary let him cry, and then, when he was more coherent, said patiently, 'All right, Mr Deakin, let's start at the very beginning, shall we, and make sure we get everything nice and clear. Now, what day was this…?' Beside him, the solicitor sighed heavily. It was clear to Hillary that sometimes the stupidity of her clients obviously depressed her.

TWO HOURS LATER, it was all down on tape and was being transcribed. Deakin had been formally charged and was looking, paradoxically, better, as he was led down to the cells. It was often the way: confession was a carthasis. It would only be later, as the true nature of his predicament came to him, that the fear and depression would take over.

In Steven's office, they all celebrated with a mug of coffee. Sam was elated, and Jimmy relieved to have got it over with so quickly. It wasn't often it happened as sweetly as that, and he for one, could appreciate a quick, clean, confession.

Geoff Rhumer glanced uneasily at Steven, who nodded and sighed.

'Hillary, we've hit a snag,' Steven began. 'One of our

suspects wasn't in his place of residence. And he hasn't turned up for his shift, either,' he added grimly.

Hillary's head shot up. 'Who?' Geoff hesitated for a moment and then tossed her a folder. Hillary opened it up and stared down at the photograph inside.

'His name's Thomas Warrington,' Steven said, and explained the circumstances surrounding his newly bought caravan and why he hadn't slept that night in his parents' place.

Hillary stared down at the PC in uniform, noting the cat-green eyes, the square-chinned, handsome face. 'We're not sure it's him yet,' Geoff carried on. 'We're still interrogating the other four. But…well, to be honest, none of them are looking good for it. One has an alibi for the time of the attack on you. One had a bout of illness and was hospitalized around the time that Gillian Tinkerton was being stalked. And the other two just don't smell right to me.'

Hillary nodded. 'OK,' she said flatly.

'We'll keep looking for him and bring him in the moment he surfaces,' Steven added.

'OK,' she said again, and handed the file back.

'We have no reason to suppose that he knows we're on to him,' Geoff added.

'No.'

'He'll probably just walk in here for his next shift, and we'll be waiting with open arms,' he tried again.

'OK.'

Steven shifted in his seat. 'Are you all right?'

Hillary smiled. 'I'm fine,' she said dismissively. 'And right now, we've got a pile of paperwork on Deakin to follow up on.' She finished her coffee and rose. Jimmy and Sam hastily followed suit.

The two senior officers watched them depart, and Geoff sighed. 'She doesn't say much, does she?' he asked ironically.

'I'd feel happier if she bawled us out a bit. She must be simmering that Warrington's slipped through the net.' Steven nodded, grimly. He too, didn't like it when Hillary Greene went quiet.

It never boded well.

HILLARY SET SAM and Jimmy to dotting the i's and crossing the t's on the Deakin case, and went back to her office.

There she sat, morosely staring at the pile of paperwork in her in-tray, and trying not to see a pair of cat green eyes smiling back at her. But the truth was, the moment she'd seen his face, she'd known it was him. She could feel once more the weight of his arm draped around her shoulders and the touch of cold steel against her neck. His breath, warm against her neck.

She shuddered.

He was still out there. Maybe he knew about the pick up of the other four officers. Maybe not. Maybe he hadn't turned up at work because he was too absorbed in his new toy. Then again, maybe, like most predators, he'd sensed something in the wind and had gone to ground. Either way, sitting and brooding about it wouldn't do her a damned bit of good. She needed to get her mind firmly back on to other things.

She reached for a random file. It was the one that dealt with the crosses that had been sent to her during her last investigation. She studied the photographs of them—all crude, obviously handmade wooden crosses, with the initials of the three missing girls burned into them.

Of course, none of them was missing any longer, though, she thought with a triumphant smile of satisfaction. Gilly was with her parents right now, probably being stuffed full of coconut cake and Meg Vickary was living it large in Spain. And at some point, she'd have to inform Judy Yelland's parents about her fate, and the thought of returning to that cold, loveless house depressed her. Then she remembered Mrs Yelland's plea for information, and knew she had to go back there soon.

But not right now. She was simply feeling too drained. Besides, it was better to wait for official confirmation of ID.

Her eyes rested on the last photograph—the last cross to be delivered to her. She'd found it waiting for her on the doorstep of a witness she'd gone back to question, unlike the other two, which had been delivered— Her thoughts suddenly came to a scratching halt.

The cross had been *waiting* for her on the doorstep of the witness. She hadn't found it *after* she'd interviewed her witness, so Tom Warrington hadn't been following her, or watched her go into a house and then left the cross on the doorstep for when she'd come out. No. The cross had been waiting for her *before* she'd entered the house.

It could mean only one thing.

'Bloody hell!' Hillary yelped and, grabbing the photo, shot through into the other office. Jimmy looked up, took one look at her taunt face and blazing eyes, and froze. Hillary stared at him, and shook her head. Then she looked across at Sam.

'Sam,' she said, her voice whipping across the room as hard as diamonds. Jimmy wasn't surprised to see the lad go suddenly pale. 'On our last case, did you tell anyone about our movements?'

'Guv?' Sam gulped.

'Did you discuss it with any of your mates?' she demanded impatiently. 'Do you have any friends here on the force?'

'Some, guv,' Sam said, clearly bewildered. 'But I never discuss our cases with them. You told me not to.' Hillary took a deep shaking breath. Yes, she had told him that. And he would have obeyed her, he was a good lad. Jimmy wouldn't have talked, and she knew damned well she hadn't, and that Steven hadn't.

Besides, Tom Warrington was a ladies' man, or thought of himself as such and so.... Hillary went suddenly cold. She was aware that Jimmy had come to stand beside her, and had taken the photograph from her hand. Its significance made no sense to him but standing beside her he could tell she was as tense as a drawn bowstring. She was almost vibrating with it.

'What's up, guv?' But Hillary was staring, wide-eyed and white as milk, at Vivienne's still empty seat.

'Where the hell,' she finally croaked, 'is Vivienne?'

TWELVE

'SHE'S PROBABLY JUST running late,' Sam said, then blushed as he realized how stupid that sounded. If true, she'd be running almost a whole day late. 'Or perhaps she's not well and isn't coming in today,' he corrected.

'Did she seem unwell yesterday?' Hillary demanded, her voice still incredibly tight. Something in her eye made the young lad pale.

'Not really,' he admitted softly.

Hillary turned on her heel and headed for Steven's office, Jimmy right behind her. She knocked but went straight in. Steven was on the phone, but after one surprised look at her tight, white face, quickly ended the conversation and hung up.

'I think we have a problem. With Vivienne,' she said.

Steven blinked. Of course they had a problem with the girl, he thought, she was totally unsuitable, but now hardly seemed to be the time to deal with it. Geoff Rhumer and his team were currently tracking down a hot lead on where Tom Warrington might have parked his new camper van, and they still had Deakin to process.

As if reading his thoughts, Hillary shook her head impatiently.

'No, I mean a real problem. She hasn't shown up today. I think she's been feeding Tom Warrington information on my cases.' Behind her, Jimmy muttered something, and Steven got to his feet.

'Think or know?' he said flatly. He knew Hillary wasn't the sort to throw around unsubstantiated accusations.

'I should have realized it before. She's got a new fella. She's been sort of hinting and bragging about him for a bit, but I haven't been taking any notice. If I had, I might have wondered why, if he was so hot, she hadn't found a way to introduce him to us and show off.' Steven shrugged.

'That's hardly proof she's been seeing Warrington,' he pointed out.

'Of course it isn't,' Hillary said irritably. She was feeling sick to her stomach, and knew she had to get it together fast. 'It was the last of the crosses that did it. I should have realized before. You remember, the one that was waiting for me on the doorstep of the witness in our last case? I went to interview her and it was waiting for me.'

'Right. So?'

'It was waiting for me when I *arrived*,' Hillary repeated. And when both Steven and Jimmy looked at her, puzzled, stressed again, 'It was *waiting for me* on the doorstep. So how did Warrington know where I was going in order to get there ahead of me and plant it?'

Jimmy swore, and instantly twigged. 'Somebody must have told him.'

'I didn't,' Hillary snapped. 'Did you?'

'Hell, no. And not the lad either,' Jimmy said, glanced at Steven and then swore again. 'It had to have been Vivienne.'

'What do we know about our stalker—about Warrington?' Hillary pressed, and this time it was Steven who answered.

'He likes the ladies. If he were looking for a weak link in your team, he'd go for a woman first. A young and pretty one like Vivienne would be bound to catch his eye.'

'And Warrington's good-looking, fit and on the job. Vivienne would have been easy prey. She hasn't come in to work today, although she's due; and she hasn't called in sick, or I would have been notified. Add to that mix the fact that Warrington hasn't shown up either and....' She paused and took a deep breath. But the sick feeling in her stomach roiled uneasily. She didn't say it, but then she didn't need to. Everyone in the room was thinking the same thing.

If Hillary was right, then the girl could be dead already. They all knew that Warrington had been working himself up to actually killing someone, ever since he'd taken a knife to Hillary's throat. Vivienne, being under Hillary's supervision, was the ideal target. What could be more satisfying for him, and the sick, twisted games that he was playing, than to snatch one of Hillary's own, right from under her nose?

'Oh shit,' Jimmy said softly. Then jumped, as the door to Steven's office burst open and Rhumer shot in.

'We think we've found him,' he said, too excited by his own news to sense the atmosphere in the room. 'A neighbour of the Warringtons is a drinking buddy with a local farmer. Apparently, he lets Warrington use a bit of scrap land in one of his fields. He reckons it deters tractor thieves and sheep rustlers, would you believe it, to have a copper in uniform seen regularly on his land. And we're looking for a cheap, rent-free place where Warrington might have parked his van, right?'

'Where is it,' Steven snapped, reaching for his coat.

'Not a couple of miles away,' Rhumer said, flushed with success.

'Right, let's go and check it out. Bring a couple of your team with you,' Steven said. 'Grab some field-glasses. We're going in softly. First we need to see if a van is there, and if it is, if it's occupied. We might have a hostage situation,' he added, as Geoff opened his mouth to ask why they just didn't go in mob-handed and nab him, as he'd been expecting Steven to suggest.

'What? Who?' he spluttered.

Steven turned and put a hand out towards Hillary and Jimmy who were both set to follow him. 'No way,' Steven said flatly. 'You two stay here.' He turned and hurried out, Rhumer still shooting questions at him as he did so.

Hillary stood silently, counting to ten. Beside her, Jimmy shifted restlessly. When she'd finished counting, she said, 'Right then, Jimmy, let's go. We'll take your car—Steven knows mine.'

Jimmy gulped. 'We're going to follow them then, guv?' he said needlessly.

''Course we are. Or rather, I am,' she qualified, turning to give him a small smile. 'I wouldn't blame you if you decided to stay here.'

Jimmy gave her a small smile back. 'Yeah, right, guv,' he said. And then muttered, 'What's the super gonna do? Fire me? I'm already retired, right?' But Hillary had already gone, and Jimmy swore again as he hurried out after her.

'WE'D BETTER NOT turn off up the farm track, guv,' Jimmy said, ten minutes later as he pulled off to the side of a narrow lane. They'd followed the superintendent's car down ever more isolated country roads until they'd seen Rhumer get out and open a five-barred gate, where a stone-track led through a field just turning green with wheat.

Hillary agreed. Steven would be bound to spot them if they stayed in the vehicle. 'How do you feel about a nice country walk in the sunshine then?' she asked cheerfully.

Jimmy grunted. About as good as he felt about disobeying a super's direct orders, indulging in an unauthorized pursuit, and then sneaking up on a possibly armed subject with a possible hostage. All without back-up.

'Always was a nature lover me, guv,' he forced himself to say, just as cheerfully. There was, after all, no way he could let her go alone as he knew she would. If Vivienne was in danger, he knew that Hillary would hold herself responsible, regardless of how inane that was. Besides, she wasn't the sort to abandon one of her own. And neither was he. If the worse did come to the worst...well, who the hell wanted to live to grow really old anyway? Jimmy remembered his own grandfather falling prey to senility and decay and shuddered.

Nah, he thought, closing the car door with the quietest of clicks and falling in behind Hillary as she made for a hedge and quickly walked, half-ducked, alongside it towards a stand of scrappy trees in a hollow. When it came right down to it, he'd rather go out with a bang than a whimper any day.

Ahead, Hillary crouched down, and pointed. Off to one side of the field, just before it came to the crest of a slight ridge in the field, she pointed to Steven's car. From their position, they could see Steven and Rhumer, and two of his men surveying the small copse with binoculars. Not that they needed them, for, even from this distance, Hillary and Jimmy could easily see a squarish-shaped blob of white that had to be a camper van parked within.

Hillary quickly surveyed the area and thought rapidly.

'Steven's going to call in for armed back-up,' she said softly. 'And probably a hostage negotiator.' It was standard procedure.

Jimmy gulped again. 'Heavy stuff, guv,' he agreed nervously.

'And *if* Vivienne is in there, and *if* she's still alive, how do you think Warrington will react to suddenly finding himself surrounded?' she asked. 'Think for a moment. He's made his move, he's got Vivienne, and either he's already killed her and is gloating over it, in which case, getting caught straight away is seriously going to dent his pride and send him bug-eyed crazy, or he hasn't actually done the deed yet, and is about to be stopped before finally fulfilling his life-time obsession.'

'Which will also send him bug-eyed crazy,' Jimmy agreed, nodding glumly. 'Either way he hasn't got anything to lose, has he?' he asked helplessly.

'No he hasn't,' Hillary agreed. 'If he's armed, he'll choose to go out in a blaze of glory. His type always do,' she said flatly.

'How many times do we see it happen? A cornered rat turning on anyone and anything in its path?'

'If he isn't armed and Vivienne's still alive, he'll kill her before being taken down, otherwise, he'll go down as an utter loser and a total tosser,' Jimmy predicted. 'A miserable, wannabe serial killer, who couldn't even take out one captured female victim. His ego will never take it.' Hillary sighed noisily.

'But Steven has to play it by the book. So he'll wait for back-up and a hostage negotiator. And in the meantime, Vivienne....' But she didn't say what could be happening to Vivienne in that camper van right now. She couldn't even let herself think about it, because if she did, she wouldn't be able to function. And she needed to function now—she needed to think clearly and choose her options, and make rational decisions like she never had before.

Without a word she turned and, crouched below hedge level, went back to the car.

'You've got stuff in the boot?' she asked, and Jimmy, not needing any clarification, nodded, almost feeling insulted.

''Course I have,' he said, opening it up. He'd been one of those keeping watch on Hillary's boat at night, and he wouldn't have done so without having something handy.

Hillary gazed down at the display. There was the good old heavy truncheon, a tyre iron, illegal pepper spray, and an even more illegal taser gun.

She didn't bother asking the old-timer where he'd managed to get *that*.

She picked it up and hefted it in her hand. 'Fully charged, right?'

'Yep.' She nodded, thought about it for a moment, and then handed it over to him. Surprised, Jimmy took it. He'd expected her to want to hold on to it—it was the most effective weapon in the arsenal. Instead, she reached for the pepper spray and put it into the large pocket of her russet-coloured jacket, where it made barely a bulge.

'We don't have much time,' she said flatly. 'Let's hope Warrington's in there and that he hasn't spotted Steven and the others yet. There's no reason he should have— the car's out of his eyeline.' Hillary turned, and headed

counter-clockwise to the way they'd previously gone.
Quickly, steadily, they crept up and around the side of
the small copse, edging closer to the white van. When
they were almost level with it, and on the far side from
where Steven and Rhumer were watching them, she hun-
kered down.

All the time they'd been creeping closer, she'd been
thinking. What they'd needed was a fairly simple plan
that stood a good chance of working. Well, she didn't
know if she'd come up with one of *those,* but she was
sure that she'd come up with something that gave Vivienne Tyrell a better chance of living through this than
an assault by an armed response unit—always provided
she was still alive.

They needed a distraction out front, and a sneaky in-
cursion from the rear. And there was only one person
that she knew of who could distract Tom Warrington
from whatever he was currently doing inside the van.

She felt sick. Her heart was racing. But it had to be
done.

She took a long, slow breath. 'OK, Jimmy, here's what
we're going to do.'

STEVEN CRAYLE SLOWLY lowered his binoculars and swore.
Beside him, Geoff Rhumer looked at him and saw that
his superior officer had gone quite white. 'What? Have
you spotted movement inside?' he asked, but realized
that the superintendent hadn't even been looking at the
camper van. He'd been distracted by something on the
other side of the site.

'No,' Steven said, crouching down behind the car.
'Look, stay here and wait for the armed response team.
Fill them in on all we have and tell them not to do any-

thing without a direct order from me.' He checked that his
radio was turned to its lowest noise setting, and shoved
it down further into his pocket.

'What? Where are you going?' a thoroughly rattled
Geoff Rhumer hissed, as he watched his superior officer scuttle away.

'Just do as I said,' Steven hissed back, and took off
at a low running crouch. Behind him, the two officers
with Rhumer watched him go.

'Shall we follow him, guv?' one of them asked uncertainly. Like the DI, they weren't happy to see the man in
charge suddenly disappear.

'What? No. You heard our orders,' Geoff said, his
palms going sweaty. He had no idea what had just happened, but one thing was for sure: if things started to go
pear-shaped, nobody was going to be able to point the
finger at him. Steven Crayle was the officer in charge,
after all. The buck stopped with him.

Rhumer, the sweat popping out on his brow, looked
over the fields towards the main roads. How much longer was the armed response unit going to be?

STEVEN CRAYLE, HIS heart in his mouth, worked quickly
around towards the back of the woods.

In front of him, coming from the opposite direction,
he caught the occasional glimpse of Jimmy Jessop, using
every bit of available cover, and sometimes going down
on his belly to crawl across the ridges of growing wheat,
as he sneaked up towards the back of the van.

But where the hell was Hillary?

When he'd first spotted movement on the other side
of the site, and saw Jessop through his viewfinder, he
knew that Hillary had to be here somewhere. He didn't

stop to question the whys and wherefores. Not now. He
only knew that he had to find her and intercept her before she put herself in harm's way.

He cursed silently and got down on all fours himself
and began edging his way towards Jessop. He should
have known that she wouldn't stay safely back at HQ.
Damn it, he should have understood at once that she'd
see it as her duty to try and save Tyrell herself.

He thought he saw the van move slightly, and froze.
He noticed that Jimmy had seen the same thing, and was
now likewise hugging the dirt.

Yes. There was definitely a slight rocking movement,
as if someone was moving around.

Then he heard it. The sound of the door opening.

Great! If Warrington was leaving, then they might
just be able to grab him without any fuss.

And then Steven Crayle's heart almost stopped beating as he heard a familiar feminine voice say clearly and
calmly, 'Hello, Tom.' Tom Warrington stood in the doorway. He was dressed in a pair of blue denim jeans with
a white shirt hanging loose over his hips. He had a bit of
a five o'clock shadow, and his hair was slightly ruffled.

He looked at Hillary with hot, eager eyes.

'You came. How did you find me?'

Hillary stood a few feet away from him, and gave a
slow, dazzling smile. 'Tom, sweetheart,' she said simply.
'Remember who you're talking to,' she chided gently.

Tom Warrington's smile widened even further. 'You're
right. Sorry. Won't you come in?' Out of the corner of
his eye, Steven saw Jessop get to his feet and run for the
back of the van. Without a thought, Steven did the same.

Jimmy Jessop's eyes widened as he flattened himself
against the back of the van's paintwork, and saw his su-

perintendent sprint quietly up to join him. Steven held a
hand to his lips and Jimmy nodded.

In truth, Jimmy had never been glad to see anyone
so much in his life.

In front of the van, Hillary Greene smiled up into Tom
Warrington's green eyes.

'Don't be silly, Tom,' Hillary said. 'You don't really
think I'm going to go inside with you, do you?'

Tom held his hands wide. 'Of course not. You're
way too smart for that. Normally, I mean. But we both
know that I've got an ace in the hole, don't we?' And
he laughed. There was something wire-taut and reck-
less about it, and it set the flesh on the back of her spine
creeping.

Hillary forced herself to laugh lightly. 'Is she still
alive?' She tried to keep her voice nonchalant, barely
even curious, but wasn't quite sure that she'd succeeded.

Tom laughed again. 'Oh, she's been learning her les-
son. I couldn't stand the way she bad-mouthed you, but
I had to put up with it before. Now she knows better.
But yeah, she's still alive. I wanted to take my time. I
thought I had plenty. But it seems I underestimated you
again. Sorry about that, sweetheart.' Suddenly Tom's
green eyes sharpened and he looked around nervously.
'You are alone, right?' Hillary frowned.

'Of course I'm alone,' she said, letting censure drip
into her voice. 'You don't think I'd want anybody else
trampling all over us, do you?'

Instantly, Tom's face cleared. 'No, of course not.
Sorry. You just took me by surprise.' At the back of the
van, Steven peered up into first one window then another,
but the curtains were drawn and he couldn't see a thing.

There was no way to confirm Warrington's assertion that Vivienne was still alive in there.

Cautiously, he began to edge to the side of the van. He could feel Jessop right behind him, and turned, and pointed to the other side of the van. Better to get Warrington in a pincer movement if possible. It doubled the chances of preventing him from getting back into the van that way. The priority now was to make sure that he couldn't get back to his hostage.

And to save Hillary Greene from getting her throat cut. Jessop nodded that he understood and began to edge back the other way.

In front of the van, Hillary thought that she saw a number of fingers appear at the side of the van and forced her eyes not to move there. She needed to keep Warrington's attention riveted on her and away from Jimmy. More importantly still, she needed to get him out of the doorway and further into the open.

'Are you saying you're not happy to see me?' she asked archly, and took a few steps back, pretending to be about to turn around and walk away. 'In that case, I'll go!'

'No!' She turned back, relieved to see that Warrington had come down the two steps and was now standing on the ground.

'Don't tease me,' Tom said, but although his voice was half-amused, half-petulant, his eyes were begin to slit together in a show of real anger.

Hillary smiled quickly and turned back to him. 'I thought you liked a bit of teasing,' she said. 'After all, fair's fair. You've been teasing me for weeks.'

Tom shrugged, but his eyes opened in a blaze of mock innocence and insolence. 'You loved it,' he crowed.

Hillary shrugged. 'But playtime's over now,' she said. And meant it. 'Aren't you going to come and claim your reward?' Tom Warrington took three steps towards her and stopped. From the right-hand side of the van, Hillary saw Jimmy Jessop's face abruptly appear and disappear. He was taking a quick look at the lie of the land, and that was understandable, but what shook Hillary was the fact that she was sure that she'd seen the fingers on the *left*-hand side of the van. How could an old man like Jimmy get from one side to the other so quickly?

'What's wrong?' Tom Warrington asked sharply, not liking the way her lovely sherry-coloured eyes flickered just then. He was feeling super-alert, and super-charged, and he wanted so much just to run to her and take her.

But he was wary.

'Why don't *you* tell *me*?' Hillary asked softly. 'You're the one over there, whilst I'm the one over here.' Tom smiled uncertainly and took another few steps towards her. As he did so, Steven Crayle moved around the left-hand side of the van and began a fast, almost silent sprint up behind Warrington.

Almost silent, but not quite.

Then three things happened at once.

Tom Warrington started to turn around, saw Steven Crayle and, with a roar, reached into his back denim pocket and came out with a flick knife.

Hillary Greene shouted a warning and launched herself forward.

Jimmy, hearing Hillary's scream of warning, shot around from the right-hand side, taser raised.

Tom Warrington was interested only in Steven Crayle. For weeks now, the elegant, superior, handsome superintendent had been nosing his way into Hillary's life, and here at last was his chance to get payback. He stepped forward, raising the knife, anticipating the moment with relish when he was able to slide it into the bastard's ribs. He felt something land on his back, and he staggered forward with the unexpected weight, bending over slightly.

He could smell Hillary's perfume, and felt her arms come around his neck. But her fingers were gouging for his eyes and he jerked his head back quickly, flexing his massive shoulders muscles and attempting to throw her off.

But she clung on, and he felt her bite his ear savagely. Something warm and sticky ran down his neck. At the same time, Crayle went low, ducked his head, and hit him straight in the lower gut with a head-ram that made the air whoosh out of his lungs.

He roared and threw his arms wide, dislodging Hillary who went flying. He reached down, inverting the knife and, through the layers of pain, pointed the blade down, towards Steven's exposed back. His arms, pumped with muscle, tensed, ready to plunge the blade home.

And then the world exploded with a bright blue light, and a zzzzzzzing sound that seemed to split his ears. He felt his whole body jerk and dance spasmodically, and then he had the sensation of falling into blackness.

He didn't see Jimmy Jessop standing over him, the discharged taser gun in his hand and a snarling, satisfied smile on his face.

COMMANDER MARCUS DONLEAVY sighed heavily and looked at the three people in front of him. It was five hours later, and he was still not sure whether to be in a good mood or a raging temper.

Whatever, he was in no mood to string this out. He

pointed a finger at Jimmy Jessop who froze like a rabbit in the spotlight.

'You,' he said. 'Get yourself down to supplies and liaise with Sergeant Fulcott. You were assigned the taser three days ago, and filled out every piece of paper needed. Remember to backdate it. I don't want any loose ends if an inquiry is convened, and people come sniffing. You acted with Superintendent Crayle's full knowledge and support. If there is an inquiry, and I'm going to do my best to ensure there's not, you'll say bugger all about anything. Got it?'

'Yes, sir,' Jimmy barked.

Donleavy nodded. 'All right then. Sod off.' Jimmy gulped and shot out of his chair. Hillary gave the commander a long level look and, just as Jimmy got to the door, he added gruffly, 'That was good work you did today, Mr Jessop.' Jimmy nodded, and shot through the door like a scalded cat. He'd always heard Donleavy was one of the good ones—a bastard, but a good one, and having seen that for himself, was in no mood to prolong the experience.

Donleavy sighed and then glanced at Crayle.

'I expect you and DI Rhumer to get your stories straight too. You planned the whole procedure. You decided that you couldn't wait for back-up. You take all the glory—and if the shit hits the fan, you take all the brown stuff too. Agreed?'

'Yes, sir,' Steven said stiffly.

Marcus Donleavy nodded. Then smiled. 'Don't worry. It'll be glory all the way. You solved two missing persons' cases, and one murder. And you rescued a colleague from danger and apprehended one sick puppy. Of course, the media will have a field day with Warrington being one of our own, but that can't be helped.'

'Sir, I think we should get the PR doctors to spin Vivienne Tyrell as the heroine of this story,' Hillary put in.

After Jimmy had put down Warrington, she'd staggered to her feet and been the first through the van door. She'd found Vivienne tied up on the bed with a black eye. She'd been in shock, of course, and was currently in the hospital being treated, but she'd managed to tell them that she hadn't been raped, and that Warrington had been ranting on and on about Hillary for most of the time.

'I know Vivienne won't be coming back to us, sir,' she carried on. 'She admitted to me she wasn't cut out for police work. But she needs to turn this experience into something positive—we owe her that. And I think that, when she's had a chance to recover, she'll be more than happy to be in the spotlight, and will be able to turn her five minutes of fame into a career opportunity, perhaps to go for something in the media. Besides, I think the top brass will be happy to have a copper—well, sort of a copper—shown in an heroic light, given the circumstances. It'll help to take the focus away from Warrington.'

Donleavy's grey eyes glittered. 'I dare say it will. And if what I've been hearing about our Miss Tyrell is true, she'll be happy to take the proper advantage of the situation. So. How exactly are you two feeling?'

Hillary rubbed her throbbing shoulder. She thought she'd wrenched it when Warrington had thrown her to the ground, but she hadn't said anything. 'I'll be fine, sir,' she said flatly.

Donleavy's eyes narrowed, but he nodded. 'And you?' He turned to Steven Crayle. 'Head butting a suspect and then getting the residue zapping from a taser gun couldn't have been a picnic.'

Steven, who had a major headache, grimaced. 'I'm fine,' he said flatly. When you had a muscle-bound suspect to tackle, the least-armoured area was the stomach. Forget about going at it with fists—that way led to broken bones and injury. Still, that didn't stop his head and neck from feeling as if they'd just been used as a battering ram. Which they had.

Donleavy, without a word, reached into his desk and came out with a packet of aspirin. He pushed it towards Hillary, who smiled grimly, and accepted the peace offering for them both.

'OK, Steven,' Donleavy said, 'today's shenanigans, if played right—and I'll make damned sure that they are played right—could mean a promotion for you. Or at the very least, bring you to the top men's attention. Chief Super sounds good, does it?'

Steven smiled wanly. Right now, bed and a stiff whisky sounded even better. 'Yes sir,' he agreed obediently.

'I don't really have to read you two the Riot Act, do I?' Marcus Donleavy demanded. 'What went down this afternoon was a right farce. You're both damned lucky it turned out as it did. Get your act together. I don't want to have a repeat performance. Etc, etc.'

Hillary nodded and rose abruptly to her feet. 'Understood, sir,' she said crisply. She was in no mood for Donleavy's heavy sarcasm right now. Besides, as a civilian, she didn't have to take it anymore.

Steven, slightly surprised by her abrupt retreat, nevertheless rose and quite happily followed her out. Without a word, they left the building together and walked slowly towards his car. No doubt, the news about the afternoon's events was spreading through the station house like wildfire, but they would have to deal with that, and any fall out from it, tomorrow.

Inside the car, he slumped wearily back against the driver's seat and sighed.

'I'm as mad as hell at you, you know,' he said listlessly, staring out in front of him at a line of similarly parked cars. 'You scared the living daylights out of me.'

'I know. I'm sorry.' Steven suddenly gave a great bark of laughter. Hillary Greene, being humble? He never thought he'd live to see the day. He turned to look at her, and saw with a pang, that she was exhausted.

And who could blame her? She'd been through hell.

Then he laughed again. 'Ah, what the hell? Do you realize, you haven't stroked that damned scar on your neck once today?'

Hillary slowly rolled her head to one side and looked at him. Her lips twitched. 'What damned scar?'

* * * * *